ADVENTURES FROM THE ICPA: *A SERIES OF SHORT STORIES*

John Francis

Library of Congress Cataloging- in-Publication Data has been applied for.
ISBN 978-0-578-35133-9

PREFACE

The ICPA saga started out as an essay for an English class when I was a high school student. It is funny to think about it now, but I was not overly enthused about the essay topic. In the end I bent the rules as much as possible while still staying within the confines of the rubric and ended up with a story about a spy preventing crime around the world. I based many of the characters on my friends at the time and everyone liked the story so much, including myself, that I kept writing. Every break from school I would write a new chapter and email it to everyone to enjoy. We even had an induction ceremony for new friends who had characters joining the storyline. As time progressed the characters grew into completely independent and new individuals with their own wonderful personalities.

When I started university, I wrote what I thought would be the final chapter of the storyline and then shelved the work for about three years. While the story was shelved, I did a lot of traveling in Europe. I lived in Spain for a short period of time and then later moved to Japan. While living in Japan I happened to come across the files for the story and decided to complete my goal of eventually publishing it. What this means is that the process to bring this work into the world from start to finish took about ten years. The beauty of the time spent on the manuscript is that I was able to rewrite large portions to include my own memories and experiences from some of the countries allowing the story to become more authentic.

I want to give a special thanks to my mother Beth, my father Bill, and brother William who continuously read this story and offered feedback throughout the whole process from start to finish. In addition to my family, I would like to thank CJ Skye, my main editor who not only helped me polish the work in terms of grammar, but also provided wonderful story suggestions that really made the piece come together. Lastly a huge thanks to all of my beta readers and a special thanks to Lauren Yehle and Daniel Zimney-Schmidt for all the love and support as I brought this manuscript into existence.

To those who are not daring in real life but have wild imaginations

A CULT, A SPY, AND AN ANGEL: JAPAN

Location: The Streets of Chicago_

It was a rainy day in Chicago, lights from various shops reflected off the asphalt in a ghostly sort of manner. People milled about the busy streets and then vanished into the curtain of mist. I, for one, was rather alert on that particular day. Something felt off. I had always been one to over analyze a situation, although something really did feel different. What the difference was, I couldn't pinpoint.

Being a member of the International Crime Prevention Agency (ICPA) was a risky job. My office had sent me to Chicago on a field assignment. I was looking for someone who was illegally selling goods on the black market. Usually, the local police dealt with these matters, but officers had noticed that there was something strange about the transactions from a specific group. After being tracked, the network used by the unknown group was spread much farther than most black-market dealings in the city. Goods and services through this particular network reached as far as Japan, Nepal, and France.

I sat huddled at the outdoor table of a corner coffee shop. The umbrella on the table wasn't doing much good due to the wind and mist spewing off the road from passing vehicles. I resigned myself to watching a lady in heels scamper out of a nearby boutique, arms full of shopping bags, and into a waiting taxi. She wasn't the criminal I was looking for, but shopping at that boutique would certainly be a fashion crime. More shadowy figures trudged through the rain.

As I continued watching, something by one of the shops caught my eye. A red-coated figure, clearly visible through the rain, darted into an alley. My heart pounded; I was extremely nervous. This was my first mission in the field as part of the agency's cross-departmental initiative to create spies with more all-around skills. I was usually the desk agent. However, instead of monitoring communications from my office like usual, I was the one who had to catch the bad guy. I pulled out my wrist communicator and paged headquarters.

"I have spotted a suspicious entity heading east of Amy's position, code one." I whispered into my wrist communicator. My voice disappeared in the damp wind.

"Repeat, over," came the voice in my earpiece.

Just as I was about to respond, someone grabbed me from behind. I flailed all I could, but the mysterious person was too strong. My limited combat training flashed through my mind, but I couldn't seem to put it into practice. I couldn't believe I had already blown my first field assignment. I squirmed and tried to free myself while being dragged into an alley where we were joined by another shadowy figure. My assailants tied up my wrists. Looking up, two men cloaked in crimson stood before me.

The taller shadowy figure began to speak. "Well, well. It looks like the little desk agent can't handle himself in the real world," came a scratchy voice behind a ski mask.

"Let me go or you'll be sorry," I said, trying to sound strong. My mind was racing so fast, I didn't really know what to do. I hadn't even been in field training for more than a week. I wondered if the two figures had obtained this information, thus spotting me as an easy target.

"Really, what could a measly desk agent even do? Hack into our brains?" came the voice again, followed by a sinister laugh.

Obviously, the kidnappers were not the brightest. I was able to swing my bound arms into the wall behind us, activating my wrist communicator to produce a small saw. Cutting my restraints, I burst free and proceeded to blind the kidnappers with pepper spray. I then ran down the alleyway. I could hear the two assailants in close pursuit as their boots splashed through the puddles.

Darting down another path, I activated a holographic map and plotted the most effective escape. They were still on my tail. Seeing a rusty fire escape on the side of a building, I shot my grappling hook up and caught the top rung. I pulled myself onto the roof. Knowing I only had a few seconds, I ran as fast as I could and jumped across a gap in the buildings vanishing from direct view. I then took advantage of the curtain of mist and disappeared. Sliding down a drainpipe, I landed back out on the main street. I headed for the nearest base, a small coffee shop. As I walked, I worried about being reprimanded for compromising the mission. I didn't catch the cult member, and I had alerted them to our presence.

I pushed my wet bangs out of my face as I looked up at the glowing neon sign that read *International Coffee*. The shop was a hole-in-the-wall type of café. Its warm light spilled out into the dark. Patrons sat at an elevated bar gazing out onto the gloomy streetscape. I pushed open the door and the smell of freshly roasted coffee wafted out. A small bell on the door jingled as I pushed though.

Inside it was warm and cheery, but there was no time to enjoy a cup of coffee; instead, I made my way casually to the door marked *Employees Only*. The sign slid over, and I scanned my fingerprint. The scanner accepted my credentials, and the door opened. Amy, the top spy in the agency, sat monitoring a wall of TV screens.

Amy looked up with a startled expression when she saw me enter. "Why are you here?"

"I ran into a little hassle with some gangsters."

"Sir Alexander, I know this is your first field assignment, but you have to be more careful. Obviously, you were doing something that got their attention." I winced at Amy's words. My goal was to prove that I could do this...that I could be just as good as a field agent.

Field agents were far more revered within the agency. They were the ones that actually fought crime. The desk agents were just there to assist. In reality, desk agents did a lot more than they got credit for but didn't have the bragging ability. Our stories were of thwarting hackers, rerouting money, and gathering intel. Field agents could boast about car chases, explosions, and near-death escapes which, even I had to admit, was far more enthralling.

"I really don't know what I could have done, Amy. I was sitting in the corner. I was completely covered. For some reason, I had a feeling they knew even before I got there, and they knew that I wasn't trained as well as other agents. I don't know why; I just have a feeling."

"I hear you. There may be more to this than it appears," Amy replied with a sigh, "It seems there is a new cult called the Spartans in this neighborhood. I think they are aiding our black-market dealer. I'm glad you're okay, but even if they acted on inside information this does constitute negligence on your part for preparation. I won't put it on your permanent record, but I am going to require you to have more training before returning to the field."

I frowned, pondering the events unfolding before my eyes. I couldn't decide if I was more concerned about the fact that the black-market dealers might have had inside information, or the fact that Amy was putting me into some sort of remedial training courses because, as I feared, I wasn't able to prove that I could be a field agent like the rest of them. So much for all my work with the cross-departmental training program.

Location: ICPA HQ_

Amy had me return to Colorado immediately after my encounter. My flight was bound for Aspen. It was the nearest airport to the location of our headquarters nestled remotely in the Rocky Mountains. As the airplane drifted through the clouds, I considered the recent developments. It hadn't been long since I had stepped up to the position of head desk agent. When it had come up that the previous head desk agent was retiring, rather than simply going off seniority, a vote went out to the team as to whom they thought would be the best replacement.

I was shocked when the team voted me in. At first, I had actually tried to decline the offer considering the large amount of responsibility, but my friend and training partner Josey had encouraged me to step outside my comfort zone and get the recognition I deserved after I had guided countless successful missions over my time at the agency. I also thought about Amy. I was thankful she didn't blame me for the mishap with the cult members, but I was still frustrated that she was putting me into training. I decided to put those feelings behind me as I checked into a hotel for the night, so I could start fresh back in the office the next day.

It felt good to be back. Everything ran normally, at least for me. After entering the office, my intern and secretary, Laurel, came to greet me.

"How's our head desk agent?" Laurel flounced over to me from across the room. "I heard that you were in a skirmish with one of the people from the cult," she stated rather matter-of-factly.

"Yes, I'm fine," I said with a smile. "You don't have to tease me so much. Pretty soon you are going to end up in the field too with this whole cross-departmental training program. You're lucky that the lead agents are testing it out first before everyone else has to do it."

"You know I love to tease you, but I really respect you for working to create the cross-departmental training program. I think it will foster a lot more respect from both sides of the agency. You already saw how hard field work is. I can't wait to get some field agents in here and have them see that we don't just relax all day behind computer screens," said Laurel.

"Sir Alexander, over here," Veronica, one of the other desk agents, waved to me. "I'm so glad you're back. I've been having issues with my computer, and I can't seem to get things sorted out, mind taking a look?"

That was one thing that had propelled me ahead in the desk agent department. I had a knack for technology. In fact, technology was what got me into the ICPA in the first place. After graduating from university, I worked as a white hat hacker. One day, while securing a company's computers, I had come across an unknown connection to their system. After some hacking, I had made my way into the ICPA mainframe and realized that something was fishy. It turned out the company that had hired me was a criminal organization trying to secure their network against the ICPA. The ICPA was extremely impressed that I was able to hack through such sophisticated security and offered me either a job or to get a new identity after having found their existence. I decided on the job.

"That should do it," I said tweaking a few settings on Veronica's computer. "If you ever have any other issues logging into that database again, let me know."

"You're such a lifesaver, thank you."

I was so glad to be back in my usual setting with Laurel and all my other desk agent friends. Here, my skills could shine, and I wasn't a newbie. Slipping into the bathroom to adjust my hair, I stared back at my own reflection. I had just turned twenty-three, but all of the recent stress had certainly made me look older. I pulled out a travel sized can of hairspray and pushed my dark brown hair to one side. Despite being short and straight, it wouldn't stay in place without a good helping of hair products. I glanced down at my tall, slim figure, smoothing out my immaculately pressed charcoal suit that contrasted with my lighter complexion.

Lastly, I adjusted my agency badge. Sir Alexander, my full name, was displayed in dark bold letters above my photo and the agency logo. Being loosely related to some ancient royal in Great Brittan had landed me with an oddly formal name, but I felt it fit my personality perfectly. Deep down inside, I knew I wasn't perfect, but if I dressed the part perhaps others would believe it, or maybe I could believe it myself.

After brushing up, I meandered my way to my office, stopping to say hi to the other desk agents along the way. My office was one of the nicest in the building; it was one of the perks of being the head desk agent. Entering my space, I took in the surroundings. The room was large with a low ceiling; I could touch it if I stood on my tiptoes. It gave the room a cozy feel. A vase of purple artificial flowers sat on my curved mahogany desk. Mauve drapes hung around the window and a comfy sofa sat in one corner. I always kept the room rather dark because it calmed me even though it was intimidating for the new recruits who came to visit for paperwork. Just as I sat, my phone gave a loud ring. Glancing at the display, I noticed it was Amy's direct line. I answered it via headset, and Amy's voice floated into my ear.

"Hi, Sir Alexander, it is good to know you are back in the office. I was hoping you could investigate a case on a set of stolen credit cards. I think the Spartans are responsible. The reason for my speculation is that there's a series of fraudulent one-dollar charges right in a row that match up across over seven hundred cards. The card companies probably don't see this specific pattern since the Spartans have disguised it well to make the cards appear stolen in isolation. You better check it out."

I smiled at the opportunity to complete a task that would hopefully gain me back some brownie points. I glanced over the information Amy had sent over in an email while we were talking. I knew that the Spartans usually charged one-dollar increments on their stolen credit cards to verify they were valid, but that was a lot of cards. To gather intel, I had to call the credit card company for access to their system. I dialed the number and ended up on hold for an inordinate amount of time. Finally, someone answered.

"This is Pricilla. How may I help you?" came the voice.

"This is Sir Alexander, a member of the International Crime Prevention Agency. I require access to your computer system," I stated. I could have hacked in myself, but there was no point of hacking into a system for which we already had security clearance. It just meant having to wait and be patient.

After telling Pricilla the secret clearance codes we give to companies, I was permitted to access the system. I looked through the recent purchases on the accounts. Our crime analytics system identified many patterns related to black market dealings, stolen cards, and other questionable purchases that all traced back to the cult.

I quickly disabled the cards so that no further transactions could occur. I had to chuckle as the image of a Spartan getting a card declined flashed through my mind. They certainly wouldn't be making any more one-dollar purchases. I wondered what they were buying with the money anyway. I looked through the list for the store name. All the purchases were from a foreign country, Japan. The name of the store was Simple Computing.

I looked up the company's website and it seemed legitimate, however that was never something one could count on. The business itself might not even be linked with the cult. They could just be using it as a front. I called the store with a masked local phone number. Also, thanks to spending time in Japan when I was a university student, I was able to fluently speak Japanese to raise even less suspicion. I asked some general questions to the person who answered the phone about the store, its hours, and the products they carried. After a little conversation a new image started to appear. The person on the phone struggled to speak Japanese, which was odd, and they had a hard time answering product questions. I decided an in-person investigation would be best.

I brought the information to Amy's attention and her response was as expected. I would be allowed to go to Japan on the condition that I took part in more combat and physical training. It still frustrated me that I couldn't just go to Japan right away. This wasn't a dangerous mission by any means. I would be collecting intel while investigating from the sidelines. Why all field agents had the idea that an assignment in the field meant running in and blowing things up was beyond me. Walking back into the desk agent department I ran into Laurel.

"So, I have to complete a bunch of remedial combat and physical training courses before I go to Japan...what are the odds I could rope you into joining me? I'll feel out of place if I'm the only desk agent there. You know how those buff field agent guys are. Such showoffs."

"I would say no, but hearing you mention this whole cross-departmental training thing I might as well join you. I have no intention of being in the field, but I can cancel my gym membership if I join you for the training classes." She laughed.

Location: ICPA HQ - Training Facility_

Laurel and I made our way over to the ICPA training facility that field agents used. It was an area of the building I rarely visited other than to deliver paperwork from time to time regarding necessary physical training that might be needed for field agents based on what the desk agent department found in our intel gathering before missions. The glass doors slid open, and Laurel and I walked up to the front desk. A buff receptionist sat behind a small computer monitor that seemed to augment his size even more.

"Ah, you must be the desk agents who are joining the training program. Amy sent me your information. Here are your cards. You can access the training facilities and workout center 24-hours a day with these."

He seemed helpful and friendly enough, but I still wasn't fully convinced about the training program.

"Your trainer is Kai. It looks like Amy has recommended a bit of karate and self-defense, so you can meet him in training room 127B. Two doors down on the left," said the secretary motioning down the hall behind him.

Laurel and I took our cards and made our way to the training room. Entering the space, we found ourselves in a ballet style room with glossy wood flooring. On the one wall was a set of floor-to-ceiling windows that overlooked the snowy mountains and on the other side was a wall of mirrors that reflected the panoramic view making the room feel bright, airy, and twice its actual size. Tumbling mats had been laid onto the floor and boxes with pads and other equipment sat along the non-mirrored wall.

I then noticed Kai. He was tall and sculpted as one would expect for a fitness instructor. His black hair was tied up in a manbun with a few strands falling down the side of his face. He wore an ICPA branded tank top, an article of clothing I didn't even know we offered, that clearly showed off his copper toned skin and physique.

"Hi, I'm Kai," he smiled reaching out his hand. When I shook it, his grip was very firm to the point it almost hurt a bit. "It's an honor to get to train you. I never thought I would be meeting the head desk agent for karate. I've heard a lot of great things about you and this whole new cross-departmental program."

I relaxed a bit. Contrary to what I expected, Kai was not the typical field agent. In fact, he seemed quite kind and genuine. Over the next two weeks, Kai taught us various forms of karate for self-defense and also cheered us on at our daily gym sessions.

After class one day I was packing up my bag. Laurel had already left before me. Kai came over to see how I was doing.

"How do you feel? You've improved a lot in your technique."

"Thanks, Kai. In addition to your classes, I've also been doing regular workouts. Things like lifting weights, running on the treadmill, and just taking some outdoor walks."

"I sense that you are trying to prove something. Perhaps that you can handle all this physical training just like the other guys?"

"You're not wrong," I sighed. "There's a bit more to it than that, but if I'm being totally honest, I was kind of dreading coming here with all the gym rats and showoffs. I'm glad you were my trainer and not one of the other guys."

"Sir Alexander, or Alex, if I may. Think of it this way. You don't have to prove you are strong enough to be a field agent. While muscle and endurance are key, it's really the mindset. That's something you had the moment you stepped in here. Good luck on your next mission. I have family and business connections in Japan, so if you need a favor, don't hesitate to ask."

The next day a memo came from Amy that Kai had cleared me in terms of physical defense ability. I was headed to Japan. Although I knew it was for intel gathering, something told me that this mission would be much more complex compared to my first.

Location: Jet A127 – Destination DIA_

Boarding my private jet, I settled in for the short flight to Denver International Airport, from which I could catch a flight to Japan. Usually, I would have flown directly in my private jet, but Laurel found some flight itineraries that were headed to Japan on one of the Spartan's computers. I was now traveling aboard the same flight as a mysterious Spartan. I hoped to follow him after he got off the plane. We took a sharp turn and my laptop almost fell off my desk. The pilot came over the intercom and said we would be landing shortly.

We landed and I exited my jet to be greeted by a guard who guided me into the airport though a back exit, so I could enter the waiting area for passengers inconspicuously. I looked over the waiting room and wondered which passenger the Spartan was. As we began to board the next flight, to my surprise I saw the same red jacket I had spotted on the rainy day before in Chicago. Thanks to Laurel I had a seat diagonal and just behind the red clad passenger's row, so I could keep track of him easily.

"Welcome aboard Flight 493 with non-stop service to Haneda, Tokyo," came a flight attendant's voice as passengers shuffled to their seats. "We will be departing shortly."

While I was in the air, I decided to do a bit of work. Connecting my laptop to the plane's Wi-fi, I enabled my VPN to make sure no one could snoop on my data while I was working. I opened my email to see a message waiting in my inbox. It read...

ALEX, PLEASE STOP BY AND SEE ME WHILE YOU ARE IN JAPAN. I HAVE NOT SEEN ANYONE FROM THE AGENCY IN A VERY LONG TIME, YOUR FRIEND JOSEY.

Josey and I were longtime friends. We had entered the agency at the same time and were both trained under Amy. About a year earlier, Josey had taken an international field agent position and I hadn't seen her since. It wasn't uncommon to lose contact with a colleague for an extended period of time for security reasons, but suddenly receiving a vague message like this was a bit odd.

I wondered what could have happened to her, and how she knew I was coming to Japan. I kept an eye on the Spartan while pretending to watch an in-flight K-drama. The Spartan did not seem to be suspicious of me. In fact, he acted rather carefree for a high-level criminal. As he dozed off, I was able to roll a tracking device under the seat to stick to his shoes. Nothing else interesting happened during the flight, and soon we were landing in Japan.

Location: Tokyo, Japan -
Haneda Airport_

On the way out of the plane, I did my best to keep up with the Spartan, but a passenger in front of me tripped and accidentally lost the contents of their carry-on. Usually, I would have helped clean up the explosion of clothing, but I had to stay on the tail of my target. Quickly handing the disgruntled passenger a shirt that had been launched in my direction, I shimmied past with the Spartan scarcely in view. Once I had fully exited the plane, which took quite a while thanks to the clothing explosion, I found myself in Haneda International Airport. I felt rather overwhelmed, because the airport happened to be five times the size of Denver International. Keeping track of the Spartan was hard because of the enormous crowds that passed between us. I followed the GPS on my tracking device.

Just as I was catching up, my target darted to the left and stopped at a drinking fountain in a small alcove out of the direct view of most of the people in the area. I realized he had no clue I was following him. Just as I started to sneak closer the wall rotated, and he disappeared behind it. I couldn't believe it. There must have been some sort of Spartan base at the airport.

Sitting down on one of the navy vinyl chairs, I pulled out my laptop to get a closer look at the GPS readings and see if I could build a 3D schematic of the base. Sadly, the Spartan had fully disappeared off the map and there seemed to be some sort of electromagnetic interference that wouldn't allow me to figure out what was hiding below the airport. I sighed. I had already lost my target. Again, I seemed to be a failure at fieldwork. I buried my head in my hands, feeling hopeless. Then Kai came to mind. I smiled thinking about his encouragement and pulled myself together. I couldn't run after the Spartan for now, so I moved on to the next priority on my list. Josey.

I called Laurel to see if she could locate Josey for me, because the email I had received revealed no location and was met with no response. Laurel couldn't find any exact information other than the general area where Josey was last seen. I decided I would call on the help of my best friend Yuki who lived in the Minato area near Tokyo Tower. Yuki and I met when I was a student studying at Waseda University in Japan. We had a few classes together and connected right away. I caught a taxi and called her on the way over.

"Yuki, I have unexpectedly ended up in Tokyo. I need help locating someone, and also would enjoy a visit if you're free."

"On a mission again, I presume," she said over the phone. "You know you can stop by any time."

Location: Minato Ward – Yuki's Apartment_

I arrived at her apartment building which towered so high it was dizzying to look up at from the street level. Taking the elevator, I felt my ears pop from the pressure adjustment. Yuki was one of the only outsiders who knew about the ICPA and what I did for a living. I trusted her. In turn, she told me her secrets as well. We were very good friends. Amy didn't know that an outsider knew about me, but Yuki was different. A quick knock on the door and she had already whisked me inside. I was struck by the view from her living room windows. One could clearly see Tokyo Tower in the distance.

"So, this is the new place you were telling me about! You neglected to mention that your view of Tokyo Tower was so unobstructed. Your new job must be good."

"The fashion industry is hit or miss; you remember my old place back when we were at Waseda together, right? Most people in fashion can only afford a cramped one-room. Finally, I had my breakthrough. What exactly brings you to Japan this time?"

I glanced around, trying to decide if I should fully disclose what I was up to, but I decided it was fine considering I often shared most of my mission details with Yuki and it had never been a problem.

"There's a new cult that has cropped up called the Spartans. We have an important lead that they might have some sort of operation here in Tokyo. Josey might be able to help me but is nowhere to be found despite sending an oddly cryptic message. Laurel sent me her general location."

"I haven't heard that name in a while," said Yuki.

"Yeah, ever since she took that international position, I really fell out of touch with her despite the fact that we trained together. Here's the ward that she is located in."

"Interesting, that is not really a residential area. In fact, there isn't really anywhere one could stay besides a hotel, and I doubt the agency has been paying to have her live in a hotel for the past few years," Yuki said as she pulled up a map of the area on her phone.

"You are right, Laurel would have mentioned that if it were the case, also we would have that on record as well. It appears she went deep under cover recently."

"Alex, I have a sneaking suspicion and I don't think you are going to like to hear it...but I wonder if she is at the hospital. It is one of the largest buildings in that ward and really the main reason people would be in that area is either to visit someone there or receive treatment themselves."

I paused in concern. I decided though that I shouldn't get worked up. There were many reasons Josey could be stationed near or in a hospital, or if something unexpected had come up perhaps she was providing care or protection to someone at the institution.

"I think that's the best lead I've gotten so far on her location. I'll head over and check it out. I hope you don't mind me leaving so soon...I'm still technically on duty. I'll make sure to hang out a bit more after the mission is done."

"Don't worry at all, even seeing you for a short bit today was a nice surprise. Get out there and save the world, Alex." Yuki smiled as she ushered me out of her apartment.

Location: Tokyo Hospital_

Armed with my new lead, I caught another taxi and made my way to the hospital. Stepping out of the vehicle, I approached the automatic doors which slid out of my way as I entered the massive building. I hoped that Josey was okay considering that this was a hospital and try as I might to rationalize the situation, I still had a feeling that something was wrong. The secretary at the desk bowed and asked how she could help.

"Do you have a patient under the name of Josey Scott?" I asked, showing my badge.

She glanced at her computer and then gave me a card with the room number written in Japanese. I was able to make out what it said-- first floor, room 105. I followed the signs to the correct room and walked in to find Josey. I nearly fainted at the sight of her. She used to be a rather tall, strong looking lady, but now she looked frail and sick. Her once voluminous brown hair had turned into thin sparse strands, her eyes had sunken in, and it looked as if her skin had been stretched directly over her bones.

"Are you okay?" I stammered.

"Yes, I'm fine. It's so good to see you, Alex."

I was glad her smile had not left. It brought life back into her face. I needed to see that life because at that moment I felt as if I was looking at death.

"I suppose you're wondering what happened to me," she sighed.

Josey then relayed a rather scary story. She was on the tail of a Spartan when she followed him behind a drinking fountain at the airport and got sprayed with a mist of an unknown chemical. She ended up in the hospital and was not recovering well.

"I saw a Spartan go behind the same drinking fountain, but I did not follow him," I whispered.

Josey looked straight into my eyes. "That's why I needed to see you."

In her typical fashion, Josey moved right along to business. She showed me the research that she had done on the Spartans while she had been staying in the hospital, and a way for me to catch them without getting sprayed with the toxic chemical.

"Are you going to *die?*" I asked without thinking.

Josey smiled and told me she didn't know, but in case she did, I should visit as often as possible, and she would help me with my mission. I nearly broke down into tears.

"I came here to gather intel, Josey. I don't know how I am going to handle things now that I know you aren't well."

"Alex, take a moment and let go of the perfectionism. Your performance on this assignment is not going to change how I think of you. You are my friend and the person I trust most to complete this important task. All I ask is that you try, not that you succeed flawlessly."

Location: The Streets of Tokyo_

Back outside the hospital, I recollected my senses. If Josey wanted me to complete the mission, I would complete the mission. Despite what she said, I would put all of my effort and energy into perfectly exposing the cult. They hurt someone I loved, and I could not let that go unpunished. I followed my next lead looking for what appeared to be an unguarded back entrance to the Spartan's secret lair, which seemed to be connected to Simple Computing.

I walked around, observing the wildly colorful streets of Tokyo. Electro style music floated through the air and bright LED signs glared off the pavement. I made my way to Daimon station and boarded the Asakusa line. After a quick transfer to the Chuo line, I squeezed myself off at the Kichijoji stop. The train station was elevated above the neighborhood below. Glancing down, I saw my next destination; a dimly lit street lined with izakayas and bars.

In the suburbs of Tokyo, the buildings were squeezed together, creating a sort of labyrinth. Exiting the station, I found myself shimmying through the maze of buildings in the dim light, taking in the scent of gyoza and other delicious snacks. Sadly, I didn't have time to indulge. I slipped into one of the alleyways and kicked a trashcan. The unguarded entrance opened to reveal a code pad.

"Cracking the code will be a cinch," I said to myself.

In a few seconds, I had the door open. A gloomy tunnel stood before me. It was certainly not the most inviting. Usually when I entered one of our bases, there was a white futuristic looking hallway. I guess that showed the difference between a spy agency and a criminal organization. I whipped out a pair of sunglasses and my invisible light.

The glasses allowed only me to see the light so the hall appeared bright to me and not anyone else who may have been lurking in the shadows. I didn't want to enter the tunnel, but for the sake of preventing future chaos, I did. The tunnel led to an industrial looking door with a voice check. I quickly pulled out a recorded voice sample of a Spartan and the door creaked open. There in front of me was a nicely kept balcony with black furnishings—a rather drastic change from the tunnel I had just walked through.

I slipped to the edge of the balcony to discover a cavernous underground chamber. It appeared to be some sort of auditorium with a small stage, banquet-style seating, and dim lighting. A perfect location for a sinister meeting. The room was filled with Spartans. Every single person sported his or her red attire at tables covered in white linen with red flowers for centerpieces. A large chandelier glinted over those conspiring below. I stayed crouched out of sight but leaned closer to see what I could hear. A Spartan came onto the stage and started a prepared speech.

"My fellow Spartans, as your leader I hope to see that we'll eventually control most of the world market. We've been investing laundered cash as well as dealing goods on the black market and have accumulated trillions of dollars in profits. Using these profits, we will be able to bribe government officials into letting us run various sectors as well."

I couldn't believe it. I had stumbled onto a high-level cult meeting, and I had accidentally located the leader of the group as well. I quickly snapped a few photos of him to the best of my ability. Hopefully we could run them through the system and see if this man had been involved in any other crime before. I then made my way for the door before I overstayed my welcome. Sadly, the door squeaked as I opened it.

"Wait, who is on the balcony?"

With my cover blown, I ran through the tunnel, and fumbled for the next-door handle. Bursting through the door, I entered the alleyway. Darting onto the street, I hailed the first taxi that drove by just as the Spartans poured into the alleyway.

Location: The Streets of Tokyo_

It was a bit too close for my liking. I thought about the events as we drove down the highly crowded streets. I arrived at the hospital without being followed and relayed my story to Josey.

"You've got to report this," Josey said urgently.

I looked at my friend who appeared even worse than when I saw her just two hours earlier.

"I will," I started for the door.

"I'm coming with you," Josey said.

"Josey, you are not in the condition to be joining me on such a mission. Rest, I'll report what happened to the police and see if I can get any other leads. I have a picture of their leader so hopefully they can track him down." I looked back at her. She had that look that I remembered seeing when something was wrong. Usually, it meant that we had compromised our cover, but in this case, I knew what she was going to say before she even told me.

"I am going to die," she said rather calmly.

I couldn't take it anymore and burst into tears. "How much longer do you have?" I wailed.

"Only a few more days – and don't cry; I want to spend the rest of my time with you."

That made me feel a little better. If these were Josey's last few days, then we would make the best of it and solve this case together. I knew Josey had read my mind.

"Now you see why I requested to come on one last mission. I have enough strength left in me to do this. Where do we start?" she asked.

Location: Tokyo Governmental Building_

Having Josey in a better mood helped me avoid thinking about the fact that we might not have many...or any future missions together. I pushed the thoughts aside as our train pulled into Shinjuku station. Stepping onto the platform, we were immediately whisked into the hordes of salary men making their way to the office. Shinjuku station was enormous. The underground tunnels were so extensive that some even had stores and restaurants lining the sides.

"I swear we already passed this dessert shop before," said Josey.

"I think you're right. This place is such a maze. I think we need to take that exit ahead instead," I replied.

After finally navigating our way out of Shinjuku station, we weaved our way through the bustling streets toward the governmental campus in the area. After passing by some cute boba tea shops and an abundance of hotels, we arrived at a very tall skyscraper that towered above the other buildings in the area. We ascended the stairs and approached the entrance.

Once inside, a stylish lobby sat before us. The lobby had a glossy granite floor polished to such perfection it created a mirror image. There were plush chairs and an assortment of lamps that gave the room a warm glow and eliminated the need for fluorescent lighting. A secretary sat at a curved black marble desk. We walked up feeling rather intimidated by the elegant furnishings.

"May I help you?" the secretary asked sarcastically.

I could not figure out why she seemed so annoyed with our appearance. And it was certainly not Japanese custom to interact with guests in such a manner. Obviously, this institution did not get many visitors judging by the pristine condition of the floor.

"Yes. We are here to speak with your security authorities," I stated, pulling out my badge.

She looked at us like we were crazy.

"Okay, it may be a while. Feel free to relax in our waiting area," she said, motioning to the lobby. I could tell that she would have rather had us leave. I sat in a chair and nearly sank down a foot. After about thirty minutes, the secretary told us that we could meet with some of the security officials. We got a key card to go up to the more secure floors of the building for our meeting. Josey pressed the up button and the elevator doors opened to reveal another immaculate space.

"Wow, it's so clean I could do my makeup in here without a mirror," said Josey.

I looked at the walls and saw my reflection staring back at me. There were no fingerprints on a single inch of the brass.

"There is something strange about how unvisited this building is," I said. "I mean, wouldn't you have a few other people and dirt enter on a daily basis?"

I could tell Josey was contemplating that as we rode up in the elevator.

Josey's brows furrowed together, and I could tell she was thinking. "You know, now that you mention it, I haven't seen anyone else besides the secretary the whole time we've been here." Just then, the elevator screeched to a halt. At first, I thought we had reached our destination, but the doors never opened. After realizing we were stuck, I reached for the phone in the elevator only to find it missing.

"Josey," I said in panic. "I think we just walked into a trap. Think about it. There was no one here, the secretary was not friendly, and now we are stuck in an elevator that just happens not to have a phone or emergency button."

I contacted Laurel with my wrist communicator while Josey pried off the wall panel and fiddled with the door wires.

"Laurel just confirmed this building is under the ownership of Simple Computing," I said with wide eyes. "We should have checked it earlier, but it appeared to be a governmental facility. Here I go again, failing to be a field agent."

"Alex, as much as you want to prove yourself, you do have to realize you are new at this. We all make mistakes. I should have been more on my game myself, but there's no time to lose. We have to find a way out of here."

After a brief planning session, we decided to use Josey's laser cutter to make a hatch in the top of the enclosure. Josey cut a square out of the ceiling, and I threw a rope up and snagged the elevator pulley system. We used the rope and climbed up into the dark elevator shaft. There were slits of light we could see from the doors above.

"Let's try to get up to the next level," I whispered.

Josey and I shot our grappling hooks up to the next door and scaled the wall.

"There must be an emergency release lever somewhere..." said Josey.

After fumbling around in the dark, we found the lever and released the door, jumping out just in time to see the elevator come up and nearly flatten us.

"Someone is definitely trying to stop us," I breathed.

Location: (Actually) Spartan HQ _

As I stood up, someone grabbed me from behind just like in Chicago.

"I guess our little desk agent was able to prove himself as more of a field agent than I thought. I never expected you to get this far."

"Who are you and what do you have against us?" I yelled, trying to free myself.

The attacker allowed his Spartan goons keep hold of my wrists and ankles.

"The name's Mac, and I'm motivated by money. Money is what makes the world turn. The more you have the more you can control. One country's leader at a time."

"You are a threat to society, and you will be met with appropriate cost." I retorted.

"I wouldn't be so sure of that," laughed Mac. His goons threw Josey and I into an empty conference room and tied us to some chairs. He also confiscated our wrist communicators.

"We'll be back to question you shortly," said Mac, closing the door as he departed.

"Great, what now?" I asked Josey.

She smiled and clicked her shoes together. A laser emerged. "I always come prepared."

After freeing ourselves, we glanced around the room. There wasn't an easy way out that would not have alerted the Spartans in the hallway.

"We can cut a hole in the window and make our way to another floor," pondered Josey. "I bet there's a payphone somewhere in this building. Many Japanese establishments still have them."

"True, I replied. We could probably find one in the lobby."

Using some braided phone cables in the room, we started to scale down the side of the skyscraper. It was super risky as the cables could have broken at any moment, but they held long enough for us to get to the floor below and break through the window. We then took a different elevator back to the lobby.

"Josey, I need you to distract the secretary while I make a call."

"You've got it." Josey ran over to the desk. "I am so sorry to bother you, but we got lost and weren't able to find the security center."

I slipped over to an alcove with some vending machines and sure enough, a green boxy payphone was attached to the wall. I picked the lock on the vending machine and snagged some coins to pop into the phone. I dialed the number I had memorized.

29

"Kai, it's Alex. We're in a bit of a sticky situation. Any chance you could get someone over to Shinjuku and fast?"

"For you, I can make that happen," his voice replied.

I joined Josey at the desk to keep stalling. The secretary seemed to be losing her patience. "I told you, ma'am, it's floor fifty-five. The desk is right there, I don't know how you missed it."

As we talked, a group of black vehicles pulled up and a bunch of burly men pushed through the door.

"You Alex?" grunted the tallest one.

"Yes," I replied nervously.

"Kai sent us, sounds like you need a little assistance."

The secretary put up her hands as one of the men stayed with her to make sure she didn't alert Mac. We boarded the one working elevator and made our way to the floor where Mac was last seen.

"The police are on the way," the one man alerted me. When the doors opened Mac happened to be right there.

"Hey Mac," I yelled. "Surprise!"

The group easily took down Mac and his bodyguards. The police arrived shortly to arrest Mac and scour the Spartan base.

Location: Tokyo Hospital_

The next day, I sat by Josey in the hospital, and we watched the news which had a huge story on the cult base found in one of Tokyo's main skyscrapers, but none of that seemed to matter. I was more focused on Josey. The previous day's activity had made her even sicker than before.

"Alex, I want to thank you for letting me come on the mission with you. It will be my last mission, and you helped make it the best one ever."

"Thank you," I whispered through my tears.

I was holding Josey's hand, and it suddenly went limp. That was the end.

Location: ICPA HQ_

I returned to Colorado, still feeling down after Josey's funeral. Laurel brought me my mail and a cup of matcha. I managed to smile. As much as everything had ended perfectly in terms of finding the leader of the Spartans, it didn't save Josey. I didn't know why in my mind I thought if I had perfectly completed the mission, it would have somehow saved her, but it didn't. She was gone.

"I think you should read this," Laurel said as she handed me a letter. She patted me on the shoulder as she left.

I read the return address and noticed Josey's name. Tearing open the letter, I began to read.

DEAR ALEX,

YOU HAVE ALWAYS BEEN MY BEST FRIEND SINCE WE BOTH ENTERED THE AGENCY AS ROOKIES. DO YOU REMEMBER WHEN WE FAILED THAT TRAINING COURSE TOGETHER? THAT WAS SO MUCH FUN EVEN THOUGH AMY GAVE US A BAD GRADE. I REMEMBER WHEN WE WENT ON OUR FIRST MISSION TOGETHER IN LA AND NEARLY GOT RAN OVER BY A BUS. ONE OF MY FAVORITE MEMORIES WAS WHEN WE WENT TO FRANCE AND CAUGHT THE ART THIEF. I HOPE YOU WILL REMEMBER OUR MISSIONS TOGETHER. PLEASE DO NOT THINK ABOUT MY DEATH, AS IT WILL ONLY HURT. THINK ABOUT MY LIFE AND THE FUN WE HAD TOGETHER. DON'T STOP LIVING JUST BECAUSE I AM NOT HERE. I WILL ALWAYS BE IN YOUR HEART.

JOSEY

I looked up in bewilderment and tears. How could Josey have written me? I then turned around just in time to see Josey outlined in light with wings and yes, her wrist communicator. A spy angel, I thought to myself with a smile as Josey waved and then disappeared. I would never forget Josey. I took her advice and celebrated her life instead of mourning her death. Josey's lessons in courage continued to help me become a better spy, especially as I started to embark on more field assignments.

MOUNTAINEERING: NEPAL

Location: ICPA HQ_

I sat at my desk working through my usual agency tasks. A few messages from Amy and Laurel about new recruits and a bunch of advertisements filled my screen. I had just finished my mission to Japan where my friend Josey and I caught the leader of the Spartans; he was no longer a threat... or so we thought. Since Josey had passed away, it had been hard for me to come back to work, so I was granted a few months off. During my break, I spent my time in Japan and even bought a vacation home there, keeping the memory of Josey alive in my heart. I was also able to rely on my best friend Yuki for support. I had now started to move forward to the next chapter of my life. As I sat pondering those events, an email appeared in my inbox from Amy. It read:

Dear Sir Alexander,

I have an important new recruit to bring to your attention. She goes by Agent G. I brought her on to assist with the ever-growing threat of the Spartans. Please get acquainted with her, as I am sure you will be working together in the future. Also, I am considering placing you back in the field since your fieldwork was stellar on your last mission. I hope you are starting to feel better now that you are back. We are all here to support you. —Amy

I was glad to hear from Amy, and it was exciting that she would have me work in the field again. I guessed for better or worse the successful mission would further the cross-departmental program; additionally, I had to admit fieldwork was beginning to grow on me since my last mission. The new field agent on the other hand...I had my doubts.

I decided to get started on entering the new spies into the database. I opened the program and typed my username and password. The screen read *invalid*. It seemed odd. The database must have been down, but there wasn't any scheduled maintenance. Laurel would know. I walked into the hall that connected our offices and stopped at a window to see what the weather was like. Still snowy, the mountains looked bleak in the winter storm as flurries spun through the air and dark evergreen trees hunched under the weight of the snow. I arrived at Laurel's desk where she was working on filing spy records.

"Hey Laurel, is the database undergoing an update?"

She set down the mass of papers she held and looked at me with a worried expression.

"Not to my knowledge, but let me check," she said in a rather tense tone.

I could tell something was wrong, especially when Laurel was upset.

"It is," she gasped, "but it shouldn't be."

I thought about what we could do to find out what happened. I ran a code on her computer that only Amy and I knew. The code let us debug the databases and computer systems. The screen read... *Database locked out. Invalid login attempt 20 times.* All the spies knew the password, and none of us would have tried to log in twenty times. "Laurel, someone is trying to hack into our files," I stated as calmly as possible. I knew what question would come next.

"What should we do?"

I knew I needed to lock down the computer system and use our backup server in Nepal as quickly as possible. I ran to the server room and used my keycard to enter. Once inside, I switched off all the systems and flipped a lever to activate the default backup system.

"*Rebooting, please wait,*" came and automated voice.

The system control room lighting turned orange to indicate that we were running on the backup computer system. I ran back to Laurel's office.

"I fixed the problem for now," I said breathlessly.

She made an attempt to smile. "Yes, you fixed that problem, but now all our phones are down; we only have our emergency line and..." she broke off as the lights flickered. "Now we're on backup battery power, great," she finished.

I needed to find Amy, and fast. I ran down the now dim hallways to Amy's office. I burst in and found her rapidly typing on her computer. She looked up quickly when I entered.

"What's going on, Sir Alexander?" she asked with wide eyes.

I hated to be the one to deliver the bad news. "We are on battery power. Our phones are down, and I just switched over our computers to our backup server," I said grimly.

Location: ICPA HQ – Amy's Office_

I could tell Amy was just as worried as I was. I searched my mind for any possible solution when I remembered that we could hack into the Spartan's communication system to retrieve recent messages and phone calls.

"Amy, I know what we can do to get a better idea of what is going on. We need to access the Spartan's communication system."

Amy went to a plant in her office. The plant sat on a table of finished, dark oak with a single light casting a warm glow on the decoration. She pulled the plant toward her, and the wall lifted to reveal her secret laboratory—something only a few spies in the agency knew about. I walked into the laboratory with her. The walls were bright white and computer equipment, flasks, and other spare electronics cluttered the lab tables. Amy stopped in front of a large black box with a phone attachment. We had set up that piece of equipment to hack into the Spartan's computer and communication systems. Amy slowly lifted the phone and a computer monitor nearby lit up to reveal messages and audio recordings.

"The Spartans are becoming more sophisticated, they've encrypted some of their messages," Amy said.

Sure enough, there were a series of messages that appeared in random symbols with the words *encrypted*. I knew just what to do. Scanning the document, I uploaded the private encryption key we had stolen from a Spartan base. Once I uploaded the key, the file read in English. All the parts that could not be decrypted showed up in random letters. Amy and I quickly started to read the transmission.

AGENT, WE ARE SENDING YOU TO THE ICPA'S BASE IN THE ROCKY MOUNTAINS. WEARING THE DISGUISE OF A SPY, WE NEED YOU TO SHUT DOWN AS MUCH OF THE AGENCY AS POSSIBLE. FIRST THE COMPUTERS AND PHONES, THEN SEE IF YOU CAN GET RID OF THE POWER. WE KNOW THAT THE ICPA IS PREPARED FOR ANYTHING, SO DO YOUR BEST.

Amy and I glanced at each other. I could tell from the look on her face that she was clearly concerned.

"Amy, we need to put the base in lockdown."

Amy walked to a door inside the lab and scanned her fingerprint. The door swished open to a room with a red button. Pressing the button, Amy put the base into lockdown. The lights turned amber to indicate the emergency. All the spies in the agency knew exactly what to do, which would make the intruder stand out by comparison. Soon after Amy and I had initiated the lockdown, our security system identified an unknown "object" in one of the hallways. Amy pressed a button on her wrist communicator and a hologram flickered to life unveiling the location of our intruder.

"He is in hall 127," I stated, even though it was obvious.

We rushed to the area where the intruder was last spotted and found him trying to pry open a window.

"Not the best way to escape. I would use the door instead," Amy joked.

The Spartan jerked around so fast he almost fell over. Amy quickly shot him with sleeping spray, and the Spartan fell over in exhaustion almost instantly.

Location: ICPA HQ — Interrogation Office_

We had taken our intruder to the interrogation chamber where he sat ready to answer our questions. When he awoke, he was still a little groggy.

Amy asked, "Who sent you here?"

Without thinking, he looked at her like she should have already known and said, "Mac, of course. Who'd you think sent me?"

He didn't catch himself in time; we now knew Mac was not where we thought he was. Our intruder was starting to come to his senses and noticed that he was not in a Spartan base, but we had already prepared for this situation. Our latest addition to the sleeping spray was an aftereffect that made the person forget where they were temporarily so we could get them to tell the truth.

"Where am I?" the Spartan asked.

Amy and I smiled at each other. "You're in the Spartan base at Tokyo Haneda Airport," Amy said.

Our intruder smiled with relief and recapped the whole story that we had just witnessed.

"Really? That sounds awful," Amy acted.

He giggled for no apparent reason. After a series of questions, Amy and I made our way back to the offices. I was worried that this whole situation would come back at me. Gossip would fly around the agency about how I hadn't taken proper precautions when choosing the location for Mac's imprisonment, or that I hadn't adequately informed the officials holding him of how dangerous he could be.

"Sir Alexander, this isn't good. Mac has broken out of captivity and is now leading the Spartans once more," Amy sighed. "You caught Mac once; would you be willing to do it again? I mean, you've got the experience."

I was surprised Amy was so ready for me to go back into the field. Thankfully she hadn't placed the blame on me. I wasn't so sure what the rest of the field agent department would say. I could already imagine them talking about how none of this would have happened if we had sent a "real" field agent. I thought about this for a while and dove into a flash back of when Josey and I had caught Mac the first time. Mac was a scary person; he was tough, always dressed in black, and just had this air of negative energy around him.

"I guess I can do that," I said still wondering if I really could or not.

I could tell Amy was really counting on me, so I didn't want to let her down, and to be honest, I didn't want to let myself down either.

Location: ICPA HQ - Amy's Office_

The next thing I knew, I found myself sitting in Amy's office for a briefing on my next mission.

"We've located Mac in Nepal," Amy said, deep in thought.

I worried to myself about the fact that our science labs and remote servers were located there. We hadn't been able to switch back to our default computer system yet and the last thing we needed was a problem with the backup too. Amy must have seen my face because she added a few words of encouragement.

"I'm sure the servers are fine," she said almost too fast.

I hoped they were too. Then a thought wedged its way to the front of my mind. If I was going into the mountains of Nepal, I would need a new wardrobe considering I did not have any heavy winter spy gear.

"Amy, I need a new outfit," I said.

That was where the amazing Double J came into the plan.

Location: ICPA HQ - Agent Double J's Design Studio_

I made my way to the west wing of the building where I knew Agent Double J awaited my arrival. Nobody needed to know exactly where the clothing and outfit department was; the spies simply said you would know where it was when you got there. I saw what they meant. Although I was close with the head agent of the clothing and gear department since we often planned what gear and outfits spies would need for missions, this was my first excursion to her office.

After walking along the white futuristic hallway and passing door after door, there was an alcove with amber lighting. Two cylindrical lamps sat on either side of the curved chrome door. It was quite the entrance. I walked up to the door feeling rather intimidated. I scanned my fingerprint and the chrome panels slid open.

Once inside, I felt like I was certainly not in an office. I felt as if I had been transported to another world. Everything was a tan alabaster color with dusty pink accents, and low lighting illuminated the space. A curved staircase on the right led to another floor. The curvature of the stairs surrounded a pink chaise lounge crowded with an assortment of pillows. Directly in front of me was a foyer with a mural of the Rocky Mountains at sunrise painted in pastel pinks. A crystal chandelier hung above tying the whole extravagant space together. I knew when Agent Double J was coming before I even saw her, because I heard her heels click on the rosy, marble floor.

"Sir Alexander, so good to see you again," she trilled.

I stared at the space in awe. "Wow, you have quite the abode here."

She glanced around the matching interior and chuckled, patting me on the shoulder. "I couldn't sit in an office all day like you do. So, what kind of outfit are we looking for?"

"Something Nepal style," I said.

She smiled and led me through the foyer to the entrance of the outfitting room. After a few more security procedures, the glass doors separating the space from the rest of the suite glided open. I looked around when we entered. Mannequins stood in transparent cases modeling clothing and bolts of fabric sat organized by color on the back wall. In front of us was a table with various patterns. Agent Double J was responsible for creating outfits and gear for spies across the agency for various missions. Her unique abilities with fabric science allowed her to create fabrics that covered a multitude of situations helping spies stay safe and fashionable at the same time.

"I would like something in the color purple," I said, "After all, purple is my favorite color."

Agent Double J walked over to the bolts of fabric and then turned around. "Purple will be far too noticeable in the snow. Thankfully, I have created a fabric that can change colors, in your case from purple to white, with the touch of a button."

She was too good; we measured my height, waist, and arm span for the new attire. After we finished, Agent Double J let me try on my tailored outfit. A plum purple, tightfitting coat covered my top half. The coat had chrome-plated rings around the upper part of the sleeves. My snow pants were black with matching purple stripes down the sides, and the boots were black with purple laces.

"I *love* it," I exclaimed.

"Oh, and don't just judge a book by its cover," Agent Double J said, "This outfit has a few tricks up its sleeve. If you press the button on the wrist the outfit will change from purple and black to white with cream-colored accents to help you easily blend into the snow surroundings of Nepal. It's also fire, acid, heat, cold, bullet, and radiation proof. Oh, and it will not fade or change in composition if you end up in a situation with any of the things I listed."

"It's perfect. Looks like I'm ready for my mission."

Location: Denver Apartment_

That night, I dreamt of Mac. I was trying to reach for Josey as she slipped away into darkness, but Mac stopped me. I couldn't get to her as she slid away. Next, he turned to me and drew a knife. I woke up in a cold sweat gasping for air.

Pushing open my curtains, I gazed over the glittering Denver skyline. The clock read three in the morning. My primary residence was in one of the city's premier luxury apartments. I could hardly afford it alongside my apartment in Japan, but there was something about having a nice place to live that was very important to me. Thank goodness the agency provided travel allowance for the chartered flights to Aspen.

I wandered over to the kitchen and poured myself a glass of water. My cat Maru hopped off his tower, thinking it was time to get up. He was a Siberian Forest cat, the only kind of cat I could have with my allergies. Popping a few sleeping pills would hopefully get me some rest. Of course, I didn't take any hard-core sleeping medications, just the over-the-counter stuff.

Maru snuggled up next to me on the bed and I watched the skyline a bit more while thinking of Josey. My heart hurt whenever I thought about her despite knowing she was happy and finally at rest. I finally felt myself slipping back into the realm of the unconscious.

Location: Apartment & ICPA HQ - Jet Hangar_

The next day, I woke up to the sun streaming through my window since I had forgotten to close the curtains. I opened my refrigerator to find it almost empty. I didn't often come down to stay in my apartment. Even though there were chartered flights for those of us that lived in the city, it was often easier to use the agency provided sleeping quarters and just stay up in Aspen during the week. Scraping together the little food I had, I finished my breakfast in no time. After a quick thirty-minute flight, I found myself walking up to the agency headquarters.

It was the day I was actually going on my mission. I wondered what adventures awaited. Amy had told me she was bringing on some help, including the new field agent. I wasn't very enthused to have to bring another field agent with us on the trip. Agent G was probably someone with all brawn and no brains. I walked to the briefing room, running into Kai on the way. He wished me well with a high-five.

"Another field mission I see - impressive."

I gave him a thumbs up and quickly made my way to the meeting space. Once I entered, three other spies as well as Amy greeted me.

"As I mentioned, I thought you might need a little help on this mission, not because you can't handle yourself, but to help keep everyone safe," Amy said.

Even though I was a bit apprehensive about the field agent situation, I was still excited to meet my team for the mission. Amy had informed me that this would be my field team going forward on any other future assignments as well.

First was Bruce. He was the jet pilot, a hybrid position between field and desk agent. Our extraction team needed to be both tough and smart to effectively get agents to and from places safely. Bruce seemed to be a rough, burly guy with a soft heart. He had a close-cut beard, shaved head, and wore all black with dark shaded glasses. Very much the typical secret-service look. I could tell his type right away and I was relieved that under his façade he seemed to be kind. I had heard many things about Bruce in the agency. He was one of the most skilled pilots and was rumored to have performed one of the riskiest extraction operations the agency had ever accomplished.

Next was Veronica our desk agent. She was very stately, and I knew she liked everything just so since we already worked together, and I had helped train her in the desk agent department. I was excited to have a skilled and organized desk agent to assist us on the mission. She was tall with long black hair and always dressed fashionably. Today, she had her hair pinned up in a bun with large, silver hoop earrings. Her black pencil skirt contrasted with her silver bracelets that clinked together as she typed away on her laptop.

Last was Agent G. I was shocked. Instead of a bulky field agent bro, she was a woman. She was tall, thin, and very in shape. Even though she had a smaller frame, I was positive she could outdo any of the field agent guys when it came to physical training tests. Unlike my other two counterparts she was joining this mission on special assignment from the defense department in case we needed extra protection.

I could tell she was outgoing and ready to get started before we had even finished the briefing. Agent G had a fun personality and had already made us laugh a few times throughout the meeting. Within the agency the field agents were known to be funny, bold, and carefree while the desk agents were often considered more serious and cautious, but of course those were only stereotypes.

"All right, now for the mission," Amy said solemnly. "Sir Alexander, Bruce will get you to the drop point at Tribhuvan International Airport. It's your job to blend in and find any information you can. Agent G, you will parachute into the mountains and check on our backup computer servers. Veronica, it's your job to get them where they need to be and quickly while relaying any important information."

So, we were off. My team and I boarded the jet and prepared for takeoff. It was an amazing sight. Our hangar had been built into the top of the mountain which housed our base. We started to move toward the wall, and it slid apart letting in snow and wind.

"Hold on guys, this is going to be a bumpy takeoff," Bruce yelled over the intercom.

We braced ourselves, Bruce got on the runway, we sped ahead and lifted off the ground. After we made it out of the hangar, I looked back to see a hole in the side of the mountain close and disappear.

"Everyone, may I have your attention please," said Veronica. "Agent G will be parachuting into the mountains of Nepal first, then I'll drop off Sir Alexander at the airport."

"Perfect," I said.

It was great to be able to take an ICPA jet whenever we were able since the jets were equipped with many amenities. This particular jet had a meeting room where we could hold briefings as well as sleeping quarters that were able to house everyone on board. The main meeting room in the jet was lined with plush white couches and mauve throw pillows. A fold-away table could be placed in the middle of the room when needed and small vases of flowers sat on side tables at the ends of the room. On the limited wall space there were abstract pieces of art.

"Since we have a sixteen-hour flight, I think I'll take a rest," I said to the crew.

Entering my quarters, I was pleased to see that although they were small, they were certainly comfortable. A bed sat to my right and a small chair and desk sat to the left with windows overlooking the clouds and sky. Activating the curtains, the room became dim, and I laid down to doze off. I was awoken by Bruce's voice on the intercom again.

"Veronica, we are nearing the drop zone. Please prepare the agents."

I walked into the main area where Veronica was preparing Agent G's gear. She and I helped Agent G into her outfit, and she performed an equipment check. Veronica went to the airlock space in the plane and opened it. After securing Agent G inside, she activated the outer door. Agent G gracefully jumped out of the plane without any indication of fear.

"I couldn't do that," I said, looking over to Veronica.

She nodded her head in agreement. After closing the door, we both sat together at the briefing table and awaited our landing at Tribhuvan International Airport.

"Agent G to plane," came a voice over our radio system.

Veronica and I ran to the radio.

"This is plane, we acknowledge you," Veronica spoke into the transmitter.

There was a pause and both of us did not know what to think; something strange was going on. Then the system crackled to life again.

"I was just heading up the mountain when I spotted some sort of base. It appears to be some kind of covert facility. I'm sending you my location. I'll go and investigate to see what I can find. Agent G out."

The line went dead. Veronica and I looked at a computer screen with a digital map of Nepal. A red dot appeared where Agent G had marked the mysterious facility. Soon after, we landed at Tribhuvan International Airport. I stepped off the plane in the stylish outfit Double J had made me. Making my way through the terminal, I eventually found myself outside. I wondered where to start. I called Veronica on my wrist communicator.

"Sir Alexander, to Veronica. Where is a good place to find a Spartan?"

"The café down the street should be a good place to start. We believe it's a base of theirs, and we have reports from locals indicating that many red-clad individuals frequent the location."

"All right, thanks. Sir Alexander out."

I made my way down the beautiful streets of Nepal. It was a mixture of old and new architecture. Massive stone buildings stood right next to newer, wooden ones. I found the café and stepped inside. It was cozy with red accents. Not surprisingly, there was also a glut of red-coated people. I ordered a drink and sat at a table where I could catch some of the conversation.

"Do you think the ICPA has caught on to us again?" asked a Spartan.

I perked up my ears; they were talking about our agency. They certainly weren't being very careful discussing such matters in public.

"Yes, the other day one of the rookies broke in, but they caught him and somehow got him to tell them about Mac's escape," another Spartan replied. I pressed the button on my wrist communicator to mark the café as a base. Someone must have caught the radio signals and knew they were from the ICPA.

"Did you detect that?" a Spartan asked.

The others nodded and the group scanned the restaurant.

"If only I was dressed in red like them," I muttered under my breath.

I looked around for an escape, but there did not appear to be any other way out. Just then my shirt beeped, and an electronic voice came through my earpiece.

"*Acknowledged, clothing color scheme detected.*"

My coat, pants, and boots turned red like the Spartans. I realized my clothing had more than just two color options. The Spartans continued to search, until one pointed at me.

"That one over there isn't dressed like the rest of us. Look at his coat. Far too stylish for our outfit guidelines."

I got up and ran out the door.

"Match surroundings," I gasped when I was outside.

My coat, pants, and boots turned grey and brown. The Spartans, still looking for a red-coated figure, lost me in the crowd.

Location: The Streets of Nepal_

I realized I wouldn't be able to find any more information from the café, it was time for a new lead. I decided to find the hotel down the street where Veronica had discovered that the Spartans were having a conference.

"Hey Veronica, I think I will try to get into the conference at that hotel," I said, speaking into my wrist communicator.

"Roger that. We'll meet you at the International Steak House down the street. Veronica out."

I made my way to the International Steak House. Our bases disguised as businesses generally started with "international." Patrons thought nothing of it, but it helped ICPA agents locate safe havens around the world. The base was just a few blocks away from the hotel. At these bases, there were rooms for the spies on missions among other amenities.

I entered the restaurant and made my way into the kitchen. There was a small cleaning closet in the back of the room. I opened the door to find a bunch of mops, brooms, and a vacuum. I realized I forgot to scan my card. Scanning my card, the closet's contents slid aside to reveal an elevator. I stepped inside and pressed the only button. The elevator went up so fast I nearly fell over. When the doors opened, I found myself in the upper level of the restaurant, which had been converted into a base. I spotted Veronica and Bruce at a table in the corner.

"Hey, guys," I said.

They both looked up from their papers and smiled.

"We hear you want to sneak into a Spartan conference. Double J was kind enough to send you a disguise." Bruce said as he held up a package.

We opened the package to find an exact replica of a Spartan's gear.

"Wow, that was fast," I said.

Veronica went on to explain how they had it airmailed to them through the large network of ICPA transportation equipment allowing it to arrive in almost no time.

I started to put on the gear and noticed that the tag read fire and bulletproof. I was glad she added those features to this outfit too. "How do I look?" I asked.

Veronica and Bruce stepped back and smiled. "Like a Spartan," Veronica stated plainly as she took a picture with her phone. "I am sending a picture to Laurel. She is going to get a kick out of this."

Location: Nepal – Spartan Conference_

After dressing, I rode down another elevator, which dropped me off in an alley behind the base. I walked to the hotel and sat in the lobby. After waiting for a while, other Spartans started to show up and make their way to the conference room. Following their lead, I walked into the event space, and who but Mac sat at the head of the table.

"Yo, Jeff," Mac yelled to another Spartan.

They all were all so interested in seeing each other and catching up they didn't seem to notice me. After a while, they took their seats, and I sat as well. The meeting began.

"So here I am, safe and sound," laughed Mac.

All the Spartans cheered. One of the Spartans from the restaurant earlier stood up to announce new developments. "Mac, I believe that the ICPA is after you again. We met one of their agents in our base today. They got away before we could catch them."

"Who do you believe it was?" asked Mac.

The Spartans looked at each other and shrugged.

"I bet they're here to find me and check on their backup servers," said Mac. "They will not get away this time. I'll capture them all, and no one will know about our next plan."

The meeting ended without any other interesting or helpful leads. I ran back to the International Steak House. Once I was safe inside, I threw off the Spartan gear and relayed the information to my fellow spies.

"That's disturbing; I don't know what to think," said Veronica. We went over possible plans of how to catch Mac, and we all agreed that I should accompany Agent G in the mountains to catch him. Veronica sent Agent G the coordinates for our rendezvous. We all decided to go to bed early to prepare for the next day.

Location: The Himalayas_

I woke early and put on my snow gear from Agent Double J. It was time to meet up with the others. I walked into the lobby to find them ready to go.

"We're going to fly you up to the mountains, Sir Alexander," said Bruce.

He was such a nice guy; I could have driven myself, but Bruce was set on flying me at least halfway up. We drove to Tribhuvan International Airport and boarded our jet. After about ten minutes, we were over the drop zone where Agent G was supposed to meet us.

"We guessed that you'd rather not parachute so we have a jet pack for you," said Veronica.

"Thanks, you know me well," I said, shrugging the straps over my shoulders. "This is a lot heavier than I expected."

I stepped into the airlock and jumped after the outer door opened. I hated free falling, so I turned on the jet pack and gently landed. It was a bit too thrilling for me even with the assistance of the jetpack. I set off on snowshoes up the mountain. I trudged along and eventually made it to the rendezvous coordinates, but Agent G was nowhere to be found. I was a bit early, so I wasn't too worried. The terrain was difficult to traverse. Perhaps she was just running a bit behind schedule. After waiting for a while longer Agent G still had not shown up. I paged Veronica. "Any information on Agent G's location?" I asked.

"I can't make contact with her, but she appears to be nearby. I'm sending you her exact location now."

I wondered if Agent G was in some sort of trouble. Perhaps she had fallen into a crevasse or ended up in an altercation with the local wildlife. In any case she wasn't too far away, so I made my way to the coordinates Veronica sent. I started to get a bad feeling when I could see buildings in the distance. As I approached, a plane swopped down and shot at me. I found out that my coat was *very* bulletproof, because it deflected each bullet.

I quickly changed the color of my suit to white and the plane stopped shooting. I knew that they couldn't see me from that altitude. I flipped off my snowshoes and snuck up to the main gate of the building in front of me. It must have been part of the facility Agent G had mentioned earlier. I couldn't tell whom it belonged to from the outside. While the plane firing at me could signify the Spartans, it could also have been some sort of secure government facility judging from the bunker style architecture.

The gate had a computer screen with a code pad on it. With my computer skills, I successfully hacked the system and the gate opened. Once inside the courtyard area, I made my way up to the main door. It was clear I couldn't go through the main entrance. I looked to the right to see an air vent. I pulled out a screwdriver and pried off the panel. The vent was far too small for me. I needed to find another way in.

I scanned the building with my wrist communicator, and it revealed a main hallway. To get in I would need access to the roof. Luckily, there was a maintenance ladder on the side of the structure. I nimbly climbed onto the roof. I tried to picture where the hall would be and pulled out a special blade. Making a hole in the roof, I quickly jumped through. I landed inside along with a bunch of snow. A dark hall loomed before me. Using my holo-map, I found the room where Agent G was located.

"And who might you be?" came a voice.

I turned to find a patrol. He pressed a button on his arm that made the alarm system go into frenzy. I threw on a pair of sound canceling earphones and ran to find Agent G.

Location: Nepal - Remote facility_

It was hard to navigate the building due to its gloomy hallways. I ran into walls several times. Right when my wrist communicator indicated I was near Agent G; I ran into what I thought was another wall. Instead of a wall, it turned out to be a person, Mac. He tied my arms behind me so fast, I could not escape. I realized I had been lured into a trap.

"You won't be needing this," he smirked, swiping my wrist communicator.

I was now without any means of communication, besides writing notes, which would not be easy considering my hands were bound behind my back.

"Looking for Agent G?" he asked laughing. "A poor decision on your part. Now both of you are in my custody and nobody is coming to save you."

"I would not be so sure of that," I hissed.

Mac barely glanced at me. I wished there was something I could do, but Mac was so strong, I could not break free, and my words had no effect on him.

"You know, you've come a long way since you last caught me. I remember very clearly you and your friend calling for help and backup, but not this time. You came on your own to confront me," Mac rambled.

"I did not come to see you; I came to save my friend," I said.

Mac looked like he was getting tired of talking, and I must say I was not the best audience for him.

"Enough stalling, now you get to see your friend again," Mac jeered.

Two of his men came and dragged me down the hall to a small room where Agent G sat tied to a chair. She was unharmed which was good in one sense, but on the other hand I knew that meant they had questioned her or would shortly.

"Sir Alexander, I'm so sorry I led you into a trap," Agent G sobbed.

The Spartans tied me to a chair next to Agent G's, and then left, locking the door behind them. I looked around the room for an escape but there was none.

"Okay, first we need to get out of these ropes."

Agent G looked at me sadly and shook her head.

"It's no use, Sir Alexander, they are far too strong, and even if we did escape there's no way to get out of the room."

I would not give up. No matter what, we were escaping that trap. I had the determination to do it. I just had to think more like a field agent. That was the trick.

"Agent G, when I worked with Josey, we would get into all sorts of sticky situations. I remember one time we were stuck in a completely metal room with no air supply, and we still found a way out. If we could survive that, you and I can survive this."

Hope flooded back into Agent G's face. "Okay, let's come up with a plan."

The plan turned out to be more complicated than I expected. The first objective was to get out of the chairs.

As I sat pondering, I noticed a blinking light. The light was coming from Agent G. "Agent G, you still have your wrist communicator. They didn't destroy it."

She looked down at her arm to see it in perfect condition. "I guess you're right, and it still works unlike yours. I hadn't noticed since I was panicking."

Because of the angle of our chairs, Agent G was able to use her wrist communicator laser to cut one of my ropes. She cut the right one because it unraveled all my restraints. I then removed her wrist communicator and used it to free her as well.

"Now, to get out of the room," Agent G stated puzzled.

I looked around... the door was not going to work, because there were guards on either side in the hallway. As I was looking around a draft of air hit my back. I looked up to see a large vent.

"I found a way out," I announced. "I can't believe they fell for the oldest trick in the book. Who leaves an air vent that large in a detention cell?"

Agent G pulled off a bracket from the folding chair in the room and we used it to take off the vent.

"There's only one problem. My wrist communicator detects a laser net over the opening," Agent G said in despair.

"Don't worry, I think I can buy us some time. You see when Mac caught me, he took my wrist communicator. Every one of our communication devices can be remotely self-destructed. When I destroy it, Mac will call his men for assistance. We will have enough time to get through the vent while they are busy helping him and cleaning up." With Agent G's wrist communicator, I activated mine as a small bomb.

"*The remote device will destruct in 5...4...3...2...1,*" an automated voice announced.

We heard an explosion and many urgent footsteps. Agent G and I slid into the ventilation system.

"Quick disarm the security system," Agent G whispered.

"I'm trying," I found the wires to the lasers and mixed them up causing the system to deactivate. "Call Bruce and Veronica for help," I whispered.

Agent G quickly activated her SOS beacon. Both she and I made our way along the ventilation system. Every so many yards, light came from a vent, but none were daylight. After a while, we approached a vent from which we could hear yelling. Agent G and I peered down into a big office. Black leather chairs sat on a white wool carpet, and abstract stone sculptures lurked in the dim lighting around the room. We knew where we were right away. Mac's office. We scanned the room and found Mac yelling at a Spartan standing by a now destroyed control panel.

"What were you thinking?" Mac yelled. "Most of the wrist communicators are bombs, and now look, we can't see our prisoners because the explosion destroyed the screen for the security camera."

Agent G and I looked at each other in question. There was a security camera? Good thing we escaped while they weren't watching. Just then, a Spartan ran into Mac's office.

"Boss, the prisoners have escaped," the visitor stammered.

Mac stopped yelling for a second to comprehend this statement, and then he started to yell again. During the commotion, Agent G and I slipped past the air vent. After we made our way a little further in the ventilation system, we heard a metal clanging sound and voices.

"They're onto us," breathed Agent G. A few Spartans had entered the ventilation system.

"What do we do?" I questioned in a panic.

Agent G scanned the walls and found an opening not too far from us, but there was no time to get there. She used her laser to cut a hole in the roof. Agent G and I jumped up on top of the building.

"Look, there's Bruce and Veronica," I shouted.

A helicopter hovered overhead and dropped down a ladder that Agent G and I grabbed onto. We were then pulled away from the Spartan base. Luckily, I had on my bulletproof coat because a few bullets hit me as we flew away.

Location: Nepal – International Steakhouse_

We arrived back at the International Steak House in no time. Bruce, Veronica, Agent G, and I sat around a table with cups of warm tea.

"We have to capture Mac. With him on the loose, we'll keep running into more trouble," Agent G said.

Everyone agreed, but the question we all had was how? In a few hours we came up with the perfect plan. My job was to start the chain of events by paging Veronica on an unencrypted channel that the Spartans were clearly monitoring

"Hi Veronica. I just wanted to let you know that all our servers are secure, and Agent G is just leaving Base 21. Have a nice day."

During my conversation, Agent G was in the mountains waiting there as bait to draw in the Spartans. I heard a click on the radio channel and knew that the Spartans were listening in. Our chain reaction was starting. I ran to the plane where Bruce and Veronica were waiting.

"Ready!" I yelled.

We took off quickly, I looked below to see a squad of police cars headed for the mountains. Everything was going as planned. Once we were in the mountains, we released three police officers on parachute. Now all I had to do was watch the scene unfold. I saw Agent G's figure in the snow; she looked like a small black dot from the altitude we were at. A little way down the mountain was a group of black dots, the police. I also noticed a bunch of red dots advancing toward Agent G. When the Spartans had almost reached Agent G, all the police charged them and then there was a big blob of red and black dots as seen from above. It was not long before Agent G jet packed to the plane, and we flew off to let the police deal with the rest.

As Bruce flew the plane back toward the airport, we all let out a collective sigh of relief.

"Nice work team," I said to everyone. "It feels great to have completed our first successful mission!"

Location: ICPA HQ_

The next day, we all sat back at the ICPA's base in Colorado. Bruce and Veronica were joking about something, and Agent G was retelling the story of our escape to Amy. I sat and just took in the moment when my fellow spies and I could relax and just share stories.

"You did it again, Sir Alexander," complimented Amy.

I knew that this would not be my last mission; it would not be long before the Spartans would act up again. After all the excitement it was time for another vacation. Amy graciously approved my request and I set off for what I hoped would be a relaxing time at my vacation apartment in Japan. As I packed my suitcase, I thought about the fact that maybe I had what it would take to be a field agent, just maybe.

DECEPTION UNDER THE SURFACE: SPAIN

Location: Tokyo, Japan – Vacation Apartment_

I gazed over the Tokyo skyline while working on my laptop. I was enjoying spending some time at my new vacation home in Japan. Yuki had helped me find an apartment in the Shinjuku area famous for its restaurants, nightlife, and being a business center. I also liked how convenient everything was compared to living in America. All I had to do was step outside and there was a wealth of things do, plus my apartment was not far from the Yamanote train line so getting anywhere was a breeze. After my previous mission, I was exhausted. Nepal was a cold place, and it was good to be back where the weather was more temperate. As I sat considering whether I would go to meet a friend for coffee, my phone rang. I looked at the caller ID and noticed it was Amy.

"Hey, Amy," I chirped, trying to mask the concern in my voice.

"Hi, Sir Alexander. I'm so sorry to bother you on vacation, but the Spartans just invaded one of our sister organizations in Santander Spain. It appears Mac was able to outsmart the local authorities in Nepal where we had him arrested. You are one of our few Spanish speaking agents so..."

It was the end of my vacation. I started packing the second I heard the word "Spartans."

"I'm on my way, Amy." I hung up.

To be honest, I still wasn't confident in the field and the thought of having to travel to Spain on a mission didn't really appeal to me at the moment. I looked around my apartment; it was a small two-room abode with a modest kitchen. The apartment was on the thirty-second floor of a skyscraper. I paid a small fortune to have a good view, but it was worth waking up to the skyline through the floor-to-ceiling windows each morning.

I didn't know how long I would be gone. My plants would need to be watered; the mail would pile up, and, of course, my cat Maru would need to be fed. I decided to go next door to ask Yuki if I could drop off Maru and the plants at her place for a bit.

Location: Yuki's Apartment_

Yuki was kind enough to help me out whenever I went on missions and when I was working in America. I caught a taxi to her building in Minato. Once inside, I pressed her doorbell.

"One sec, Alex, I'll be right there," she called from inside. When she opened the door, she had brought some Pino. She gave me a box before I even asked if I could have some.

"You know me too well." I laughed.

She smiled and motioned me in.

"Yuki, would you be willing to take care of Maru and my plants for about a week? I have a business trip to Spain, so I won't be able to bring anything with me."

"No worries. I'll take care of Maru, your plants, and mail." She laughed.

After we got caught up and I had given Yuki my spare key, I returned to my apartment and booked a flight. Afterward, I took the elevator thirty-two floors down to the lobby.

Outside the glass doors, the hustle and bustle of people milled about. I took a deep breath and walked outside. The weather was nice, and it seemed to be a great day to fly. I caught another taxi and started off to Haneda Airport. I sighed, thinking of the 650-yen base fare. Super expensive, but sometimes one didn't have a choice.

After about fifteen minutes, I noticed a red car had been following my cab the entire time. I ducked and told the driver to drop me off a little before the airport entrance.

When we arrived, I slipped into a nearby crowd of people. I watched, and, to my relief, it was not a Spartan who stepped out of the red car.

I entered the airport, checked in, and got through security with no problems. While I waited, I gave Kai a call.

"Hey there, I'm headed back into the field yet again if you can believe it," I said this time allowing my frustration to show a bit more than on my call with Amy.

"Alex, don't be discouraged. Just like it took you practice mastering all of the training we did in class, it is going to take practice to become a better and better field agent. I'm sure Amy is sending you because she has faith you can do it," he replied through the phone.

Chatting with Kai helped the time pass and before I knew it, I was boarding the plane. The flight to Spain was long, but uneventful.

Location: The Streets of Santander

When the plane landed, I walked out into the local airport. After changing flights, the airport in Santander felt miniscule by comparison to the one in Madrid. I waited for my bag to come out and stepped out into the warm humid air.

Waiting for a taxi, I paged Amy on my wrist communicator. "So, where am I off to?" I inquired.

"You will need catch a taxi to Santander Bank; the agency is housed in the upper levels of the building. The doors will probably be closed and locked because I am positive the Spartans are holding the agents hostage." I cringed, knowing this was not the kind of mission I was up to at the moment. "Also, I think you are not ready to do this alone so contact Laurel and see what agents are nearby to help."

I paged Laurel to see if she could find me any information on a possible partner. "Hey, Laurel, do you know of any agents in Spain?" I inquired.

"Sure do, I've marked them on your map."

I looked at a holo-map of Spain. There were two pinpointed places, one close to me and the other about 100 miles away. Choosing the closer target, I headed off.

Location: Agent Double J's Clothing Shop_

I called a taxi and gave them the location I had found from my wrist communicator. He sped along the seaside into the more populated area of the city. It was a beautiful day and driving right alongside the ocean was calming. There wasn't much to obscure the view so I could see all the way to the horizon. Houses with red clay tile roofs were perched on the hillside.

After a short ten-minute ride, we pulled up to a clothing shop – one that sold some of Spain's finest clothing, in fact. The store was on the main street in the bay area. Restaurants sat out on the pier and shops in colonial buildings made of stone with iron embellishments ran along the other side of the street. Looking at the store's sign, I recognized the brand right away; it was one of Agent Double J's boutiques. I quickly made my way inside. Mannequins stood around, modeling elegant pieces. Each masterpiece had a single spotlight on it.

I wandered through the store for a while and acted like I was shopping until I saw Agent Double J. She recognized me right away and ran over.

"Welcome to Spain!" She smiled. "What luck that I was here for a showcase and not back in Colorado at the base." Her smile faded, as she could tell I was not here on vacation.

"Agent Double J, we have a situation. There's a group of our colleagues being held hostage in the bank down the street."

Agent Double J did not hesitate to help; she got her manager to run the store while she would be gone. Then she got on her spy gear.

"Okay, I'm ready," she said.

Location: The Streets of Santander_

We walked down the street, breathing in the seaside air. We passed a small ice-cream shop on the way. The shop doors were propped open, and one could easily see all of the delicious flavors for sale.

"It's hard to believe anything could be wrong; everything is so calm and beautiful," I said. "We are totally stopping by that ice-cream shop after we are done with everything."

Agent Double Jay laughed.

We arrived at the bank. The building was at an intersection and took up most of the block. The main entrance was directly on the corner surrounded by ornate stonework. An ATM had been retrofitted in the much more traditional looking building and looked rather out of place with the more historic architecture.

"I wonder what they have set up in the lobby. I mean, they can't say they're closed today. If we disguise ourselves as regular customers, maybe we could find a way in," I pondered.

Agent Double J pulled out a stylish handbag and two wigs and outfits. We slipped into an alleyway to change. I pulled on the dress shirt khakis, and leather shoes over my gear and popped on the wig. Agent Double J sported a sundress with sandals.

"I think we look local enough to fit in," I said.

Location: Bank (ICPA Sister Organization) _

I nodded and held my breath as we opened the heavy wooden front doors. To our surprise, the bank was still in full operation. Spartans stood at the teller booths, and elevator music drifted through the lobby. Agent Double J and I walked across the white and green tiled floors up to a bronze clad teller booth. I pulled out a fake check and asked if I could get a few euros.

"Of course," said the Spartan. He cashed the check and gave me the euros I had asked for.

It was certainly the most civil I had ever seen one of them. So, the Spartans were operating the bank so it would not look suspicious. Agent Double J and I sat in the lobby and counted our euros as we whispered.

"Do you see a way we could get into the back?" I asked.

Agent Double Jay pulled up a map of the building on her phone. "It looks like we could cut through the wall over there."

I looked at the wall about fifteen feet away. I pulled a purple detonator out of my pocket and pressed a small button on it. The detonator flashed for a second as I rolled it across the floor.

"Hold your breath." I muttered as the detonator clinked onto the polished marble.

The detonator made a small clicking noise, and the room grew dense with purple fog. I heard the Spartans pass out. Agent Double J and I ran over to the wall and cut through it with our lasers. We hid behind a plant in the next room.

"What was that?" a voice yelled.

A Spartan walked around the corner and glanced over. He saw the hole in the wall and purple smoke. "ICPA," he mumbled.

Location: Alleyway_

Agent Double J and I darted around the corner into a small corridor. The hall led up some stairs to an outdoor breezeway with beautiful archways and flower baskets. I peeked over the edge and saw movement through a window on the third story. It was our fellow spies being held captive.

"Up there," I jerked my head toward the window.

Agent Double J looked up to the window and nodded. She launched a grappling hook up above the window, and it lodged its pointy metal tines in the stone wall. We held onto the cord and swung over the alleyway. I almost got hit in the head with some laundry hanging in the breeze. We swung back and forth letting out the line until we were just below the window we needed to enter.

"My arms are killing me. Could you hurry up?" I complained.

"One sec," Agent Double J whispered.

We scaled the wall. When we were close to the window, I threw a small tool and the glass shattered into glittering pieces.

Location: Bank (ICPA Sister Organization) _

"Intruders again!" yelled a voice from inside.

Agent Double J and I jumped into a fair-sized room with marble floors and some green velvet couches around the perimeter of the captive spies. The room matched traditional style of the rest of the building.

"Alright, it's go time!" I shouted.

We pulled out some gear. I flipped out a small device on my wrist and sprayed a Spartan in the face with sleeping mist. Agent Double J kicked a Spartan into a nearby room and closed the door, sealing it with her laser. Another Spartan charged at me; I slid out of the way just in time to see him crash into a mirror on the wall.

Just as Agent Double J and I were tying up the last Spartan soldier, the doors to the main hall slid open and in walked Mac. We started for the window with a group of Spartans running close behind us. I tripped one, and Agent Double J shot another with a tranquilizer dart. To our dismay, the remaining Spartans dog-piled us, then walked us over to Mac as we struggled in their firm grips.

Location: Bank - Mac's office_

"Look who I've caught again," cheered Mac.

I frowned and tried to pull away from one of the Spartans holding my arms, but to no avail. Mac had us escorted to his "personal office," even though it was our base. Our wrists were bound in front of us, and we were tied to chairs like many other times.

"This almost seems cliché." I laughed to Agent Double J.

Mac clearly did not think my joke was funny. "Silence or I will gag you both so I can't hear your sarcasm," he barked.

Mac seemed like he had nothing to do but blab about his latest accomplishments. I remembered I could tap into the building's control system on my wrist communicator; however, I couldn't easily move my hands to see it since my arms were tied to the chair. I wiggled my wrists around in the restraints enough that I could press the button on my wrist communicator. Before Mac could take it away, I had already overcharged the generators on the lower floor. We heard a loud crash, and the room shook.

"You!" Mac yelled, running into the hall.

We got the opportunity we needed. Agent Double J used her backup laser to cut the ropes that tied us together. We ran to an open window and jumped out, activating our paragliders to easily sail to safety.

Location: The Streets of Santander_

As soon as we landed, we darted down the street as fast as we could and ducked into a nearby alley.

"That was a little too close," I gasped.

Agent Double J nodded. We needed a different way in, one that would not draw much attention. We decided it was best to page Amy and see if there were any other avenues.

"Sir Alexander, I am extremely disappointed in you. The tactics you used were childish and you ended up getting caught by Mac. Now they know we are on to them, and this mission is going to become that much harder."

"I'm sorry, Amy, you know I am new at this, and Agent Double J isn't a field agent either, but she was the closest person to help," I said through my wrist communicator. A knot had worked its way into my throat, and I held back my tears.

"That was a poor choice on your part. You should have known you needed to be with a field agent. Agent A is nearby, and Bruce can get her to you by supersonic jet shortly. In the meantime, please don't do anything else to compromise the mission."

I sat down on a bench dejectedly. Agent Double J put her hand on my shoulder.

"I thought I knew what I was doing. Amy said to find someone to help, I didn't think it had to be another field agent, but I guess she is right. I'm not good at my job and don't know what I am doing. I should have known."

"Stop giving yourself such a hard time. As you said, you are new at this, and while Amy was clearly upset, she didn't remove you from the mission which obviously means she still trusts you. She just knows that you and me both need a bit more help," Agent Double J consoled.

"Whoever this Agent A is, he better not be one of those field agent guys who thinks he's 'all that,'" I said. "I don't have patience to deal with an arrogant person on this mission."

Location: Alleyway_

As Amy said, Bruce was on call with a private jet, so Agent A arrived in no time. To my surprise, Agent A was a female agent. She was short and petite with long straight brown hair. What surprised me even more was her relaxed personality. Rather than give me a hard time about failing to lead the mission, she jumped in right away to problem solving. Yet another time I had misjudged a field agent based off stereotypes. I made a mental note to myself to be more openminded going forward.

"You know what, Sir Alexander? There's a network of tunnels that run under the base," Agent A said.

I knew of the tunnels to which she was referring. The tunnels were used for city maintenance, and we spies had counterfeited them for secret travel. The only problem was they were not heavily used, and many had been untraveled for years. There were no public maps, and very few spies actually knew their way around the labyrinth.

"I had considered that, but they are a maze and despite the fact that I speak Spanish, it wouldn't be much use for navigating secret tunnels," I said.

"Lucky for you, I have studied the ICPA tunnel systems in many countries extensively, including Spain," Agent A responded calmly. She then led us down another alleyway to the nearest entrance. There was a mossy brick wall with what looked like a large drain; a thick metal grate covered the opening.

Agent A pressed a brick above the drain, and it slid away to reveal a keyhole. She inserted the key, and the heavy grate creaked as it inched up. In the distance, I heard water dripping. Agent Double J was kind enough to bring along some waterproof garments in anticipation of possibly using the tunnels. I slipped on the jumpsuit and felt a little better. Agent A then proceeded to hand each of us an oxygen mask.

"Just in case," she said gravely.

Location: The ICPA Tunnels

I swallowed hard. This was not going to be fun. I watched as Agent A shimmied into the drain; next, Agent Double J disappeared. I ducked. Damp air, reeking like swamp water, blew in my face. The inside of the drain was slippery with green algae.

I held my breath, even though I wore an oxygen mask. I kept my eyes on Agent Double J's headlamp as we inched through the tunnel.

After a while, we came to an overhead hatch with a ladder. We slipped our way up into a dark room with a small window overlooking a plaza where a small carnival was taking place. Street vendors had set up stalls and rides. Families strolled about with ice cream and cotton candy.

I heard Agent A close and lock the hatch in the floor. I exhaled loudly as the tension in my body decreased. A small staircase with iron railings curved up the perimeter of the room. We changed out of our jumpsuits. Agent A led the way up the staircase. At the top of the stairs were double doors. However, when we slid the doors out of the way, we exited through a large armoire.

"Wow, that was quite the secret passage," I exclaimed.

Agent Double J nodded.

"Where are we now?" inquired Agent Double J.

Agent A pulled out a holo-map. "We're on the seventh floor, above where I believe the Spartans are housing a temporary base," she whispered.

I pulled out a small knife and prepared to cut a hole in the floor.

"There's no need for that; we can use the secret passageways to spy on them," Agent A interrupted.

"Fine by me," I said. "I'd much rather use a passageway than get caught again."

Agent A lifted a vase of flowers on a nearby table, and a mirror on the wall creaked open. I again felt somewhat weary to enter.

"No worries, the most you'll find in here are a few old cobwebs," comforted Agent A.

I did my best to smile as I stepped into the cold passageway. We inched our way along a catwalk between the walls. After climbing down a steep flight of stone stairs, we reached a small opening that looked into the room where the Spartans had their makeshift base. Agent A peered through the crevasse.

"There are about twenty from what I can see," she whispered.

I got out my gear and mentally prepared myself for anther showdown.

"We need to take out their security system... Let's see, in the corner is the main computer. Sir Alexander, that's your job. Agent Double J and I will cover you," she instructed.

Location: Bank (ICPA Sister Organization)

Agent A pulled a lever on the wall, and a sculpture slid away to reveal our location. I ran to the computer; however, there were Spartans on my tail. I turned and kicked one in the chest and tripped two others. I took out a sleep detonator and threw it on the ground, eliminating four more. The last three charged at me and latched onto my arms and legs.

"A little help here," I yelled to my fellow spies.

Agent Double J and Agent A ran over and pried the Spartans from my arms.

I dashed to the computer and hacked in. I disabled the radio communications and turned to help Agents A and Double J with the rest of the Spartans. It only took a few minutes, and we had captured the base.

"We need to get back to the third floor where the spies are being held captive," said Agent A.

We slipped back into the passageway and made our descent. It was dark, and I tripped a few times. I also got a few spider webs in my face. After we slid our way through the walls, we ended up at the room that Agent Double J and I had already been to. The spies were no longer there. There weren't even any Spartans.

"Don't go out there; it could be a trap," I cautioned.

Agent A looked around and evaluated the situation. "It's odd that they would create a trap here. I mean, you ran away, so they probably think you're too afraid to come back. Let's go out there anyway."

Location: Bank (ICPA Sister Organization)_

We slid over a painting and stepped into the room. No spies. The door Agent Double J had sealed shut was now open, and the Spartan was gone.

"This is creepy," whispered Agent Double J.

The room was a mess. One window was shattered on the floor, and there was a door off its hinges. The curtains drifted in the breeze in a ghostly sort of manner.

"We'll have to figure out where they've been moved. I mean, they couldn't have gone across the globe in the last hour," I said.

We opened the door to the hallway and peered out. There was no one. We walked around the base, looking for any sign of life, but there was none. Even the "temporary HQ" and Mac's office were empty.

"Okay, what did we miss?" asked Agent A.

We were wondering how one could move hundreds of Spartans and spies to another location without anyone noticing.

"Wait, did you hear that?" I asked.

We sat and listened. Voices, they were far away. I heard them echoing from a heater vent.

"They must've discovered the tunnels," exclaimed Agent A.

Location: Bank - Mac's Office_

We ran back up to Mac's "office" to find that the Spartans had blown a hole in the wall, revealing a passageway.

"I bet they got one of the spies to crack and tell them the passages existed but didn't know where to enter," said Agent A.

"A typical Spartan solution...blow things up," I replied.

"Let's locate where they are first, then maybe we can cut them off from the front or divert them to where we can handle the situation," suggested Agent A. She pulled out her holo-map, and we looked at the large network of tunnel systems which seemed to cover all of Santander. "I spent a lot of my time with the ICPA mapping these tunnels, but I never published these maps."

"They're about right here," I said, pointing to a junction of tunnels on the map that appeared to be somewhere near the ice-cream shop Agent Double J and I had passed earlier. "We have to develop a plan to make them come out in the police station."

"The best way to do this is if we use items to block the tunnels, forcing them to wind up in the police station. We can use some of the boxes in the alleyway and some of the old cables in the tunnels," contemplated Agent Double J.

We started off in our jumpsuits and oxygen masks.

Location: Alleyway & ICPA Tunnels

"This will be complicated, so take only two boxes and push them in front of you," instructed Agent A.

We did as we were told, and Agent Double J and I each lifted up two boxes. The three of us slipped back into the tunnel system.

"We need to split up and block as many junctions in the tunnels as we can; your holo-maps will guide you," said Agent A.

I slipped off to the right, Agent Double J to the left, and Agent A to the middle. It was cold, and the green algae on the walls made me sick to my stomach. I thought I felt a fish swim by, and I jumped, but it was just my imagination. My holo-map led me with arrows to the first junction. I maneuvered my first box into the opening and secured it with some nails. The sound was so loud I was sure Mac would hear it.

I kept slipping along until I made it to the next place I needed to block off; I secured my second box. Now my mission was to see if I could find anything else to block some other less obvious openings. After sifting through junk in the water, I found some heavy wire, a tire, and a glove. I dropped the glove and watched it sink down a flooded shaft. I pulled along the tire and wire.

I found another possible escape route for Mac and his team, so I shoved the tire in the tunnel effectively blocking the entrance; next, I wove the wire over some nails to keep it in place. I secured a few more exits, then pressed the "all clear" button on my wrist communicator to alert Agent A and Agent Double J that I was finished. I made my way back into the alley.

Surprisingly, I was the first out; I sat and waited for the others. I immediately started to worry. I was sure I was the least experienced one there, so the fact that I had finished first was odd. Not only was I worried about my team's safety, but I knew if anything else went wrong I would be in bigger trouble than I already was. After about fifteen minutes, Agent Double J and Agent A appeared. I let out a sigh of relief.

"Wow, you were fast! Let's head over to the police station and alert them of the 'visitors' that are about to drop by," said Agent A.

We jogged to the police station and made it there quickly.

Location: Police Station_

"How may I help you?" asked a police officer behind a desk.

I translated and explained the situation. Agent A showed the officer where the group would emerge from: a large grate in the storage room.

"We better not let them know this is a police station," I cautioned. "They may just run back down into the tunnels."

"How about we disguise this place as a restaurant?" offered Agent Double J.

We loved the idea; Agent A ran to a restaurant down the street and borrowed some dishes and tablecloths. She even brought us some waiter and host outfits. Agent Double J pulled out the wigs from earlier, and we all sat, ready for the intruders.

"Shhh...we have no clue where we are," a voice from the storage room cautioned. Mac peeked his head out of the door.

"Cómo está?" I greeted.

Mac looked at me quizzically. "English?"

We glanced at each other and acted like we had to think about what he was saying.

"Oh, English! What are you doing in our storage closet?" I asked

"Just, some maintenance, everything looks good."

"Would you like a table? We would be happy to give you a complimentary meal for helping with the maintenance," I said.

Mac fell into our trap, as planned. "Oh, really? Well, my workers and I would love that."

I led Mac and the rest of the Spartans to different jail cells that we had outfitted to look like dining booths. Agent Double J had done a nice job disguising the cells. There was a table with a light-pink cloth overtop, as well as a bouquet of flowers in each "booth." On the tables were china plates with fancy silver cutlery. The Spartans sat down, eagerly wanting to eat dinner.

"Let me go grab some menus for you guys," I smiled. "I'm going to close this door, so you won't not be bothered by any of the other tables." I used my fluent Spanish to further the ruse as I talked with the others around me.

I closed and locked the door. Agent Double J, the police officer, and Agent A emerged from their cells and locked the doors as well.

"Good work, everyone," congratulated Agent A.

I walked to the storage closet to find the rest of our spies tied together.

"You came to save us!" shouted one of the spies after we removed their gags.

I nodded and waved over Agent A and Agent Double J to help me untangle the group.

As we untangled the spies, we heard a loud clanging. Rushing back to the cells I could hear Mac shouting. "You never brought us our menus!"

"Mac, I don't know how you fell for such an odd trick, but this isn't a restaurant. You are now in the custody of the Spanish police," I replied with a smirk.

After a pause, the Spartans began to panic, pulling on the cell doors only to find them solidly locked.

"You win this round, Sir Alexander, but I've escaped before and I'll do it again," retorted Mac.

Location: Tokyo, Japan_

The next day, I flew back to Tokyo. It felt good to continue my interrupted vacation. I smiled as I approached Yuki's apartment building. The sun glinted off the glass as I walked. I spun my way through the rotating door and took a deep breath in the lobby; it smelled like rubber and cleaning chemicals. Never had it seemed so nice to stand in that lobby.

I let the people exiting the building flow around me. I was happy. I strolled over to the elevator and was lifted up. I stepped out and ran down the hall. Doors flew by, room number 128, 129, 131, 135, 140. I knocked on Yuki's door.

She opened the door a few seconds later. A grin spread across her face when she realized it was me. "Oh, good, you're back; I was so lonely here with no one to talk to. How was the mission?" Yuki laughed.

"To be honest, I made a lot of mistakes, but as my friend Kai told me, it's just like training at the gym. Each time I do it I will improve. Amy wasn't happy with me, but we succeeded in the mission so I'm sure she will cut me some slack,"

"That's good to hear," now let's go get coffee. "You need to tell me more about Kai; you said he's handsome, any chance you could hook me up?"

We both laughed. It was good to be back on vacation.

A HOLIDAY KIDNAPPING: USA

Location: ICPA HQ_

A few months after returning to the US, I walked into my office feeling very cheery and refreshed; the holiday season was upon us. I glanced out my window to see snowflakes gently drifting out of the sky. Everything was going very well. The Spartans had not acted up in months, and all our paperwork was filed correctly, thanks to Laurel. Today was the day before the agency's winter vacation. I sat staring at my computer screen, at a complete loss as to what to do.

"I might as well go visit Laurel," I said to myself.

After a few more minutes of checking my email and phone messages, I waltzed into Laurel's office which was connected to mine, so I often dropped in to chat. The first thing I noticed was her six-foot tall Christmas tree. Laurel had completely remodeled her office just so that tree could fit on her desk.

"Good morning Laurel. I can't wait for vacation," I said. Laurel looked up from her laptop screen. She always worked on her favorite pink, well-loved laptop. I had offered to set her up with one of the ICPA computers, but she preferred her own. Of course, I had to install a bunch of extra security software to make it safe, but for Laurel it was worth it.

"Hi, Sir Alexander, I'm so excited for the ICPA Christmas party. All the agents are going to be there." Laurel said.

Laurel always planned the ICPA Christmas party. It was a big deal, and everyone loved to attend. The event was formal, and all of the agents dressed in their most fashionable attire. There was a gift exchange, awards for outstanding agents, as well as the announcement of any bonuses. The event was held in the conference hall with panoramic views of the Rocky Mountains. It was spectacular and classy in every way.

"So, which outfit should I wear? Agent Double J designed both," Laurel said motioning to two outfits hung on the coatrack behind her. "I really like this lovely red ball gown, but on the other hand this scarlet business suit is very classy."

I chuckled to myself. Laurel was so fussy about the party every year, and inevitably, both Laurel and I would end up making a trip to see Agent Double J for more outfit options.

"Why don't we go see what Agent Double J thinks? In my opinion, the dress would be best for the party."

Location: ICPA HQ – Agent Double J's Design Studio

Laurel and I made our way over to Agent Double J's studio; once we were inside, I rang the bell on Agent Double J's desk.

"I'll be right there," came a voice from the behind a sea of fabric and mannequins. Agent Double J emerged holding a hot pink dress.

"Who is that for?" I inquired.

"Why, it's for me," Agent Double J smiled as she twirled the dress around.

We all laughed. There was not a day that Agent Double J was not creating some outfit.

"We have a problem. Laurel can't decide on which outfit to wear to the ICPA Christmas Party," I said.

Agent Double J looked at both of Laurel's outfits and contemplated.

"I think the dress would be perfect for the party, especially since you're the hostess," she concluded.

Location: ICPA HQ - Desk Agent Department_

Laurel and I made our way back to our offices.

"I guess you know what you'll be wearing for the party." I smiled.

We both got back to work. When I was halfway through typing up some of my mission logs, my phone rang.

"Hi, Amy," I spoke into the receiver.

I knew something was wrong by the tone of her voice. I tensed up as she continued to speak.

"Sir Alexander, I need to talk to you and Laurel in my office, quickly," she pleaded in a tense tone.

I ran and whisked Laurel out of her office.

"Wow, you're in a hurry."

I gave her a brief overview of what Amy had said, and after I finished explaining Laurel walked faster as well.

Location: ICPA HQ - Amy's Office_

We both burst into Amy's office to find her missing. It was very eerie... all the lights were off except the desk lamp. Laurel and I both slowly crept into the space.

"Amy?" I whispered quietly.

There was no response. Laurel and I glanced at each other. We did not want to alert the whole base for fear that the intruder was still inside the office. I picked up a vase of flowers for protection, not that it would have done much, and peered behind Amy's desk, but there was no Amy. I reached over and turned on the lights.

"It looks like Amy is actually gone. It is so strange since she just called us to her office. I suspect she may have been kidnapped," I said trying to keep my voice from wavering. I wanted to seem cool and collected, but inside I was very worried.

Laurel and I called for more of our colleagues to help us search the office and dust for fingerprints.

"I am going to look in Amy's lab," I sighed.

After entering through the secret passage, I found nothing at all. Not even a single vile was out of place since yesterday. I emerged and reported that the lab appeared untouched. I felt frustrated and at a loss. If only I had gotten to her office faster, perhaps we could have stopped the intruder.

"Look, her computer is in extreme lockdown!" exclaimed Matthew, a young spy who had joined us.

Laurel and I ran over and saw the red lock on Amy's computer screen.

"I will unlock it and see if we can find any clues," I said.

Matthew watched in awe as I used a fancy set of codes to reopen Amy's computer; not many of the young spies ever got to learn those codes. On the desktop was a blank document with a few words typed in the lovely Times New Roman font.

HELP, SPARTANS INVADED. MY LOCATION IS ONLY A JUMP AWAY AT Y ;AKJGSL DGH.

It looked like someone dragged her away as she was typing the last line.

"What good does that do us?" asked Matthew.

I looked carefully at the screen.

"Her fingers were on the home row of the keyboard judging by the letters she typed minus 'Y' and 'I'," I noted.

We tried to look closer when the power went out. And I mean *out*. Usually, our backup generators would have worked, but in this instance the only lights that worked were a few dim emergency lamps in Amy's office.

"Someone does not want us to find Amy," I said.

We started to rummage through Amy's cabinets and found two flashlights to help better illuminate the room. I walked to a control panel on the wall and pressed the analyze button.

"*Multiple problems, main power off, thirty minutes of battery power remaining. Generators failed to start properly,*" came an automated voice.

"Well, I have good news and bad news, the main power is off, but it is not damaged, that means someone had to manually turn off the switch," I sighed.

"That's good news how?" inquired Laurel.

I looked around the room as everyone anticipated what I was going to say.

"We have another clue for our puzzle," I said.

I slid a bookcase over to reveal a generator that only powered Amy's office. The switch was off. I had Matthew dust for fingerprints. He found some, but they were smudged. I flipped the switch on, and the lights in the office lit up.

"Whoever broke in had to know this was here," I grimaced. "It may even be someone in our own agency. Amy would never turn off her own generator."

The spies looked at each other wide eyed.

"Our search starts now," I said to the others.

I sat at Amy's computer and scanned for her wrist communicator. It appeared on the map twenty miles from the base.

"Can I help you and Laurel find Amy?" asked Matthew sheepishly.

"Of course, you can, we are *all* going to search for her," I said.

There weren't many spies at the base because most had already gone home for the holidays. So, the teams were split into groups of twos and threes. Veronica and Agent Double J stayed at the base and monitored communications from Amy's office. Bruce and Joe manned a helicopter; lastly Laurel, Matthew and I went outside on foot to find Amy's wrist communicator and hopefully Amy.

Location: Outside the ICPA HQ_

Snow burned my face as I trudged through the sea of shrubs at my feet, the sky dark and windy. A bright spotlight appeared from Bruce and Joe's helicopter and led us along for what seemed like an eternity. We even had to scale a cliff before we came to Amy's last known location.

"I doubt that they would have scaled a cliff," I yelled over the landing helicopter. We started to scan the area. I located Amy's wrist communicator and ran to it. No Amy, just her communicator lying in the snow. I felt a tear run down my cheek and freeze to my face. Amy was in danger. Why couldn't I have just been a little faster? I could have prevented all of this! The thoughts kept rattling around in my mind as we searched for clues.

Location: ICPA Helicopter_

Inside the helicopter there was a mini lab. Matthew again dusted for fingerprints, and this time we found some. They belonged to Denel; she was Mac's personal secretary who he had recently hired.

"Strange, we have hardly ever seen Denel. In fact, I don't know if I have met her at all," I pondered aloud. I placed a call to Veronica and Agent Double J. "Hey, rerun today's security camera footage and send it to the helicopter as well."

Our computer screen turned on and we watched spies passing by Amy's office. At about 5:00:01, a girl in stiletto heels with long, light brown hair glanced around and stepped into Amy's office. At about 7:00:00 she peered out the door and then quickly went back inside. After that, Laurel and I ran into Amy's office.

"We know she is not inside, see if there is a way out of the office they could have used," I instructed Agent Double J.

"I'm on it," came her voice.

After we waited for a few minutes, Veronica came on the phone.

"Sir Alexander we were able to figure out that they went out the window. There was a piece of fabric caught in the frame. It had Amy's skin cells on it."

I held my breath. I didn't know what to do next.

Location: ICPA Helicopter_

We flew the helicopter for a few miles, scanning with the spotlight to see if anything popped out. We noticed a set of automobile tracks, which led us to a runway for a plane. None of us had ever seen this runway or knew that it existed.

"The tracks end here; scan for any signals," I commanded. There were many Spartan signals emanating from a satellite by the runway. We were able to hack into the computer remotely and found that a plane had departed a few hours ago for Florida.

"To Florida we go," I declared.

Laurel pushed Joe out of the way and steered the helicopter back toward the base.

"We're taking your private jet then," she said.

Matthew stared with huge eyes. Only Bruce and I knew that Laurel could fly a helicopter. Joe seemed offended that the ICPA intern could fly a helicopter better than him. We boarded my private jet, and Joe and Bruce exited to the cockpit, while Laurel, Matthew, and I sat on my purple couch.

As we flew along, I went over the events again in my head. Somehow Amy had been kidnapped. How could such an event have occurred in such a secure location? The whole situation had me uneasy and frustrated. I figured I would really have to put what limited field agent training I had to use.

Location: Orlando International Airport_

The next day we arrived in Florida. When we exited the plane, I immediately started to ask around to see if anyone had recently witnessed people dressed in red and a girl with blond hair. After hours, no one had an answer except for a security guard.

"Yeah, I saw em'. They walked out toward the ticket kiosk. The girl who was not in red didn't look so happy. There were two men and one other girl with her, the girl in red had brown hair," the guard recalled.

"Thank you so much. We are looking for the blonde girl; she may be in trouble. Please let us know if you see anything else," I said handing him my business card.

Wintertime Florida was a huge contrast from Colorado with snow and wind. Florida was temperate. We all sat in the airport at a loss as to what to do. Amy was somewhere in Florida, but where? It was a large state and finding Amy seemed like a huge mountain we were too exhausted to climb. Amy was the head spy and our close friend, so we continued to wander through information without finding more clues.

As I sat ready to give up, watching car after car pass by, I stared into space. I listed the color of each car in my head for something to do *blue, blue, silver, black, red, red, red, red, red.* I glanced up in surprise; only the Spartans would own so many red cars. I alerted the rest of my team, and we secretly followed the cars on foot.

"Quick, get a taxi," I hollered to Matthew

Matthew flagged down a taxi, and our team piled in. We told the taxi driver to follow the precession of red cars.

"Great, one of these types of days," groaned the taxi driver as he pulled away from the curb.

Our team rolled along for about a half-hour. Soon, we were on the verge of entering a very industrialized area. Smokestacks from factories stretched into the sky with white steam columns floating up and joining with the clouds.

"This is as far as I can take you," said the taxi driver.

We glanced at each other nervously. Laurel paid and tipped the taxi driver, and we quickly darted out of the vehicle.

Location: Industrial Area_

"I guess we are following on foot again," I sighed.

Joe, Matthew, Bruce, Laurel, and I ran from alley to alley following the red cars, until they came to a gate with guards on either side. The cars entered and the gate closed with a click. We all looked at the gate in dismay; it crossed the opening of the alley and was about twelve-feet tall.

"Great, now we'll never be able to get in," exclaimed Matthew.

Every time it seemed like we had found a lead and got closer, something would get in the way. We headed down the street and found a small auto repair business. Inside we inquired as to what was behind the gate, and if they had seen any strange behavior over the past few days.

"Actually, we've wondered about that business for a while," said one of the mechanics. "We always wondered why all their cars were red, and why they had so many guards."

"Is there some other way we could possibly get in? We are a team of private investigators," I stated.

The manager of the store led us to the back and pointed to a ladder. "This ladder leads to the roof. You should be able to go over the roof into the alley behind the gate."

"All right, here we go," I directed.

We climbed the ladder and found ourselves on the roof of the building. There was gravel spread on the surface, and TV antennas alongside various vents dotting the landscape.

Location: The Rooftops_

As we walked along, I kept thinking I heard another set of footsteps. I stopped walking. Laurel, Joe, Matthew, and Bruce stopped too.

"What's the matter?" asked Bruce.

I listened but heard nothing.

Due to my mounting concern, I decided it would be best to have a quick escape. I was sure a real field agent would have probably considered that sooner, but there was no time to lose.

"Depending on what we find, we may need a quick escape. Joe and Bruce, go get a helicopter. According to my research there should be a place where you can rent one to view the everglades not far from here. If you need money, just page headquarters. Veronica can take care of arranging things for you."

Joe and Bruce nodded heading back to the ladder.

"Okay, let's keep moving," I commanded. Laurel, Matthew, and I kept walking. We swung across alleyways, and over satellites. After two rooftops, I heard the footsteps again. "Do you hear those footsteps?" I whispered to Laurel.

Laurel and I both stopped at the same time, and we heard two more footsteps. *Click click.* Matthew glanced around nervously.

"I hear them." Laurel whispered. "Maybe we're being followed..." she trailed off as we heard the footsteps again. *Click... click.... click.* We glanced at each other and picked up the pace. The faster we moved, the faster the ghostly steps followed. We all stopped again and looked around; there was nothing. I squinted and caught the movement of something behind one of the chimneys.

"Over there, Laurel," I hissed.

Laurel spun, startled. The look on her face was unsettling.

"I saw something move behind a chimney," she said pointing in the opposite direction.

"No, I think I saw something over there," Matthew said pointing in yet a different direction.

I looked at them, puzzled because we were all pointing in opposite directions. Our group started to run.

"I should have seen this coming; it's some sort of ambush," I yelled to Laurel as we sprinted over to the alleyway.

When we were almost at the area where the Spartan base should have been, a girl in heels with a red dress walked in front of us. At first, I wondered if she was real; I was expecting a group of Spartans, not some random girl.

"It's Denel!" said Matthew.

She just stood there, unmoving, with her arms crossed. I could not figure out what was going on. "You must be the infamous ICPA team." She glared. "I finally get to meet you. Mac has told me a lot about you."

We all just stared; was she actually going to try to stop us singlehandedly?

"Take care of them, boys," she yelled.

A hoard of Spartans poured out of windows, vents, chimneys, and every other possible opening.

Our team was expecting this but still startled; there were only three of us against about fifty Spartans. I pulled out my sleeping mist and doused a few charging men. They fell sound asleep. Laurel dropped a smoke detonator on the ground making it difficult for the Spartans to see. I kept running, knocking over a Spartan here and there with ropes I lassoed around the various equipment on the roof. I saw Denel in the distance. She seemed to be enjoying the battle.

Matthew pulled a wire from some satellites on the roof and effectively lassoed together a few Spartans. Laurel was running low on ammo; I saw that all she had left was a sticky detonator and sleeping mist. She quickly stuck a group of Spartans together and took out another ten or so with the sleeping mist. Matthew used his last detonator and resorted to sleeping mist as well. I looked down and noticed that I was out of ammo too. I ran to help Matthew and Laurel, but I tripped, and a team of Spartans pounced on me. Laurel and Matthew ended up captured as well. The Spartan men pulled us struggling over to Denel.

"That was quite the show. You were able to deplete more of our troops than I expected. Now it's time to pay Mac a visit. He wanted us to finish you off, but I convinced him to keep you alive...at least for questioning." She smirked.

We started to get pulled toward the building; suddenly, the Spartans around us collapsed along with Denel. A bright light came from above us. It was coming from the helicopter. We were free thanks to the stun ray. Lucky for us it was fashioned only to affect those in red attire...a useful feature. We gave a thumbs up to Joe and Bruce and continued to run toward the Spartan HQ.

"Nice timing," I shouted to the team as we ran.

Location: Spartan HQ_

Laurel and I used our grappling hooks to scale the wall down into the alley. We crept up to the building and looked for a way in. Luckily for us, there was an open window. We stacked up some trashcans and peered in. There was a large mahogany desk, and a grand painting of Mac on the wall. Laurel and I slipped through the window and looked around again. We were in Mac's office, and he happened to be gone at the time. I ran over and locked the door. Laurel closed the window.

"All right, let's look at his computer," I said. Laurel and I hacked in and found all the information about the Spartan Base. "It looks like Amy is being held on the fifth floor. Let's disable the security system."

We disabled the security system, but to our disadvantage a loud automated voice stated, *"Security system disabled."*

Laurel and I both jumped. We would not have much time before Mac, or some other Spartan came to check out the situation. I quickly slid a bookshelf and chair in front of the window, and Laurel pushed Mac's desk in front of the door.

"That should buy us some time," gasped Laurel out of breath. A Spartan pounded on the door. Laurel picked up a heavy looking vase off the desk, although I doubted it would come in handy.

"I think I'll stick with my sleeping darts," I replied.

"Whoever is in there, you better come out *right now*," the Spartan outside yelled.

Laurel and I used our laser cutters to make a hole in the wall. We unfortunately came out in a room full of Spartans. Laurel quickly threw the surprisingly useful vase at Mac's computer, smashing it so the security could not be re-activated. We both ran through the room of Spartans into the elevator. The doors closed just before a group of them could reach us.

Location: Spartan HQ – Elevator_

"Quick, Laurel, use the emergency exit shaft," I said.

Laurel opened the hatch, and she and I exited the elevator.

"We have to get out of here before we get smashed by the elevator at the top," I said with the ceiling approaching quickly. Laurel caught the release lever with her grappling hook causing the elevator to go crashing back down to the main floor. We were both left dangling fifty feet in the air.

"All right, up we go!" shouted Laurel.

We started to scale the wall, and after five minutes we reached the fifth floor. I pushed open the door. Laurel and I rolled into the hallway.

"Let's find Amy."

We ran down the hall so quickly that I hardly noticed us fly right past Mac. Pretty soon it turned into a chase. We were not just running to get to Amy, we were also running away from Mac. When we got to Amy's cell, we opened it by using a code sypher machine, and Laurel and I ran in. I quickly closed the door before Mac could reach us.

Location: Spartan HQ – Amy's Cell_

"Aren't you the dimmest field agents I have ever seen. You just closed yourselves in a jail cell," laughed Mac. "I will come deal with you later; I have some clean-up to do thanks to you." He scowled as he ran back down the hall.

"Thanks for coming to save me," Amy said.

Laurel and I took out our laser cutters and sawed through the barred window. My heart pounded, knowing that Mac could return at any moment. The window finally fell out crashing onto the street below. I signaled Joe and Bruce. They both turned the helicopter around by our window. I shot my grappling hook. Laurel, Amy, and I climbed our way into the helicopter, as we entered, Mac appeared in the window. I quickly severed the rope before it was too late. Once we were all safe on board it dawned on me...

"Where is Matthew?" I asked nervously.

Everyone looked around. I started to panic. First and foremost, was Matthew, okay? He was only a trainee and would have been easy for the Spartans to nab.

"I knew it. I'm not cut out to be a field agent," I said in dismay. "I've committed one of the gravest offenses and lost someone on my own team."

"Sir Alexander, calm down. Panicking will get you nowhere," comforted Amy.

"I've located his commlink nearby at a department store. We will airdrop you in so you can investigate," said Bruce.

Location: Department Store_

We flew over and the helicopter dropped me on the roof. I made my way through the ventilation system until I could drop into a storage room. I exited and found Matthew with his arms full of wrapped gifts.

"Hi Matthew...what are you doing?" I asked.

Matthew relayed his story, which was very amusing despite my frustration.

"Well, you see, I didn't have time to shop for gifts for the Christmas party, so I slipped off after the battle to get gifts for everyone," he recapped.

I didn't know what to say, so I just smiled. Matthew would be a handful in the future.

Back on the plane, Bruce and Joe teased me the whole time because they were in on the gift plan as well and had dropped him off when they got the helicopter. I had improved in the field, but still had a lot to learn. I should have been keeping track of everyone on the mission. I laughed along with them, even though I was slightly concerned Amy might put another mark on my record. After a short plane ride back to Colorado, we were all home safely.

Location: ICPA HQ_

The next day was the ICPA Christmas Party. Laurel appeared in her fashionable dress as the perfect hostess. We all exchanged gifts. Matthew had something for everyone, thanks to his last-minute shopping and Amy's gift to me was letting me off with a warning for losing track of a team member.

"So, you had a good time in Florida?" asked Agent Double J. I just smiled and said, "You would not believe it."

AN UNEXPECTED CELEBRITY VISIT: SOUTH KOREA

Location: ICPA HQ_

It was good to have Amy back in the office after her recent kidnapping. All the spies were much more relaxed. Everyone except Amy, Agent Double J, and I. We were all preparing for a vacation to South Korea. While we were gone, Laurel would run the agency. I had complete trust in her, however Amy was less optimistic. I tried to help relieve the tension as much as I could. We were in my office making last minute preparations and packing our suitcases.

"Hey, Agent Double J, maybe you will get to meet Minjun while we are in South Korea," I joked.

Agent Double J had recently started listening to Korean music. She had developed a crush on Minjun, a Korean boy band member.

"I really hope so," she said in excitement. "Which outfit do you think he'd find most attractive?" she inquired jokingly holding up two different combinations.

One was a long, flowing, and hot pink dress, while the other was forest green and more form-fitting.

"I would go with the pink one," I offered.

Agent Double J slipped the dress into her suitcase. I folded my last pair of pants, and Amy hung up the phone after confirming our flight.

"All right, our flight boards in a few hours, let's get to the airport."

Location: Denver International Airport_

We all drove an unmarked ICPA vehicle to the airport. After making our way through security we found ourselves sitting in the blue and grey toned waiting area.

"Wow, I feel relieved already. It's really nice to be on vacation," exclaimed Amy.

Agent Double J and I nodded our heads in agreement. It was already starting to feel more relaxing. We had booked first class seats all the way to South Korea due to the long, strenuous flight.

"Boarding first-class passengers for flight 459 bound for Incheon, South Korea," came a voice over the speaker system.

We got our tickets out and filed into the line to board. Once on the plane, we were so excited to see the first-class cabin. The seats were wide and spacious with plush leather covers. Each seat was arranged so that it could be converted into its own private space. Sitting in my chair, I fiddled with the buttons to find I could recline, lift my feet, and even convert the chair into a bed. There were an assortment of refreshments waiting for me along with a sleek entertainment system complete with a touchscreen wireless remote.

"I don't usually fly first-class when not on business. This is such a treat," I said to my travel partners.

"I know. I think I'll order a full dinner," added Agent Double J.

We had reserved our seats in one row so we could talk on the way. Soon after the flight attendants' safety demonstration, we took off. On the flight, Agent Double J's wish about dinner came true. The dinner consisted of traditional Korean foods. I personally enjoyed the bibimbap. It was quite surprising that such a meal could be served 40,000 feet in the air. Amy and I had fun watching a Korean TV show featuring Krush, a newly debuted K-pop group.

"You know what, Sir Alexander?" said Amy, "I think that Jiho seems like the best dancer in Krush."

I glanced at her TV screen. Jiho glided across the stage easily in sync with his fellow bandmates and was certainly a skilled dancer.

"I can see why he's your favorite. He really can dance," I agreed.

Location: Incheon International Airport_

During all our fun on the flight we didn't notice a red-hooded figure until we exited the plane in Seoul.

"Did you see that guy dressed all in red?" inquired Amy.

We all looked around, but the person Amy had mentioned seemed to have vanished. I scanned the area with my wrist communicator but didn't pick up any Spartan signals.

"Relax, Amy. We are on vacation, maybe you're just a little tense," I comforted although inside I immediately went on alert.

Location: Hotel_

We caught a taxi and took off toward our hotel. It was magical to see the sparkling skyline of Seoul as we approached the city. Crossing the Han River, I snapped a few photos to post to my social media for Laurel to show the other spies back at the agency. When we arrived at the hotel, we found the suite to be very spacious with three separate rooms, one for each of us. In the common space, floor to ceiling windows overlooked the city. Popping open a bottle of sparkling water, I sunk into a chair at the table to gaze out over the city below. As I sat relaxing, Agent Double J heaved her suitcases onto the couch.

"You know that you don't need all those clothes; we're only here for five days," I laughed.

Agent Double J smiled and opened one of the suitcases. It was empty.

"I brought an extra. I mean, I'll be going shopping, and I'm sure I will find some souvenirs to bring back," she laughed.

After a quick planning session, we all went to our rooms. I fell asleep immediately; the flight had been exhausting.

I awoke early to something tapping on my window. The digital bedside clock showed it was three in the morning. I wondered what might be outside. Maybe a bird or something. I looked at the curtains and thought I saw the shadow of a person outside. Running over, I yanked open the drapes. Nothing. Just the skyline of Seoul. Not being able to sleep after the incident, I pulled out my laptop and worked on editing some of my mission records. Amy and Agent Double J awoke at about six in the morning.

"Wow, you're up early," commented Amy.

I smiled. I knew that they could tell something was bothering me, because they both just stopped and looked at me quizzically.

"I think there was someone outside my window last night. We may have someone following us," I stated gravely.

Amy and Agent Double J nodded.

"I heard someone in the hall outside our room last night; they were on a radio transmitter," added Amy.

We all sighed collectively. That was not what any of us wanted on vacation, but we all agreed that we would keep an eye out and be cautious. I flipped on the TV. I couldn't understand much since I could speak Spanish, Japanese, and English. Agent Double J was the one who was fluent in Korean.

"Hey, Agent Double J, can you translate?" I asked.

She nodded and sat next to me on the couch.

"The news reporter says there is some breaking news. The sets for Krush and MetalX got broken into last night. Some materials were stolen. Anyone who has information should call the number on the screen. Oh my, that's terrible, isn't it, Sir Alexander?" she finished.

I sat and pondered. It was rather strange. The only one who would know Amy and Agent Double J's favorite bands was the Spartan on the plane.

"You know what? We may be involved with this case. We should call the number," I said. Amy called the number on the screen, and the police station answered.

"Hi, this is Amy with the International Crime Prevention agency, preventing crime around the world. We believe we may have a lead on your story. We have three agents in South Korea right now, and they would be willing to investigate," said Amy in her business tone.

After giving her badge number she hung up the phone and gave us a thumbs up.

"They'll be here in two hours to pick us up and bring us to the scene," she said.

"Maybe you *will* get to meet Minjun," I said to Agent Double J.

Location: Seoul - Apgujeong_

The next two hours passed very slowly. After what seemed like an eternity, a police car pulled up in front of the hotel and we all piled in. Driving through Seoul was an interesting experience. The tall concrete buildings stretched up to the sky, and people milled about on the sidewalks. The meeting location was in the Apgujeong district famous for its high-end fashion stores. As we drove along, we caught glimpses of many different store windows filled with colorfully clad mannequins displaying each establishment's unique wares. I was glad to be here even if it was more of a mission than a vacation. We arrived at a TV studio made almost entirely of glass. The architecture was pretty, but it would not have kept out an intruder. Inside, the police officer led us to a waiting room where they introduced us to the head inspector on the case.

"Hello, my name is Jaemin, and I am managing this case. It's good to have an extra set of eyes. We won't waste time. I need you all to go look at the crime scenes. It's a real advantage to have you here with us. I'd like to have you interview the members of each band. To avoid stress and hopefully get more truthful accounts we would rather not have them be interviewed directly by the police. Instead, we'd like to send you in posing as foreign movie producers."

We nodded as the police ushered us to the first crime scene.

"This should be interesting, pretending to be movie producers, while trying to puzzle together all the events. We have a challenge," I said.

We entered the room with the set for the latest music video. The set was large and unique, with LED lights and a green screen. I noticed the broken window. Right next to the window on the concrete floor was a footprint which when coupled with the fingerprints matched our ICPA crime database as one of the Spartan members.

"Amy, look at this," I said showing her the record on my tablet. It was most certainly a Spartan boot print. I was glad to see that my hunch about Spartan involvement was correct. Amy nodded, took a picture of the print, and dusted the print for a lab test. We took some more dustings of other fingerprints on the set as well.

"It's time to move onto the next set," growled one of the police officers. He was clearly not happy that we were taking so long. We exited the building and drove a few blocks down to the next scene. The next studio was slightly larger. When we entered, I could tell this was MetalX's set; it was very odd. The set resembled a forest with some dead trees. It fit their style from the other videos Amy had showed me in the past. I started to walk around the studio looking for clues.

"Over here, look at this door," exclaimed Agent Double J.

Amy and I rushed over. The door's lock was clearly picked, and the paperclip was still in the keyhole.

"Wow, I wonder how they missed that?" I pondered.

In the hallway there was another boot print that matched the first. We took a picture of the print to compare and then left the facility.

"You seem to know more than the inspector himself," said the police officer changing his mood.

"We believe that we've dealt with this group of criminals before, so we have a little bit of a head start," I replied.

The police officer nodded his head in approval. After that, the police were kind enough to drop us off at the hotel. Back in our room, Agent Double J was overflowing with excitement.

"Sir Alexander, I get to interview Minjun! I'm so excited for tomorrow. What should I wear?" She smiled as she sifted through her outfits.

"Well, I wouldn't wear the ball gown. Try looking cute. Remember, you're a movie producer," I replied.

That night we all slept well, and thankfully there were no strange noises outside.

Location: Hotel_

"How do I look?" Agent Double J asked.

She was wearing a pink and white polka dotted blouse with a knee length black skirt with ruffles. She had a fashionable belt around her abdomen. As usual, she was wearing a pair of pink high heels to match.

"I think he will find you very attractive," I encouraged.

I also noticed that Amy was rather dressed up as well. She had her hair down, and she wore a black coat with a fur hood, dress pants, and high heels. Feeling underdressed, I changed into my business suit and tie.

"Let's head out," said Amy.

Location: Interview Room - Krush_

We all agreed that we looked like news or movie producers enough that it wouldn't raise any suspicion. When we arrived at the TV studio, the inspector escorted us to a conference room. After he left, I took in my surroundings. The room was large and very long. The windows overlooked the Seoul skyline on all sides of the space. There were dark mahogany accents around the room and white carpeting. We sat in black leather seats. In front of us was a long table where our interviewees would sit. There were glasses with pitchers of water and tea on each table. Before the interviews, Jaemin arrived to go over our roles.

"Good morning. I'm glad to see you here today. You have made our investigation a lot easier. Thanks to you, we actually have a relevant lead on the criminal group involved with this case. We are looking at the finger and footprints right now. I wanted to let you know that you just need to keep up your image of movie producers," encouraged Jaemin handing us some papers. "I prepared some possible questions for you as well as standard producer jargon."

We all nodded and prepared for the Members of Krush to enter. The thirteen members filed in and took their seats gravely. I glanced at Amy and noticed she had seen Jiho. I tried to locate him, and finally saw him sitting off to the right. I couldn't tell if he was looking at Amy or not.

"Thank you for making time for this interview. We are movie producers from America, and we wish to know your feelings and observations about the events over the past few days. It would make a great movie. Please feel free to share whatever you would like," I said in a very business-like voice. The interviews were conducted in a mix of English and Korean with Agent Double J translating when needed. We started at the left end of the table and worked our way to the right. Our interview turned into more of a discussion circle where everyone let out their feelings. I was glad when one of the members decided to describe what happened instead of telling us how he felt.

"Last night, I was rehearsing for the video, and I noticed a person in a red cloak outside. I did not think anything of it at the time, but they had been there almost all day," recalled Eunhyuk, the band's leader.

Apparently Jiho would not be outdone, because he gave us a very detailed description of what he remembered.

"Jeez Eunhyuk, you left out the most important details. I remember way more. First of all, the red-cloaked visitor appeared at five p.m. after we finished the fifth scene with your dance solo. I found it odd that the visitor did not do anything but stand in the mud outside. He was talking on a cell phone. That should be a lot better for a scene in a movie," Jiho smiled turning to Amy.

Eunhyuk seemed annoyed with Jiho's behavior. I could now could clearly tell that Jiho had his eye on Amy. He continued to be the most helpful, but he mainly answered Amy's questions, not Agent Double J's or mine.

"Thank you for coming today, we hope to see your latest music video soon," I said bowing to the members as they exited the room.

"I think you'll like it," Jiho smiled to Amy.

The members all exited the room. On the way out, Jiho slipped a piece of paper to Amy.

"What does your note say?" I inquired after Jiho had left.

Amy unfolded the piece of paper and read. "Please meet me in the lobby after your interviews end. And he also wrote something in Korean."

We all wondered what he had to say if he was willing to wait through our next interview.

"Look how he signed it," exclaimed Agent Double J reading the Hangul. "It means, 'Love Jiho!'"

I nudged Amy in the arm. "Looks like Jiho likes you," I teased.

Amy just blushed.

Location: Interview Room – MetalX_

The members from MetalX entered the room. I welcomed them the same way as I had the previous group. I looked at Minjun to see if he noticed Agent Double J. At first, nothing happened, but it was increasingly obvious throughout the interview that Minjun was flirting mercilessly with Agent Double J. What luck, I thought to myself, both of my friends found their soul mates in Korea.

"Do you remember anything peculiar about the night of the robbery?" inquired Agent Double J.

"Well, I remem—" started Doyun one of the other members before Minjun interrupted him.

"I can recall the whole thing," said Minjun as he gazed at Agent Double J. "Before I left the studio, I noticed a red-cloaked person loitering outside the main entrance. I said hello, but I don't think he knew Korean, because he did not respond."

"Excuse me, I was trying to say that I saw that same person standing there when I left. I exited the studio a few hours before Minjun," replied Doyun.

He seemed like a happy character. On the way out, Minjun winked at Agent Double J.

"That went well. We got some more information that definitely leads us in the direction of the Spartans." I sighed in relief while glancing over my notes.

"Yeah, we did," mused Agent Double J.

I looked up at Agent Double J and saw that she had not heard a word I said. "How about we go over and properly introduce ourselves to Jiho and Minjun," I suggested seeing I had lost both of colleagues in love land.

"You handled the interviews so professionally," laughed Amy.

We made our way to the lobby where Minjun and Jiho were waiting.

"Hello, I wanted to properly introduce my friends and I," I said smiling. "This is Agen—I mean Jay, and this is Amy." I stammered, almost blowing our cover. "I'm Alex," I added.

"That's nice," said Minjun, "Jay, that's such a pretty name. It just sounds like sunshine."

I looked away to hide my laughter. Next was Jiho's turn to flirt.

"Hi Amy, it's nice to meet you." He blushed. "Do you want to maybe go to dinner or something?"

"That would be great. I could take Jay and you could take Amy," concluded Minjun. "A double date."

"My colleagues would love that, but I have some business to take care of," I said.

Minjun seemed pleased that I was not joining them. As they were leaving, I noticed Seoham, one of the other members, try to hand Agent Double J his number. Minjun snatched it before she could see.

"Seeing as your colleagues have left you alone, I would be happy to take you to dinner," offered Eunhyuk.

"That is so kind of you, but there really is no need," I responded. "I have quite a bit to take care of with this upcoming movie. Best of luck with your comeback."

Location: The Streets of Seoul_

I was on my own considering I had "business to take care of." I actually had no clue what I was going to do since I was just trying to bow out of the situation. I should have just accepted Eunhyuk's kind offer to take me to dinner. For some reason, I always ended up pushing people away, especially when I was on a mission. To be honest, I was surprised Amy was so willing to go on a date considering it was certainly in the grey area of what was permitted by agency guidelines, but then again according to the ICPA records, we were off duty.

In the end, I decided to take in some of the city life. I changed out of my business suit and set out to do some shopping and dining. Hopping on the subway, I made my way to the Coex plaza. In the mall, I stopped by a CD store to see if I could find some limited-edition Korean CD's, and they had quite the selection. I walked down the vast isles of packaged disks; there were so many. I felt like I was wading through a sea of CD's. I really liked listening to some of the latest hits in Korea, and I bought a few from some of my favorite groups.

I then visited some of the popular fashion stores and bought a new outfit to better match the level of fashion of those around me. One thing was for sure—everywhere I turned in Seoul, it seemed that people had fashion in mind. As I strolled along doing my best to figure out what the signs meant I nearly ran into Agent Double J, Amy, Minjun, and Jiho. I quickly ducked into a nearby cosmetics store. I wondered if they decided to add some shopping to their date.

Realizing it would be best to vacate the area, I reboarded the subway and made my way to the Dongdaemun Design Plaza to see if I could take in a bit more of the local fashion. It was fun to see the unique architecture of the building and see the fashionable youth in the plaza surrounding the edifice. Even the new outfits I had purchased couldn't compare with what everyone else was wearing.

After all the shopping, I had worked up a bit of an appetite and decided to make my way to a nearby eatery. I went to one named Tavolo 24. The entryway to the restaurant led into a garden that had beautiful reflecting pools with lily pads and other unique plants. The atmosphere was welcoming and warm. A host walked me to my seat at a table that had a window overlooking another garden. I ordered a traditional dish recommended by my waiter. After two more hours of shopping and wandering around aimlessly, I decided to take the train back to the restaurant that the group decided to go to for their double date to reunite with my coworkers.

Location: Maple Tree House Restaurant_

I walked up to the building with the sign that read *Maple Tree House*. All I knew was that this was one of the best restaurants in Seoul. I stepped in and described the group I was looking for.

"Ah, yes they left a little while ago. They said they were going sightseeing," recalled the host.

I wondered where they went sight-seeing. There were many different attractions in Seoul, and it was hard to know which one they decided to go see. Perhaps they went to the Han River. I would just go back to the hotel and meet them there.

Location: Hotel_

Once I was in the hotel room, I opened my laptop. I decided to hack into the Spartan's mainframe with the extra time. I wasn't able to crack the heavy encryption for the main computer system, but I was able to get into their phone recordings. There was not too much going on: some meeting calls, food orders, and vague internal conversations with no details. I clicked on another recording, expecting it to be a pizza order.

"Hi, this is Amy, we would like three first-class plane tickets to Seoul, South Korea," came Amy's recorded voice. It was a recording of her making our flight reservations.

I gasped. The Spartans had known we were going to Korea right from the beginning. The robberies had to be their handiwork. As I sat pondering, I heard a crash in one of the bedrooms and entered to find the window broken. Glass shards covered the floor and bed, sparkling in the evening light. I ran to the phone and dialed hotel security. In no time, there were guards in the room along with me.

"So, where were you when the incident occurred?" asked one guard.

I motioned to my laptop on the table, and he nodded.

"It is strange that the intruder didn't enter," commented the guard.

I sat looking out the open window, watching the curtains fluttering. I focused my eyes; it was not just the curtains moving, there was also a red cloak right outside.

"One moment," I said to the guards. I walked into the other room and found my spy gear. I threw on my visor, designed by Laurel. This visor helped me become far more alert. I could see the temperature, time, and latest ICPA alerts. The visor would even sound an alarm if someone approached from behind me. I picked up two grappling hooks, and some magnets as well. I ran back through the room and jumped out the window.

"Where are you going? We're on the fiftieth floor," yelled the guard in dismay.

I fired my grappling hook; it wrapped around a pipe on the building across the street. Feeling my body swing around with centrifugal force, I swooped across the street. I positioned myself so I could see behind me, and there was the Spartan right outside my window. I fired the grappling hook again and swung back across the street landing just above the Spartan.

He tried to fire a tranquilizer dart at me, but I deflected it with my wristband. I noticed some police cars pull up to the hotel on the road many stories below. I quickly dropped a sleep detonator onto the Spartan. It exploded, and he fell. I let out my grappling line and started to slide down the building. When I was close to the now free-falling Spartan, I threw a sticky parachute at him. It attached to his shirt and deployed, floating him to the ground. I was shocked, but the Spartan woke up before he reached the ground. Slashing the parachute strings, he got up and darted down the street. I dropped to the ground and was immediately surrounded by police officers. I showed them my ICPA badge, and they nodded, understanding that I was trying to catch the intruder.

"You've got pretty awesome moves. We would appreciate if you could train some of our police officers," complimented one of the senior men in the group.

"I would love to," I said, clicking open my visor.

A repairman came and replaced my window later that evening. The hotel staff offered to move my room if I wished, but I politely declined. The Spartan would not be back anytime soon. I looked at the clock to see it was already eleven in the evening.

"Where could Amy and Agent Double J be?" I wondered aloud.

At one in the morning, they both returned with their arms full of shopping bags.

"Good thing you brought an extra suitcase," I exclaimed to Agent Double J.

She smiled as she heaved all her shopping bags onto the couch. "Look at this necklace Minjun got me," she said, taking it off.

I looked at the necklace; it was sterling silver, with a pink chain. On the necklace was the symbol for love in Korean.

"That is really pretty, Agent Double J," I said handing back the necklace. "What did you buy, Amy?"

"Not too much, but Jiho got me a bracelet. It's by a famous designer from here," mused Amy. "By the way, Eunhyuk sent these songpyeon for you. He met up with us before we came back."

"How kind of him. I will certainly enjoy them." I placed the rice cakes on the table, noticing they were an expensive type. "I also had my fair share of excitement while you were gallivanting about. I got a new window."

Amy and Agent Double J looked at each other with a worried expression. I told them what went on while they were on their dates.

"Are you okay?" asked Agent Double J.

"Of course, I am. And tomorrow I get to train police officers. Who needs to go on a date when I can have plenty of excitement right here?" I laughed.

The next day we were up bright and early. I had plans to go to the police station; Agent Double J and Amy set off to the dance studio.

"I will see you later this evening. Please tell everyone that I had some paperwork to complete, so I wasn't able to make it," I said.

"Sounds good, we will meet you for lunch. Minjun and Jiho want to get together for a meal today," said Agent Double J.

"Do you think they would mind me coming along? They seem to like to spend time with just you two," I commented.

"I don't think they will mind," concluded Agent Double J. "Plus Eunhyuk is joining and asked us to invite you as well so you won't be a third wheel."

I walked to the breakfast area in the hotel. There was a nice spread of traditional Korean dishes to choose from. I had a seafood salad with soup and moo saengche, a radish-based kimchi. After finishing my breakfast, I hurried outside and caught a taxi.

"Could you take me to the police station?" I asked the taxi driver.

"Yep, it isn't too far away," he replied.

Location: Police Station_

The station was tall and rather intimidating. The windows had tint and mirroring so that passersby could not see in. I walked up to the front door and pressed the bell. I waited for a few seconds, and the doors slid open. I stepped in tentatively. My objective was to find my way to room 506A. Apparently, there were so many rooms they needed "A" and "B" next to the numbers. I tiptoed my way down the hallways; it was creepy, because I hadn't come across anyone in the entire place. At last, I reached my destination. Stepping into the waiting room, I felt a sense of relief. It was small and much cheerier than the rest of the building. Three windows with white curtains overlooked the street below. A secretary busily typed away at a curved marble desk with a small antique lamp.

"Good morning," I said.

The secretary glanced up briefly from her rapid typing.

"The officers will meet you in a few minutes, please have a seat in our waiting area," she replied as fast as she typed.

I sat waiting for what seemed like an eternity. I watched the hands on the fancy gold clock tick away the minutes. Twenty, thirty, forty...

"Hello Alex, I am glad you were able to make it to train our police force. The officers are in the back waiting," said an officer peeking his head out from behind a door. I walked back through the entryway and found myself in a room with a rock-climbing wall. I guessed they wanted to learn how to use grappling hooks.

"Thank you for having me here today. I am Sir Alexander of the ICPA. Within our organization I help many recruits learn how to master using a grappling hook. It is much harder than it looks, so please pay attention," I said, starting my lecture. The officers were ready and eager to learn. The officer who met me in the waiting room acted as my translator for the class, but most of the officers were confident in English considering they were in Seoul and often helped tourists.

"First, you must know what type of grappling hook you are using. There are two main types: lodge and hook. Lodge grappling hooks will do what the name implies, they will lodge themselves into an object. These are great if the surface is wood, or rock. Remember, they will not work on metal. Lodge grappling is safer but not as easy to use. With hook-type grappling, the hooks will hook onto or wrap around just about anything, however it may take a few times to get the hook to stay," I continued. All the officers looked at what kind of hook they had at their station. Half had a regular hook, and the other half had a lodge hook.

"Okay, break into teams with the same hook type," I instructed.

The officers did as I requested and started to practice. Many of them were fairly skilled from the start, but I had to help a few with their technique. In a few hours, all the officers had mastered the skill.

"Thank you for making Seoul a safer place," said the head officer.

"It was my pleasure," I replied.

Location: The Streets of Seoul_

I stepped back out onto the streets of Seoul. It hit me at that moment. I had just taught a field agent skill to a group of police officers. It was an exhilarating realization that despite my shortcomings I was making progress. Even if the ICPA wasn't fully recognizing my growing abilities, other people were. My thoughts drifted temporarily to Kai. I really had him to thank. Without his help I wouldn't have had the skills I used at the hotel which got me the attention.

It was about time to meet Agent Double J and Amy for their lunch date at a café. I made my way back to the hotel. This time, I decided to walk after seeing how close the hotel was to the police station. The day was warm, and sun shone down in slanted segments between the skyscrapers. I plodded along for a few blocks when I thought I noticed a red cape swoop into an alleyway. I tiptoed along for a while longer, however no one ever showed up.

Location: Hotel_

I sat in the lobby and waited for Amy and Agent Double J for a while, when finally, both of my colleagues came waltzing through the door.

"Come on, Sir Alexander, you can help us get ready," said Agent Double J, whisking me from my chair.

Back in our hotel room, I helped Agent Double J and Amy with their hair and makeup for the event. Having mostly female friends growing up it was a skill I had acquired, and I had no qualms about helping my colleague get prepared to look their best. We were all quite close anyway.

"Never did I think we would be meeting and working with actual K-pop stars. Even though this isn't much of a vacation, I'm really enjoying myself," said Agent Double J.

"Me too," replied Amy, "Going on a date here and there really takes the edge off the extra work. I do feel a bit guilty bending agency policy, but we can consider it part of our disguise."

"I'm glad the two of you are getting on well in the dating world. Even though I don't have a date to share it with, I've been sightseeing and shopping in my downtime."

"Don't worry, you'll find someone someday," encouraged Amy. "All right, I think we're ready."

Agent Double J wore a pink, full-length dress, with a matching flower in her hair. She had on her signature six-inch heels. Amy wore an emerald green dress that was about knee length with a blue belt.

"You both look fabulous," I said.

"Even if you are not going on a date, you deserve to be pampered too," said Amy pulling out some cosmetics.

"Yes, I'll get his suit from the closet," added Agent Double J.

"The slate grey one," said Amy.

Before I knew it, I had been made over as well. Glancing into the mirror, I was impressed with my transformation. The girls had done my hair so that it was swept to one side in a way that made my face look narrower. Agent Double J had applied a thin layer of BB cream to my skin to give me a natural, but flawless complexion, and Amy's suit choice tied the look together with tight tailoring that highlighted my angular stature.

"You didn't have to go all out, but I appreciate the makeover," I said as we gathered our things to depart. "Why don't the two of you go ahead with your dates? I'll meet you at the restaurant."

They agreed easily since it would mean some more alone time with Minjun and Jiho.

Location: Yongsan Restaurant_

I ended up arriving at the restaurant at the same time as Eunhyuk. The facility was housed in a fancy building. It had sandstone walls with various trees growing in front of it. The building had two tall, glass doors with tree branches as handles. A planter of exotic grass by the door waved in the breeze. After entering, a hostess took us to our table.

"Thank you so much for coming along," I said to Eunhyuk, "I feel like a third wheel whenever I'm around the others."

"I am one of the few members that actually follows the company's 'no dating' rule, so I can completely relate," Eunhyuk replied.

When we arrived at the table, it was oddly empty. Agent Double J and Amy had left before me, so it was a bit strange that they weren't there. Maybe they'd taken a detour to do some sort of couple thing, whatever that might be. I certainly wasn't well versed enough in dating to even make a guess.

Eunhyuk and I decided to get started on some appetizers while we waited for the others. As we sat and chatted my wrist communicator beeped. I looked down to see a code red. A computerized voice came into my ear.

"*Spartan bomb active nearby. Please respond.*"

"Sorry Eunhyuk, do you mind if I make a quick call? I'll check in and see why the rest of our party is late."

"Go ahead," said Eunhyuk in his usual calm tone.

The restaurant staff kindly guided me to an outdoor balcony where I could use the phone. Outside, I immediately paged Amy and Double J, but there was no response. I started to feel a bit nervous, but at the same time I still couldn't rule out that they were simply enjoying their time and didn't want to be bothered, or that it was a difficult situation to answer a call. I decided it would be best to get in touch with Laurel.

"Hey, Laurel, any information on this notification I just got about an active bomb nearby?"

"It appears the Spartans have planted a bomb in the area. It's very near Amy and Doble J's wrist communicator locations. Perhaps they can get you more details."

"I've been unable to make contact with them," I said, clutching the railing. The more I learned the less positive I was about my teammates' safety. As I was talking to Laurel, I got another call. I answered it thinking it was Amy, but it was a voice I didn't recognize.

"Sir Alex, right? You have something we need. Access to the case files involving the Krush and MetalX incident. We need access to those files to erase them from existence. Provide us with your credentials. You have exactly twenty minutes to submit the information. If you don't, your friends and the general public will be in danger." The call ended before I could ask for any other details.

"Laurel, could you trace that?" I asked.

"Sorry, Sir Alexander, it appears they were using some sort of method to cloak where the message was being broadcast from, all I have is the last known location of Amy and Double J's wrist communicators. I'm sending the coordinates now."

I sank down onto the ground. I couldn't contact the police. There wasn't time for that, and I was just a desk agent. Any feelings of empowerment I had from earlier in the trip vanished. Again, I had let my team down. As I sat with my head resting on my knees, I felt a hand on my shoulder.

"Is everything okay?"

I glanced up to see Eunhyuk looking at me intently. "Amy and Jay are in trouble, and it's my fault."

Eunhyuk in his cool and relaxed fashion helped me to my feet. "I've only known you for a short time, but I can tell you are not the kind of person who lets that kind of thing happen. Don't blame yourself. That won't help them. What's going on?"

I explained the situation to the best of my ability, leaving out the part about me being involved with law enforcement.

"Well, let's go look for them," Eunhyuk said, dragging me along to his car.

Location: Warehouse District_

I guided him along until we reached the girls' last know location. It was in a warehouse district. My stomach churned. Things were not looking good at all.

"What were they doing all the way out here?" asked Eunhyuk. This certainly wasn't a spot for tourists.

As we sat, another car pulled up behind us. I turned around in shock, ready to bust out some combat moves, but to my surprise Jiho and Minjun hopped out and came rushing over.

"We saw you two frantically leaving the restaurant as we arrived. We waited a long time for Amy and Jay, but they never showed up. We thought maybe they were with you. When we saw you run out, we knew something must be wrong."

Things kept getting more complicated. I had to keep our cover from three people now, all while trying to find Amy and Double J. There was also an active bomb nearby that I had to disable in the process.

"Look, I don't know who you really are, but we are willing to help you find Amy and Jay," said Eunhyuk again putting his hand on my shoulder.

It was odd. I didn't usually make any connections with people outside of the agency. The only person I was really close with was Yuki. In terms of friendships outside of the ICPA, it was generally forbidden, but there was something about Eunhyuk. He had already managed to calm me down twice in one day.

"Okay, but you might have to sign some forms later about confidentiality," I replied. I then pulled out my wrist communicator and activated a hologram of the area. "This was their last known location."

"Looks like that warehouse over there," said Jiho motioning into the distance.

We made our way to the nondescript building. At the entrance, I lasered off the lock. Bursting into the space, we found Amy and Double J tied up and gagged.

"Are you okay?" asked Jiho and Minjun as they rushed to undo the ropes and gags.

"You shouldn't have come, it's a trap!" gasped Amy as soon as her restraints were removed.

"What do you mean? There's no one here," I replied.

"The bomb, it wasn't set for twenty minutes like they told you. It was set for ten," added Double J.

I used my wrist communicator to find the location of the explosive. Sure, enough there were only four minutes remaining. Judging by the size of the bomb it would make a pretty large explosion.

Jiho and Minjun had already ushered Amy and Double J out of the structure, but I couldn't just follow along without doing something to disable the ticking clock in front of me. I exhaled a deep breath. As much as field agents were trained to do this kind of thing, the inner workings of an explosive were basically just a small computer...that was a desk agent's expertise.

I looked at the logic board, timer, and wires attaching everything together. It was clear that whoever constructed the device had used nonstandard wires to make it impossible to know which one to cut. It would simply be a game of chance. The time ticked down to three minutes.

To my surprise, I felt a presence next to me. It was Eunhyuk.

"What are you still doing here? Join the others while you can."

"You've got this," he smiled. How he could stay so calm and supportive in a situation like this was beyond me.

There wasn't any time to waste arguing with him, so I zoned in. By examining the logic board connected to the timer, I realized that it might be possible to stop the timer or reset it to a longer amount of time. Stopping the timer could be risky since the board could register that the same as the timer running out, thus triggering an explosion. Instead, something else caught my eye.

Whoever had built the contraption had programmed the clock using a port on the computer chip. Being a desk agent, I had a multitude of connections available on my wrist communicator, and I was in luck. I had one that matched. Plugging into the board I used some simple code to add time to the clock so that it now read ninety-nine minutes.

"I knew you could do it!" said Eunhyuk.

I let out a deep breath. Sirens could be heard approaching. Apparently one of the guys must have called law enforcement. To my surprise, Jaemin walked in.

"It looks like you are a bit in over your head," he said.

"I certainly could use an actual bomb squad," I replied in relief.

The squad arrived shortly and was able to defuse the explosive easily using their equipment.

"Thanks to you, this didn't go off," said Jaemin. "I'm impressed yet again."

I smiled, feeling a small ounce of my confidence return. I still couldn't shake the feeling that it was my fault for not having gone with Amy and Double J in the first place.

Location: Police Station_

Back at the police station, I gave as much information about the situation as possible. Thankfully, Jaemin was able to explain to the band members that we were simply part of the law enforcement in an undercover investigation thus keeping the identity of the ICPA a secret.

I sat in one of those uncomfortable plastic chairs, waiting for everyone to get through questioning. The bandmembers had to sign non-disclosure and confidentiality agreements due to having seen a bit of the investigation. Thankfully, they were all cooperative and didn't have any reservations.

"Look at you, quick thinking," congratulated Amy sitting down next to me.

"Thanks, but this whole thing could have been avoided if I had just come along with you," I sighed.

"Sir Alexander, you know as good as I do that could have made things worse. Imagine if you were captured too. The bomb probably would have detonated." Amy patted me on the back.

"She's right, you know," added Double J joining the two of us.

I smiled at my team members, knowing that as much as I was hard on myself, it was true that I had done my best.

"Turns out, the Spartans were behind the robbery," said Jaemin, "I'm glad the ICPA came to help."

"As we say, 'preventing crime *around* the world,'" I smiled.

"We are here to help," added Amy.

Location: Incheon International Airport_

The end of our vacation came faster than we expected. Over the next few days Amy, Agent Double J, Jiho, and Minjun had a lot of fun in Seoul and thanks to Eunhyuk's company I was able to enjoy everything too. At the end of our trip, both of my colleagues had a teary goodbye with their newfound friends.

"Come and visit me often," said Minjun.

"Here's my number, call, text, or video chat," smiled Jiho handing a piece of paper to Amy. After that vacation, I had a hunch that Amy and Agent Double J would want to move to Korea.

"Stay in touch," said Eunhyuk giving me a quick hug before we boarded our flight. "And remember to count on your friends when you need help."

"You know what?" hinted Agent Double J on our plane ride back.

"What?" I responded.

"We should have a base in South Korea."

"I agree," said Amy.

"I will look into the paperwork," I said.

Pretty soon there would be a base in South Korea. It was convenient for me as well since I had my apartment nearby in Japan. We would all visit quite often on "business trips." However, I was usually the only one who actually worked. My colleagues usually went on dates. I knew now that Korea was much safer thanks to the ICPA, and in the process I had gained my second friend outside the agency. Eunhyuk continued to be a voice of support to me as I continued down the path of learning to be a field agent.

THE DANGERS OF PASSION AND EXPLOSIVES: FRANCE

Location: ICPA HQ_

I glanced out my office window to see a fine mist enveloping the yellowing Aspen trees on the mountainside. A deer and her fawn sprinted across the meadow below to find shelter in a nearby thicket of trees. It was the kind of day where it's hard to drag yourself out of bed and drive to work. Pulling myself away from the scenery outside, I stared back at my computer screen. I could not comprehend how many new spies there were to enter into the database and how many of them there were to verify. I picked up my phone and dialed Laurel even though her office was next door.

"Hey, Sir Alexander. How are you?" came Laurel's voice. I could not figure out how Laurel could stay so bright and happy on such a dull day.

"I am absolutely shot. How many new spies could there be?" I asked exasperatedly.

"There are about seventy-five," replied Laurel.

"Thanks," I forced a smile. Back to work. For a few more hours, I sat slaving away at entering the spies when I happily noticed that it was lunchtime. I ran out of my office and down the hall to the break room. The room had a cheery feeling, and I was glad to get away from my office for a bit.

"Hi Amy, good to see you," I replied sitting. Both of us being heads of different and often opposing departments meant we had gotten to know each other quite well through the cross departmental training program, so we often ate lunch together and enjoyed talking about the latest gossip in the agency.

"I heard that Agent Double J might be getting married to some K-pop star!" gushed Veronica.

"Whatever. They've only been dating a few months," commented Laurel. The desk agents were usually the ones who were up on the latest information since we monitored all communications.

"She is not getting married," I said, confirming Laurel's statement. In no time, our hour lunch break had passed.

"Hey, Sir Alexander, stop by my office when you can. I have information on the Spartans we need to go over," said Amy.

"Sure thing," I replied as I headed back to my office. Once inside, I locked my computer and told Laurel to send all my calls to voicemail.

"Where you headed?" inquired Laurel.

"I have a meeting with Amy about some Spartan stuff," I replied.

"Don't take too long, I'm not answering your calls all day," she joked.

Location: ICPA HQ - Amy's Office and Lab

I walked up a few flights of stairs and arrived at Amy's office. I scanned my fingerprint and the doors swished open.

"Like the fingerprint scanner?" asked Amy. We had recently installed it after Amy's kidnapping to prevent the event from reoccurring.

"It's pretty nifty. So, what's the news?" Amy opened her laptop and showed me some information on a new weapon the Spartans were developing.

"That's strange. I wonder what it does?" I pondered aloud.

"It looks pretty destructive," commented Amy. We decided to investigate a little more and entered Amy's laboratory through the secret passage.

"I got another computer with new software set up by the infiltration department. It is supposedly better at hacking into Spartan based operating systems," Amy said gesturing to the new computer.

"Cool, mind if I give it a try?" I asked.

"Go for it," replied Amy. I opened the computer's interface. The sleek controls and menus were quite impressive. I started to hack into the new base's computer to get some more information.

"Hey Amy, it looks like the weapon is housed in Paris, France," I said.

"We should have an intelligence meeting to go over this new information," concluded Amy. She picked up the intercom microphone and made an announcement: "All intelligence members, please report to Amy's office for an urgent briefing." Amy and I exited her secret lab and waited for the rest of the committee. This was where the desk agents really got to shine. The intelligence team was made up of primarily desk agents with a couple field and gear specialists as well to provide suggestions based on the information the desk agents found.

The cross departmental program was especially important for this team since it would be far more efficient to have a committee made of members that could understand all aspects of a mission and quickly and accurately build teams for missions based off of intel, field skills, and gear needed. As I pondered this, Amy spoke up.

"Sir Alexander, I'm troubled. In the past, the Spartans have engaged in more childish mischief. Nothing of the scale of a massive weapon."

"I agree, but we should remain calm until after the intelligence meeting just in case it is not as bad as we think. There is no use overreacting if it happens to be something more harmless than we presume."

"I hope you're right."

Location: ICPA HQ – Intelligence Room

On the right side of Amy's office was a tinted glass door with sculptures on both sides. Amy slid her keycard into its scanner and the door disintegrated into thin air. The two of us, along with the intelligence members who had arrived, stepped through the strange door into a room lined with windows showing the snowy landscape outside. Holographic screens were embedded in the conference table showing the latest information. We took our seats with Amy sitting at the head of the table. Activating a switch on the table, the windows tinted themselves, obscuring any view of the outside. A large projector screen descended from the ceiling to reveal the schematics of the newly discovered weapon.

"We have a new case. The Spartans are developing a weapon in Paris, France. Not much more information is available about the plan. Sir Alexander and I will keep investigating, but we would like your help as well," stated Amy gravely. The spies turned in their chairs and started to use the holo-computers around the room for research. Amy and I supervised.

"I have some new information!" exclaimed Matthew, nearly jumping out of his chair. Matthew was one of the younger spies who we always had trouble keeping under control. He was too energetic for a desk agent, but too loud to be a field agent.

"Yes, Matthew?" I smiled, trying to keep my cool.

"I intercepted a *highly* encrypted email from the base in Paris to Mac with the latest statistics and information regarding the new weapon," said Matthew proudly. All the spies rushed to his screen. The message read:

GOOD AFTERNOON BOSS. THE WEAPON IS ALMOST FINISHED. WE HAVE IT AIMED AT THE ICPA MAIN BASE IN COLORADO. THE BEST PART IS THAT THE WEAPON IS ENGINEERED TO BE VIRTUALLY SILENT SO NO ONE WILL EVEN KNOW WHAT HAPPENED ONCE WE ENGAGE THE LAUNCH.

The room flew into a flurry of panic. One of the spies nearly set the base into extreme lockdown.

"Everyone, calm down," commanded Amy, "We are not going to panic; we are going to solve this problem." Everyone calmed down a bit, but it was still unnerving to know that there was a weapon pointed at the building we were standing in. After the spies had cooled down, Amy sent them back to their regular tasks. She turned to me with one of her serious faces. I knew it meant I was heading to Paris.

Location: Agent Double J's Design Studio_

I made my way to Agent Double J's Studio later that day. I walked in to find her already working on outfits for the mission.

"I am a bit nervous for this mission, I have never disabled a gigantic weapon before," I said.

"Oh, don't worry. These new garments are fire, explosion, water, and bulletproof as usual," said Agent Double J.

"I guess you can never be too safe," I tried to laugh.

"Very true."

Amy wandered in as we were talking. "Hey guys, since this is one of those big missions, I wanted to give you the list of who is going." She sighed. "Since I can only trust the top spies in the agency it will be me, Laurel, Agent Double J, and Sir Alexander. In this way, we can have expertise from each of the main departments." We all nodded. It was unusual to bring spies that were not usually working in the field, but this was going to be one of our most risky missions yet, and we could only trust a limited number of people. I did have to give myself a little bit of a pat on the back since Laurel and I had both worked hard with dual training programs and although we were desk agents, we could still effectively navigate fieldwork for the most part.

Location: Conference Room & Plane_

The next day, Amy called our team together to devise a plan.

"All right, team, this is going to be one complicated mission, but I believe that I have found a way we can sneak into Paris without the Spartans even knowing," Amy started. We all looked at each other quizzically. "I have had our mechanics and infiltration departments develop a special type of jet for this mission. A jet we can safely crash."

I dropped a stack of paperwork I was holding, Laurel gasped, and Agent Double J bit her lip.

"Don't worry, we will be fine, but for the plan, we need to 'crash' the plane," said Amy trying to calm us down. "First, we will let the Spartans know we are on the way. We will let them shoot at our plane and start to crash. At about 3,000 feet, we will all be ejected out of the plane. Agent Double J has added a camouflage setting to our spy gear, so we will be practically invisible while falling. Our parachutes have the same camouflage technology."

We all tentatively walked into the plane hangar after our briefing. I looked at the jet we would be taking. It seemed sturdy enough, so I decided to put aside my fear and climb aboard. Inside, we had plenty of amenities to keep us occupied. There was a TV, a workstation with a laptop, and a viewing room with a nice set of comfy chairs.

"This might not be so bad after all," smiled Laurel.

Amy and Laurel walked into the cockpit while Agent Double J and I sat in the back seats. Usually, we would have had Bruce fly, but since the plane had to be destroyed, we couldn't risk bringing an extra agent. Amy, being a field agent, was already an adept pilot, and Laurel had taken flight training specifically for the mission.

"Ready for takeoff, flight attendants please prepare for crosscheck," Amy's voice floated over the intercom. I smiled at her little joke and got up to check the doors and other instruments in the back.

"All doors armed," I replied over the speaker system. I sat just as the plane lifted off the ground. Amy and Laurel walked back to brief us on the next part of our faux crash landing.

"Don't worry, the plane is on autopilot right now," reassured Amy. "The ICPA should be sending an unencrypted email that will reveal our coordinates to the Spartans so they can come shoot us down."

"I feel great already," I retorted.

"We will all step into this capsule when the alarm sounds," instructed Amy, gesturing to a small escape pod looking device.

Even after working more in the field, it was hard to me to psych myself up for the plane crash. Working in the field sure was exhausting. After many hours had passed, Amy ran an equipment check. We all had our parachutes and oxygen masks. We sat and nervously watched the clouds soar past. Right when I was starting to calm down, the alarm sounded, and red lights illuminated the cabin.

"It's go-time!" shouted Amy over the alarm. We all ran to the escape capsule. The doors swished open, and we piled in. Amy pressed the seal button.

"*Doors armed please stand by,*" came an electronic voice.

We all waited for the blow.

"When the plane explodes, the capsule will drop until we reach 3,000 feet. I will then pull the release lever and we will parachute the rest of the way down," instructed Amy. I kept watching the small window on the door. The whole room jolted, and black smoke covered the window. I felt the plane snap apart. We all lifted off the floor as the capsule started to fall. My ears were in utter pain due to our speedy descent.

"Okay, here we go," shouted Amy. She reached to a box and opened it. Inside was a red lever. When activated, the capsule split in half. Wind rushed into my face and the temperature dropped. We all started to free-fall. When we were able, we joined hands in a circle. Amy guided us away from the falling debris. When we came closer to the ground, everyone let go of each other and deployed his or her parachute. I could hardly see my colleagues because of our camouflaged gear. We all landed safely and quickly ran to regroup.

"That went better than expected," commented Amy. The rest of us could not talk because we were in such shock. Our team started to make our way toward Paris, which was about ten miles away. The walk was very long, so we caught a taxi on the edge of the road as soon as we could.

"I almost didn't see you, your clothes blend in so well," commented the driver, "In fact, they blend to the seat too."

We all just smiled.

Location: Paris, France_

It didn't take us long to arrive in Paris, which was a relief since the taxi wasn't cheap. I gazed out the window at the great architecture and waterways. Everyone I had ever met had said Paris was beautiful; they were correct. It contrasted with a lot of other countries I had visited on past field assignments in that most of the buildings were made of stone rather than wood or other materials. The architecture was also quite ornate, and it was easy to see that there was a deep history in the city. Driving down the street, we saw the Eiffel Tower in the distance. I reflected on how Paris was also the city of love. I wondered if any of us might find our true love here, excluding Agent Double J who already had a boyfriend. It certainly wouldn't be me. Even an entire city dedicated to love probably wouldn't probably be enough to overcome by bad luck with amour.

I snapped out of my daydreaming to the taxi driver's voice. "All right, here you go, the International Coffee House," announced the taxi driver. We made our way into the establishment. There were a few customers in the shop. They did not notice us, because we were still in our camouflage.

"Over here," I called, motioning to a plant. We all stood around the plant. It sat in semi-circle cut into the floor, which rotated until we were standing in another room. The secret passage led to one of our bases. We changed into our casual clothes. After everyone changed, we met around a table in the conference room.

"I am so glad we have bases all over the world. It makes things so much easier," commented Agent Double J. Amy passed out the files to get us ready for the plan of action.

"Each of us will go out and see if we can find any information about the Spartans, or the new weapon," instructed Amy. "There must be someone around who knows a little about where the new weapon might be housed. We will meet back here at eight p.m. to go over our findings."

Location: The Streets of Paris_

We exited the secret base and set out to find the mysterious location of the weapon. We decided to use a buddy system just in case anyone got into trouble. Laurel and I were team one, and Agent Double J and Amy made team two. The teams split up. Laurel and I headed toward the city center, and Amy and Agent Double J toward the outskirts.

"It is a nice day to be walking," I commented to Laurel.

"It sure is. I can't wait to start investigating. This is my first official field mission," exclaimed Laurel in excitement. "If you don't count rescuing Amy." I pulled out a map so we could plan where we wanted to go. We both decided to stop at some of the major restaurants and anywhere where there was a lot of red color, that being the Spartans favorite hue. As we walked, we happened upon a flower shop. It would have appeared fairly normal, but almost all the flowers were a scarlet red.

"I believe we have reached an unexpected destination," commented Laurel.

"Time to investigate," I said. We both walked into the store to see who was running it. A tough guy dressed all in red stood behind the counter. I had to hold back my laugh. The Spartans owned a *flower shop?* It was so unlike them, seeming far too feminine, but they must have decided to take some drastic measures to disguise any bases involved with the weapon operation.

"Welcome to the Scarlet Flower Shop," droned the Spartan. Laurel and I exchanged an amused glance.

"Hi, we were looking to buy some purple flowers," The Spartan heaved himself out of his chair.

"I'll have to look in the back." He sighed, acting like it was a lot of work to move. Once he exited the room, Laurel and I stepped behind the counter and started poking around.

"Look, Sir Alexander! There is a button with an S on it under the cash register," gasped Laurel.

"Do you have your detonators ready?" I asked. Laurel nodded. I pressed the button and a rack of flowers slid aside revealing a door. I plugged in my laptop into a nearby security port and hacked the security code.

"All right, we don't have any purple—," the Spartan started to say when he saw us by the secret door.

"Wait! You can't go in there!" he yelled. Laurel threw a sticky detonator at him, and he stuck to the floor. We both quickly ran into the elevator and closed the door.

Location: Spartan Base_

"I bet he has already notified the other Spartans in this base," I cautioned. We both pulled out a few more detonators. When the doors slid open, a group of Spartans were waiting for us. Laurel sprayed a Spartan in the face with sleeping mist. I tripped two more Spartans, sticking them to the ground with adhesive. The last two Spartans charged me, and I fell over. They started to pull me across the room when they both fell to the floor. Laurel had shot both with tranquilizer darts.

"Quick, let's disguise ourselves," I said putting on one of the Spartan capes. After we had put on the rest of the Spartan gear, Laurel and I both agreed that we looked enough like everyone else that the Spartans probably would not notice.

"What happened here?" a Spartan shouted walking in.

"There were two ICPA agents who snuck in and sabotaged our troops," I replied.

"We must find them before they escape," commanded the Spartan. Laurel and I followed the Spartan back to a lounge type room. Spartans sat around, playing pool and watching TV.

"Laurel, see if you can find a way to the control room on your holo-map," I whispered.

"I'm on it," she replied. We both sat on one of the red couches while Laurel secretly looked at her map.

"I found it," she whispered in excitement. "It is down that hall." We glanced to see a small hallway in the corner of the room. We walked in to find a labyrinth of passageways and then followed Laurel's holo-map toward the control room. As we were walking down the stairs, I stepped down and felt the stair move below me. It was a trap. Water started to flow down the tunnel. Laurel and I put on oxygen masks. I shot my grappling hook into a wall at the end of the tunnel. We pulled ourselves along the wire until we reached the end of the passageway. Laurel pushed a button on the wall and a door slid open. We both tumbled into the control room with a wave of water. There happened to only be one Spartan working, so we easily knocked him out and proceeded to hack into the computer.

"What's this?" I inquired looking at the screen. "It looks like the weapon is housed right underneath the Eiffel Tower!"

"What an odd place; it would be so obvious," commented Laurel. I went through some more information on the weapon. It appeared to be a special type of missile that would make almost no noise. The missile's trajectory was clearly the ICPA main base and was set to launch in two days.

"Laurel, we need to save this information to a flash drive and show it to Amy right away," I said. Laurel pulled out an ICPA flash drive that fit into Spartan computers. I downloaded all the data.

"Let's get out of here," urged Laurel.

"I totally agree," I replied. We both ran back through the labyrinth of hallways into the Spartan lounge.

"Stop right there!" a voice shouted. It was the Spartan that Laurel and I had stuck to the floor before we entered the base. He had apparently freed himself.

"Those are ICPA agents. Get them before they escape," he yelled. Laurel and I ran for the elevator. I tripped and somersaulted across the floor. Laurel threw me the flash drive. One of the Spartans grabbed my arm and pried the disk out of my hand. Laurel ran by and whisked it out of his grasp. Eventually, we both made it to the elevator. I opened the doors, while Laurel fended off the Spartans. At the last second, she slipped through the doors as they were closing.

"That was close," said Laurel. We both sat, exhausted, when we heard an announcement over the intercom.

"*Base in lockdown, all doors and elevators not operational,*" said the electronic voice.

"Great. I guess we'll have to get out the hard way," I groaned. Laurel and I cut out the top of the elevator and scaled the shaft just like on many other missions. In fact, it was so common for agents to end up in precarious elevator or lift based situations that we had extensive training on handling such events. When we reached the top, I overrode the security setting allowing us to exit. We both ran back out onto the streets toward the International Coffee House.

Location: ICPA Base_

"Amy, you will be amazed at the information we found," I said as soon as we entered the base. Agent Double J and Amy were sitting at the table, looking rather defeated.

"Good, because we didn't find anything," sighed Amy. Laurel and I showed our findings.

"We don't have much time. We will need to disable the missile before it's too late. That means we are headed to the Eiffel Tower," responded Amy.

The next day we set out. "To the Eiffel Tower we go," I said to the group. We walked through the beautiful streets of Paris. Our destination loomed in the distance.

"Before we put in a day's work, why don't we have breakfast at one of the cafés or a bakery?" suggested Agent Double J.

"Well, I suppose," said Amy. Our group found a bakery on one of the streets. The shop was small and smelled sweet with a hint of coffee. A menagerie of fresh French pastries was spread out beckoning us to consume them. I had my sights on the *Pain Au Chocolat* right away. After ordering in broken French, the kind shop owner thew in a few extra goodies for us for free. We sat on a nearby bench taking in the street view while enjoying our breakfast. Our group had started eating when a young man walked up.

"Hello, Miss," he smiled at Laurel. "My name is Nick."

"Hi," she blushed.

"Mind if I offer you this coffee to go with your breakfast?" he asked. Laurel was too flustered to respond.

"I take that as a yes," laughed Nick handing her a cup of coffee from a local shop. Agent Double J, Amy, and I sat on one bench while Nick and Laurel moved to another.

"Oh my! It looks like Laurel has found a potential suitor in the city of love," I said. We sat and ate our breakfast while listening in on Laurel and Nick's conversation.

Location: The Streets of Pairs

After we finished eating, Nick departed. We were bursting with questions for Laurel.

"Did he give you his num—?"

"Where does he wor—?"

"How old—?" We both talked at once.

"I don't know all of that. We just met," laughed Laurel. We gossiped as we walked toward the Eiffel Tower in the distance. On the way, we passed a curious street performer with a group of rabbits. I wanted to stop and see what the attraction was all about, but fearing pick pockets, and a lack of time, we kept onward toward the tower. When we arrived, a staff member asked if we were interested in ascending the architectural edifice.

"Thanks, but actually we have a few questions for you," I said.

"Certainly," commented the employee.

"Have you seen anyone, especially dressed in red, frequent your facility?" I inquired.

"Funny, I thought you would be curious about the history of the tower. It was actually built in 1889," smiled the employee.

"What about our first question?" I prompted.

"Sorry, I tend to get carried away - yes. It must be a fashion trend or something these days, many of them stop by every day. I'm sure you can find someone dressed in red today. Enjoy your visit. If you have any questions about the tower, feel free to ask. I am afraid I can't give you much fashion advice though," finished the employee, walking away.

"Hey look, isn't that Nick?" I asked Laurel. We glanced at a young man all in red quickly duck behind a wall nearby.

"I hope not. He is dressed in red. I bet it's a Spartan," said Laurel. We all ran to the gray, concrete wall and peeked behind.

"I wonder where he went. There is nothing back here," I said.

"Look, a piece of red fabric is caught in this trashcan," said Agent Double J. Amy slid the trashcan over, revealing a button underneath. She stepped on the button and an elevator slid out of the ground.

"Would you look at that," I exclaimed. We piled in and descended to the Spartan Base.

Location: Spartan Base - Main Hallway_

The doors slid open, and we quickly slipped behind some nearby crates.

"This looks like what I imagine Area 51 would be like," commented Amy. We nodded in agreement. We appeared to be in an underground warehouse. There were crates piled around and a missile in the process of completion. The missile was in front of a door, which I guessed led to a tunnel to go outside. I took a closer look at the crates in front of us. They had a label affixed that said *EXPLOSIVE* in big red letters.

"Um, guys, we are standing behind crates of explosives," I hissed. We glanced around nervously. As we waited, I spotted Mac walking onto the floor where the missile was sitting.

"Hurry up, you useless slugs! This thing needs to be done by tomorrow!" he yelled. I shuddered. They were truly planning the end of the ICPA. Little did they know we were here, witnessing the preparations. That was something I never understood about the Spartans. Did they think we would not figure out what they were up to? Suddenly, a familiar person walked by. It was Nick from earlier.

"Oh my!" gasped Laurel. She had grown a crush on a Spartan. I reached over to comfort her, and she just ran away back into the elevator leaving the three of us alone.

"We need to help Laurel; without her fully focused on the mission things could get even more complicated," Amy sighed. We ran back into the elevator and rode up to find Laurel sobbing, sitting with her back against the concrete wall.

"It's okay. There are plenty more guys out there who are way better," comforted Agent Double J, patting Laurel on the back.

"I know...but...I just got carried away thinking I had gotten lucky. It was so romantic and in *Paris*!" Laurel sobbed. We walked back over to the road and took a taxi back to the ICPA base. After two hours Laurel still was not improving. Amy pulled the rest of the team aside.

"They both need to know the truth about each other. It's our only hope," frowned Amy.

"I wonder if he will be near the bakery again tomorrow morning?" I questioned.

"He will have to be," said Amy. "I have a special mission for the both of you."

Location: The Streets of Paris_

Agent Double J and I had the task of getting Nick to the bakery in the morning so that he and Laurel could both divulge their true identities to each other. Amy had gotten Nick's number off Laurel's phone, so Agent Double J and I could make a call. We walked through the streets of Paris looking for a payphone.

"I hope this does not cause a disaster," I sighed.

"We will do our best to keep the situation under control," said Agent Double J. It took us forever to find a payphone, but we finally spotted one on a street corner. We quickly ran over and dropped in a few Euros. I listened to Agent Double J as she made the call.

"Hi Nick, this is one of Laurel's friends. She is rather busy, so she asked me to call you. She would like to meet at the bakery near where we first met you tomorrow. Good. See you there," trilled Agent Double J.

"That part is done," I sighed. We both plodded back to the base.

Location: ICPA Base & Café_

My alarm went off at five a.m. I drowsily tried to figure out why I had set it so early, and then I remembered. Today was the day Laurel would confront Nick. I shuddered. Nick did not seem as dangerous as other Spartans from our previous encounters, but one never could be too safe. I slipped out of bed and pulled on my ICPA gear. Laurel was already up, rehearsing what she would say with Amy.

"I don't know if I can do this," sighed Laurel.

"You have to," replied Amy. Agent Double J and I just stood still watching Laurel. We felt bad for her but did not know what we could do to help.

"Are you ready?" asked Amy.

"I guess I have no choice," said Laurel. We all set off to the bakery. That day was very cloudy, and a light mist covered Paris in a thin layer of icy water. It was great to finally reach the bakery; it was much warmer inside. When we entered, Nick was sitting at a table in the corner.

"Good morning, Laurel. Is something wrong?" he inquired.

"Laurel has something to tell you," I said looking away.

Laurel took a deep breath and stepped forward from the group. "Nick, I need to tell you that I work in law enforcement," Laurel whispered. She then sat in a nearby chair.

"You do?" he asked nervously.

"I came across information tying you to a cult," replied Laurel weakly.

"I don't think it is a good idea to keep seeing each other," stated Nick. He then got up and left. Laurel burst into tears.

"I don't understand," she sobbed. "One day, I think I have found a halfway decent guy, and the next, he ends up having a dirty secret."

"I think this probably happens more in Paris than you think," I offered. We all stood around Laurel, not knowing what to do, when Amy decided it was time to get going.

"Well, Nick or no Nick, we have to stop that missile today no matter what," she ordered. Laurel nodded and wiped her tears.

"Okay, I am ready to go," she smiled forcefully.

"That's the spirit!" I encouraged.

Location: Eiffel Tower/Spartan Base_

Our group returned to the Eiffel Tower where another tour guide intercepted us for the second time. We politely excused ourselves and took the secret entrance into the Spartan base.

"Look, they have not launched the missile yet," exclaimed Agent Double J. We still had some time. Our only problem was there was a large layer of glass separating us from the missile.

"If we break the glass, we will most certainly trigger some sort of alarm," contemplated Amy.

"We could find a way to the control room and abort the launch," offered Laurel.

"Yes, but that room is most likely full of Spartans. I think we should find the electrical room and short out the launch system," I suggested.

"Here, let's split into teams. Amy and Laurel can take the control room, and Sir Alexander and I will take the electrical room," directed

Agent Double J. We all agreed and set off on our respective goals. Agent Double J and I ran down the hall toward the electrical room following our holo-maps. After a long run, we reached our destination. We ducked behind some crates in the hall when we saw two Spartan guards standing on both sides of the door.

"What should we do?" I asked.

"We have our weapons," commented Agent Double J.

"I guess it's our only choice," I replied. I pulled out a sleeping detonator and rolled it across the floor. One of the guards picked it up and was about to disable it when the room erupted in purple mist, putting the Spartans to sleep. Agent Double J and I ran for the door and hacked in by using a smartcard we had developed that held a bunch of Spartan encryption keys allowing access to many of their facilities. Once inside, I sealed the large silver entrance behind us.

"Okay, first we need to figure out which wires control what things," I said.

"We could use this computer," said Agent Double J. In the corner of the room was a computer that controlled the electrical infrastructure. We looked at the screen. There was a map of the building showing what wires controlled what rooms, and if the rooms currently had power.

"It looks like the missile is the green wiring," commented Agent Double J. I pulled out a pair of scissors and cut the green wires in the room.

"Can you tell if it disabled the missile?" I asked Agent Double J.

"Yes, but it looks like they have a backup generator for the missile system," she stated nervously. I should have known; it made total sense. As I was contemplating the situation, an alarm went off and the electrical room's lighting turned red. *Intruder alert! Intruder alert!* An electronic voice boomed over the speaker system.

"I bet we triggered the alarm system when we cut the wires," I pondered aloud as banging emanated from the door.

"Who's in there? Come out right now or we will open the door for you," came a Spartan voice from in the hallway. My wrist communicator beeped, it was Amy and Laurel.

"Sir Alexander, we are in a bit of a sticky situation up here. We have been attacked by a group of Spartans. See if you can get up to wing D5 on the second floor, Amy out."

"I wonder if there is another way we can get out of this room?" I questioned as the banging on the door grew louder.

"There!" exclaimed Agent Double J pointing to a small skylight on the ceiling. We both stacked up some of the wiring racks and climbed our way up to the skylight. When I broke through the glass, we both found ourselves exiting from a drain at the base of the Eiffel Tower.

"Just doing some maintenance," I nodded to a passerby.

"Where exactly is wing D5?" inquired Agent Double J. We both looked at our holo-maps.

"It looks like it is on the right of the missile chamber," I commented. Agent Double J and I ran over to about where we expected the room to be, and sure enough there was a drain on the floor. We both hopped in and found ourselves in the main control room. There were about twenty Spartans.

"Quick, get them before they intercede our mission," yelled the head Spartan. I pulled out a sleep detonator, but it was too late. A group of Spartans had completely restrained me. I looked over to see Agent Double J in a similar situation.

"Mac will not be pleased," said one of the Spartans as they dragged us out into the hall and tied us up with Amy and Laurel.

"I'm sorry, guys. Agent Double J and I were coming to rescue you; I guess that didn't work out," I said. I glanced down the hall to see Mac running toward us.

"Ha! Caught you again. This time you won't escape. I have guards." Spartans dressed in red armor with electro-blades stood on both sides of our nemesis. I had never seen Spartan guards before, so I assumed they were a new addition.

"Come on, let's walk and talk," Mac smirked as the guards untied us and removed our weapons. We made our way to the missile chamber.

"I wanted to let you know, the ICPA is done for. It will no longer exist with the touch of a button. This button," smirked Mac pulling out a small remote.

"You wouldn't dare," Amy shouted.

"Really, it would be so simple. The entire agency gone, and the only ones left to deal with would be you four," Mac laughed. "It is great to have the upper hand this time." Mac dramatically held the remote in front of our faces, and to our dismay he pressed the button. The large door of the chamber opened, and the missile charged up and shot out. Laurel collapsed onto the ground in fear. Amy stood frozen, tears rolled down Agent Double J's face, and I leaned against the wall so I wouldn't fall over.

"It's over. There is nothing you can do now but sit and wait for the news," Mac laughed as he walked out of the room, "I have better things to do. *Guards*, keep them from leaving." I sat with the rest of my team.

"I can't believe it, Sir Alexander. Everything we created over the past few years, just gone," stated Amy in shock. I had no idea what to say.

"Maybe there's still a chance we can save everyone," I comforted, but I had no idea what we could do. We all just sat in silence, until a voice echoed through the missile chamber.

"Mac has requested I bring the prisoners to the cells." Nick, Laurel's ex-crush, walked into the room. The guards escorted Nick and the rest of us along the hallway.

"We could have been together! Now you are taking me to a jail cell," Laurel shouted to Nick.

"Don't worry, things between us are still possible," he said dropping a sleep detonator onto the ground, knocking out the guards, "C'mon, we don't have much time." We stood in shock that Nick was helping us escape. A group of Spartans rounded the corner.

"Look, they are escaping," one shouted. Nick returned our weapons, and we went to work knocking over, tying together, and putting to sleep the Spartans around us.

"Let's get to the hangar," commanded Nick. I could not tell if we could trust him or not, but it was our only chance to save the agency. We bolted down the hallway, following Nick. We made it to the hangar in no time. The room was huge. It housed all sorts of black planes and jets I had never seen before.

"We will take this one," shouted Nick. In front of us stood a strange thin plane with spiky wings. Its design screamed Spartan, but we all piled in anyway.

"Let Laurel fly, she knows what she is doing," I commanded.

"Fine by me, sweetheart," Nick said smiling at Laurel.

"Now is not the time for flirting," I said as we sped out of the hangar.

Location: Spartan Plane_

We lifted off the ground and exited through the tunnel that ended up coming out behind a fountain on the other side.

"Okay, I have reduced the speed of the missile so we should be able to catch up to it and shoot it down before it reaches the base," instructed Nick. Laurel pushed on the throttle, and we soared through the sky.

"Alex, you and Agent Double J go monitor the controls on the back wall. Amy, you get to man the turret. Laurel and I will pilot the plane," instructed Nick. I sat at the strange controls and did my best to figure out what they did.

These were the moments where my confidence in the field wavered a bit. Here we were escaping the Spartan base with someone we couldn't fully trust, and it was my job to monitor controls I was never trained to use. I took a deep breath and tried to center myself. All of the controls were in French. Although it was similar to Spanish in some respects, I could only pick out a few words. I rummaged around and found the multilingual guidebook and frantically flipped to the English section.

On the page, there was a diagram of all the controls with English labels. I thought to myself about the fact that the manufacturer probably wasn't expecting the guide to have to be used in an emergency situation. As I sat nervously tinkering with the various buttons, an alarm sounded, and an image of a missile appeared on my screen.

"Hey Nick, the missile is just up ahead," I shouted anxiously. There was still a chance to save our agents. I found the correct buttons just in time and locked onto the flying weapon.

"I will order an evacuation of the base, just in case," said Amy. Laurel flew the plane right up beside the missile.

"The missile will have a large shock wave, so the second you shoot it we will have to veer the plane away from the explosion and drop about a few hundred feet in altitude," instructed Nick. I looked on my screen and adjusted the settings to lock the turrets onto the missile.

"Go for it, Amy," I yelled. Amy fired a few times.

"I got it!" yelled Amy in excitement. The plane veered to the left, and we started to fall. That was the second time in the last few days we had to free-fall. As the Spartans had said, the missile made no sound when it exploded. Laurel leveled out the plane, and we soared back up to altitude.

"Let's land at the ICPA base; we should check on the spies," I suggested.

"I will let them know that we are arriving in a Spartan plane," commented Agent Double J. After a long flight, we saw the ICPA base below us. It was safe and sound.

Location: ICPA HQ_

We landed in the secret hangar inside one of the mountains. The inside of the base was eerily quiet. The lights were dim, and the doors were locked after the evacuation. There were also large lead doors sealed in case the base did get hit. Amy deactivated the doors one by one as we made our way to her office.

"So, this is the infamous ICPA headquarters," said Nick admiring the facility.

"Yes, but you will have to be questioned before you are released, and even then, we may have to wipe your memory," commented Amy.

"No!" cried Laurel, "You can't do that." Amy looked at the two of them, they were cute together; even I thought so.

"Well... you see...Amy, I want to become an ICPA agent and leave my Spartan past behind me," smiled Nick sheepishly.

"It will take a lot of paperwork and a background check, but it can be arranged," said Amy. "You also have to be monitored and won't have much access until we can trust you."

"Oh great, this means I have to create paperwork for agents transferred from the Spartans," I joked. We all stood together relieved when Amy pressed the "all clear" button. The base returned to normal.

Location: ICPA HQ - Conference Room_

The next day we had a small ceremony to welcome our first Spartan defector. Nick looked so proud arriving in his new ICPA uniform. Laurel stood at the front of the room to award him with a medal and certificate.

"Today, fellow spies, we have a very special occasion," announced Amy from the podium, "A former Spartan has defected to the ICPA, and he has taken an oath to leave behind his Spartan past and be committed to preventing crime *around* the world." The room erupted into applause. Nick leaned over and kissed Laurel on the check. After the ceremony, I sat and started to fill out Nicks paperwork. It was good to have a former Spartan on our staff; he would know some of the Spartan techniques. Future missions would be much easier with Nick along. I worried that we would have to protect him, because if Mac got him back, who knew what would become of him? I did not say anything to Laurel, however, because I did not want her to worry about her new friend.

Location: ICPA HQ - Desk Agent Department_

That night, I stayed late to finish up the last bit of paperwork and to get the base back in order. Amy walked by my office on her way out.

"Hey, Sir Alexander, what are you still doing here?" she asked. We usually left the base about the same time.

"I don't know, Amy. I guess the events over the past few days have been very troubling. The Spartans have never tried to destroy us before. They are definitely stepping up their game. Mac is still on the loose after multiple missions. It is just stressing me out," I replied.

"Would you like to take a few weeks off?" asked Amy, "You can spend some time at your vacation home in Japan to relax." I gratefully accepted her offer and bought a plane ticket that night. I sent a quick text to Yuki to let her know I would be back for a while. I then started to close down my office when I noticed that I was not alone. I walked to Laurel's office to find her and Nick talking.

"How late do you plan to stay?" I laughed. "Did Amy check on you guys on her way out?"

"No worries, we are going on our first date tonight," said Laurel.

"Then you better get going," I said. After everyone had left, I walked through the empty desk agent area. I was so glad the base was okay. I knew that my flight left tomorrow, but I had a strange feeling I would be back very soon.

Location: Flight to Japan_

The next day on the flight to Tokyo, I was watching the news. The reporter was very excited.

"Breaking news. A missile from somewhere in Europe was rapidly speeding toward the USA when we caught this footage," exclaimed the reporter. I watched the footage and noticed our plane, a small black dot, veer off to the left of the screen.

"We think the missile was shot down. Whoever was able to stop this terrorist act, on behalf of civil society. Thank you," finished the reporter.

I knew it was the ICPA to thank. I also had to congratulate myself, despite the situation I had been much calmer and more confident in the field than before. I could see myself starting grow as a field agent.

DARKNESS IN PLAIN SIGHT: CANADA

Location: ICPA HQ_

After my brief vacation in Japan, I had returned to Denver. As I got ready for the day, I called Kai on the phone.

"You won't believe it, but I think I am actually improving as a field agent," I boasted.

"I heard about the Paris mission. It sounds like you really held your own in the field on that trip," came his voice through the receiver.

"I would like to say so. I'm coming back into the office today. Yuki sent me with some Japanese sweets, so I'll bring you a few."

It was a normal day at the agency when I arrived. I made my way up the long flight of stairs. At the top, I talked with Jeff at the security check-in before admission into the building. I stepped into the Desk Agent Suite. That was my domain. Right in front of me sat a desk with the Desk Agent General Secretary, Barbra. On her left and right were dividers that sectioned off the room going all the way to the back wall. It was much like a regular office; we had cubicles, desks, and a few plants around the large room. The sound of typing filled the air as all the agents busily hacked, emailed, and researched on the ICPA computers. I walked past all of this to the right of the room toward my office. On the way there, Veronica stepped out of her cubicle.

"Good morning, Sir Alexander. I have just finished all Nick's paperwork. He is now officially an ICPA agent." She smiled proudly. "Also, you have a visitor waiting in your office."

"I'm sure Laurel will be very happy to hear that," I replied as I strode to my office. Kai was there, wearing his signature ICPA tank top.

"So, what do you have for me?" he smiled patting me on the back, a bit too hard as one would expect from a body builder.

"I've got some konpeito. I know you said you were craving it. Yuki and I also visited the Tottori Sand Dunes, so I picked up some 20th Century Pear flavored goodies too."

"You're the best, Alex!" Kai embraced me in a bear hug.

"Enough idling around," I teased.

"Okay fine, I do have a few classes this morning. Thanks again for the treats. Let's grab lunch soon now that you're back in," Kai smiled and waved as he left my office. The next thing I knew, Veronica slipped in.

"You know how much we all appreciate you getting Kai up here more often," she laughed. "Such a handsome guy. Look at you making friends in different departments. I never would have expected you to have a friend in the training facility."

"It's the new me," I responded.

I could finally get to work after everyone left my office. I noticed that I had a voicemail. I sat and heaved a stack of paperwork to the opposite side of my desk. The red light on my phone stared at me. I picked up the headset and entered my password.

"You have one new message, first unheard message," stated the electronic voice. "Hey, Alex this is Nick. I was working in the lab on floor twenty-seven when some strange things started happening. It seemed as if the security system shut down for a short period of time, because all the doors unlocked for about twenty seconds. Since I'm new, I don't know if this is normal, but I just wanted to let you know." I did not know what to think.

That wasn't supposed to happen. I decided to check in with Ken at the Security Center. I stepped out of my office into the futuristic ICPA hallways. The security center was in the middle of the building, so the quickest way to get there was to take a tram. I walked a few doors down and found the one I was looking for. A small picture of a metro was on the middle of the door. I entered my code and the door slid out of the way, revealing a tram next to a small platform.

The vehicle was open air and had seats all the way around it. The tram itself was attached to a small rail. I hopped onto one of the seats and buckled in. The tram started to move and picked up great speed. My hair whipped in the breeze, and I felt butterflies in my stomach as I looped around on my way down the track. I arrived at the security center in no time.

Location: ICPA HQ - Security Center_

I walked up to the heavily armed door on the Security Center and scanned my fingerprint. The doors swished open, and I walked in to find a huge multi-level cylindrical room with interspersed walkways crisscrossing through the atrium at various levels. Agents were busily monitoring screens and other equipment. The lighting in the room was dim with a blue hue, and the cavernous space made the sounds of typing echo. Directly ahead sat a reception area.

"Does anyone know where I can find Ken?" I asked. The room fell silent, and a young agent walked over to me. He avoided any eye contact but replied,

"I know where he is, follow me." I followed the young agent to a small elevator in the exact center of the room encased in glass that ascended through the middle of the space. We boarded and rode up, watching the platforms and spies below grow smaller and smaller. The young spy did not say a word the entire time. The elevator slowed and lurched when we reached the top. The doors swished open, and the young spy motioned me out.

I stepped into a very dark office with gold, black, and jade coloring. Bronze abstract sculptures lined the room illuminated in brighter light. The air was cold and eerie. The elevator door swished shut behind me, and I noticed that the young spy did not enter the office with me. It was very strange. I wondered if he was scared of the space or of Ken. I walked forward and massive glass doors slid to the side, revealing a large chair and desk. The back of the chair was facing me.

"What is the interruption this time?" a voice groaned, "It better be good."

I stood rather startled. Ken must have thought I was the young spy who had not entered. That was no way to treat a fellow agent.

"I had some questions about the security system this morning," I stated firmly. Ken whirled in his chair when he recognized that I was not the young spy.

"Ah, what can I do for you, Sir Alexander?" asked Ken clearly embarrassed. He was a rather arrogant spy who liked to act like he controlled the agency. However, he did not want Amy to know, so he was always better behaved when she or I were there, but we heard many stories through the grapevine. Ken was about thirty with longer brown hair. I could tell he considered himself a fashionista as he always wore tight fitted suits that showed off his stature. He had chiseled features and long hair that he wore with his bangs covering a bit of his face. Many of the spies at the agency found him rather dashing despite his less than friendly demeanor.

"It seems to me at about 07:00 hours the security system shut down for about twenty seconds. The locks on the doors were disarmed during that time, perhaps in the lab on floor twenty-seven?" I finished.

"As you well know, Sir Alexander, nothing in the entire agency gets past my watch. This is because I am *always watching*. The spies here know nothing of how much I see and the information I have access to. You are not in the position to tell me that I am not *watching*," Ken yelled. He swished his long bangs out of his face.

"I was not trying to offend you, but a spy did report this happening, so I am fairly sure it did," I said trying to keep my patience.

"You do not have the proper authorization to view the records, and I know that nothing happened. The ICPA is one of the most secure bases in the world. Leave it to me. I know what is going on," Ken glared. "Now go. I need to keep *watching* to make sure nothing happens, every second you waste could allow an intruder in." Ken swiveled back in his chair, and I left feeling rather strange about Ken's behavior. He almost seemed a bit suspicious. I decided my only choice was to go talk to Amy. She could help.

Location: ICPA HQ - Amy's Office_

I made my way back to Amy's office. When I entered, she was typing her recent records from our Paris mission.

"Hey Amy, could you get me into the security records? I think there was a breech, but Ken won't let me see them," I sighed.

"Of course," said Amy. She turned her computer so I could see. We both hacked into the records.

"Wait. Ken won't even let you see the records?" I inquired.

"Nope, but I hack in from time to time," she said. The pages of records did not show much but after some scrolling, I found a red entry marked "breech." The entry was deleted.

"What does this mean?" I asked. Did this mean that Ken had deleted the entry so Amy and I would not know? Was he expecting us to hack into the system? Just as Amy and I were contemplating these events, there was a loud knocking at the door. Amy opened it, and Ken burst in.

"Why in the world did you hack into the security database? I found traces of a breech that linked to this computer. There is nothing there for your eyes!" he yelled.

"Do you know who you are talking to? This is Amy, head of the agency. Why doesn't she have access to the database?" I asked.

"I am the only one with access, because with anyone else having access to it, it means they are *watching* too, and as you well know, Sir Alexander, I am the *only* one who can be *watching*!" yelled Ken. I looked at Ken in astonishment. Why in the world would Amy and I looking at the database be such an issue, and why was Ken so worked up? Laurel came running into Amy's office in tears.

"What seems to be the problem?" I asked.

"I went to talk to Nick and found the lab broken in, and...Nick is missing," babbled Laurel though her tears. Amy and I glanced at each other. Was this part of the Spartan's plan, and was Nick really on our side? So many questions poured into my mind. I turned to ask Ken if he had seen anything on the tapes, but strangely, Ken was gone.

"Where is Ken?" I asked Amy.

"He just walked out," stammered Amy. We both had the same thought. Was Ken working for the Spartans? If so, our entire organization could be in jeopardy. We had to find out what was going on, and fast.

"Laurel, when did you last see Nick?" I asked. I wanted to start investigating right away. I sensed the Spartans were involved in the situation.

"It looks like you have this investigation under control, Sir Alexander; I am leaving the main investigation you, because I have to monitor the other current missions," said Amy. I knew that I could not do this mission on my own, so I decided to contact Agent Double J after I finished questioning Laurel.

"I saw him this morning right before he went to work in the lab," sobbed Laurel.

"Did you notice anything strange before or after he left?" I asked.

"No, he seemed fine beforehand, but after he left the lock on my office door unlocked for a few seconds then relocked; I don't know if that puts any light on what you might be looking for," sighed Laurel.

Location: Agent Double J's Design Studio_

I walked quickly down the hallway to Agent Double J's Studio. When I entered, I could tell that she knew that we had a mission.

"What are we trying to solve this time?" she asked. I was about to tell her when I heard the lock on the door automatically click open.

"Did you hear the security system disarm? I think there is someone in our agency working against us. It may be Nick, but I also have suspicions about others," I whispered.

"Why are you whispering?" asked Agent Double J.

"You never know who is *watching*," I replied. I could tell Agent Double J knew right away I was talking about Ken with my emphasis of "watching," Ken's favorite phrase.

"First we need to find a safe place to talk, we need to know what all Ken can actually see," I suggested.

"I guess we are off to the security center then," said Agent Double J.

Location: ICPA Security Center_

We both made our way to the Security Center again using the trams. Once we arrived, we decided not to use the door and instead found another way in.

"I think I saw some windows from another room in Ken's office," I recalled. Agent Double J pulled out her holo-map, and sure enough there was a window in Ken's office that overlooked the Security Center. Agent Double J and I cut off a ventilation grate and found ourselves behind a control board; I peeked around the corner and saw that we were all clear. We both used our grappling hooks to scale the wall quickly, so the other spies would not know we were there. Once at the top, I disabled the window's security wires, and we both slipped into Ken's office.

Ken sat monitoring some computer screens on his desk. Agent Double J and I scooted along the wall and hid behind some of the bronze statues. We were about to go to the door to the surveillance room when I bumped one of the statues and a gold marble fell off. It rolled across the floor. Ken got up and walked over slowly. I knew we had been caught, and I had no excuse for being in his office. Ken lifted his fist. I winced, getting ready for the impact, but Ken simply replaced the marble.

"I had to stop monitoring the system for *this*! Wow what a day," he sighed, making his way back to the desk. Agent Double J and I looked at each other, relieved. I scanned my fingerprint on the door while Agent Double J shot the button to the elevator. They both opened at the same time Ken looked up at the elevator door while we slipped into the surveillance room.

"Careful, we don't have much time," I cautioned. Agent Double J and I started to look at the screens trying to find a place that was away from camera or audio recording.

"Amy's office does not seem to be on here, I don't know why I did not think of it before," exclaimed Agent Double J. We started to head for the door when it opened. Both of us dove beneath one of the control tables.

"I never thought that something could get past me, but I feel like there might be someone else here," floated Ken's voice. Agent Double J and I remained dead still. After Ken had walked around a while, he left the room.

"That was close," I whispered to Agent Double J. We both quickly exited and ran to Amy's office.

"Hey Amy, can we use your office to meet for our mission? It is the only place that is not under Ken's watch," I said.

"Sure, you can. Top secret."

Location: ICPA HQ - Lab on floor 27_

"I guess our next stop is the lab on floor twenty-seven," said Agent Double J. We both took the express elevator up a few floors and arrived at the lab that had been broken into. Ken already had an investigation crew scavenging for clues.

"Have you found anything?" I inquired.

"Ken told us to only tell him the evidence to make sure no one else is watching," said one of the spies.

"You can tell us; if Ken gives you grief because of it, let Amy know and we can put an end to it," I assured the group.

"In that case, we did find some strange Spartan boot prints, and this note," the spy said handing me the piece of paper. It read,

127 WEST STREET

CANADA

"I guess it would not hurt to find out where exactly this place is," I remarked. Agent Double J and I brought the piece of paper back to Amy's secret lab and analyzed it to see what we could find. There were fingerprint marks that matched some records in our system. They belonged to Denel, Mac's personal assistant.

"Nick may be in Canada now working with the Spartans," I sighed. It seemed like the only possibility, but I did not want to jump to conclusions without an investigation.

"I guess we need to find all of the 'West Streets' in Canada," groaned Agent Double J.

It took us a few days to narrow down a list of West Streets that the Spartans could have connections with. It was not easy, but we only had about five streets to visit in various parts of the country. We set off to find Nick and Denel later in the afternoon. A flight up into Ontario was our first stop.

Location: Ontario, Canada

"Wow, it's chilly up here," said Agent Double J as we stepped out of the airport. We caught a taxi to the nearest 127 West Street. When we arrived, I did not feel like it was the right place. A small candy shop sat on the corner of the street decorated in pink and purple.

"This seems way off," I chuckled to Agent Double J.

"I guess it never hurts to check, you remember how you found a base in the flower shop in Pairs. Plus, if it is not the right place at least we can get some candy," Agent Double J laughed. When we stepped inside, I felt like I recognized the girl working behind the counter.

"How may I help you?" the girl smiled. I now knew that I had seen her before, but I just could not place her. Was she Bruce's ex–

girlfriend? No, she was too tall. The girl walked over to a jar of candy on the shelf.

"Our special today is the mint twist," she suggested.

"Actually, before we make a purchase we were wondering if you have seen any suspicious activity around here, like a lot of people wearing red perhaps?" I probed.

"Oh, who are you to be asking?" she smirked.

"We are team of private investigators," I said.

"In that case, we can't have you around," the girl stated ominously. It hit me the girl was Denel. She pulled a lever and a cage encompassed Agent Double J and I.

"Perfect. Now I have three of you," she cheered. Both Agent Double J and I glanced at each other. I could tell she was wondering who the third agent was as well.

Location: Spartan Detainment Center_

We arrived at what appeared to be a building converted into a spy detainment center. The cells were not actually too bad. There was carpeting, a couch, and a window with bars drilled into the original frame. The window overlooked a quaint little garden below.

"Wow. This is not what I expected a Spartan detainment facility to be like," I admitted.

"Yes, it's much nicer than I pictured," replied Agent Double J. Denel walked into the room.

"Just because we are Spartans does not mean we are not civilized," she said. "You two are under our protection now." Protection? Hardly, we were in their prison. What kind of protection was that? What were they keeping us safe from?

"Make yourselves at home, you may be here for a while," giggled Denel. She clicked her way out of the room in her heels.

"There has to be a way out of here. There always is. The Spartans usually fail to think of every possibility," I glanced around the room. There were no ventilation grates, and there were no openings except for the door and the barred window.

"Did she take your weapons?" I asked Agent Double J. She nodded. It appeared we were going to be in custody for a while. At least, until I could acquire a screwdriver to remove the bars on the window. A few hours later, Denel arrived with our diner, which I did not eat for fear it was poison, but I did acquire the back of a fork.

"Look Agent Double J, we can use this to remove the screws," I said. I had removed two when I heard Denel clicking down the hallway. I quickly dumped the food on my plate in the trash and set the fork on top.

"Hungry, were we?" she laughed.

It wasn't fun being in Spartan confinement, even considering that it was not as bad as we expected. The main thing was it left me alone with my thoughts. What would a field agent do? I kept asking myself. I felt for certain that they would have found a way out almost instantly, not having to rely on the back of a fork to unscrew the window.

"I can tell what you are thinking about," said Agent Double J. "Don't worry about if you are a good enough field agent right now. The important part is you found a plan to get us out of here and it's working."

With regained confidence I did the only thing I could and had patience. Meal after meal passed, and I unscrewed a few screws each time. Eventually, the bars came off the window.

"Quick, Agent Double J, let's hop out the window before Denel comes back," I whispered. We both helped each other out of the window. I touched my feet to the grass in the small garden.

"Let's find our gear," suggested Agent Double J. We both snuck around the front of the building and entered through an unbarred window.

"Who are you?" exclaimed a Spartan guard spilling his coffee. I lunged at him and pinned his arms around his back while Agent Double J knocked him over pinning down his feet. I pushed his face into the carpet, so he could not scream.

"Okay, we are not going to hurt you, we just need to know where our gear is," I stated calmly. I let the Spartan lift his face off the ground.

"Sorry, sorry! Don't hurt me, please just take your gear; it's in Denel's office. I will get you in and that's it. No promises," stammered the Spartan. He led us to Denel's office quietly. I noticed Agent Double J steal his tranquilizer darts off his belt. When we were almost to the office the Spartan took off running down the hall. Agent Double J shot a dart hitting him square in the back.

"Nice thinking," I complimented.

"We only have a short bit of time before he wakes up. Let's get moving," replied Agent Double J. We picked the lock on Denel's office and entered.

The office matched Denel's personality. It was very organized. Black and white prints were hung fastidiously on the walls to complement the black office furniture with white accent pillows. Of course, to denote that we were still in a Spartan facility a vase of red flowers perched on the corner of the desk.

"I bet they are in this safe," exclaimed Agent Double J bending over to look at the small safe under Denel's desk.

"It is probably rigged, there has to be another way to open it," I hesitated. I started rummaging through Denel's desk to see if I could find anything. I finally found a sticky note under her computer monitor with the code. We entered the code and opened the vault.

"What is all of this?" asked Agent Double J. Inside the safe were shoes, jewelry, and Denel's wallet.

"Apparently our gear is somewhere else," I concluded. We scavenged the office and finally found our gear behind a secret mirror on the wall. We started to exit when Denel walked in. Agent Double J and I hid behind her long desk.

"I told you we should have kept them with Nick at the real detainment facility. I know it's all the way in Alberta, but still, they would not have escaped. This is your fault!" Denel yelled into her cell phone. Agent Double J rolled a sleep detonator under Denel's desk as she sat. A purple cloud engulfed the room, and Denel slumped in her chair fast asleep.

"Let's go," exclaimed Agent Double J. We both ran out the front doors of the building and down the street to safety.

Location: The Streets of Ontario_

We found refuge in a nearby bar, seeking safety in numbers. Agent Double J programmed our garments to match the people in the room. To anyone in the bar we looked like regulars.

"Nick is in need of our help," I stated without a plan.

"Once we get to Alberta, we can ask around and hopefully find the real detainment center," replied Agent Double J. I called the airport and found the next flight to Calgary left the next day at ten a.m. I booked two seats.

"So, what's the news?" inquired Agent Double J after I hung up.

"Our flight leaves tomorrow at ten a.m. We have some time to enjoy the local culture and avoid Denel. I'm sure they are looking for us," I responded. We both stepped out onto the streets of Ontario and caught a taxi to the nearby city of Cambridge. It was nice to relax a bit even though we had a case at hand. I smiled as I watched the landscape whiz by. After we arrived in Cambridge, Agent Double J and I aimlessly wandered around for a while when we noticed a sign advertising a conservatory where visitors could see rice paper butterflies.

"Let's check that out," said Agent Double J. We walked for a few blocks and came upon the building. Inside, it was warm and humid, a very different temperature from outdoors.

"Look, Sir Alexander, there is one of the butterflies," said Agent Double J running over to get a better view. The butterfly was thin-winged, and it had black and white coloring.

"It's very elegant," I agreed. We both enjoyed looking at the various species of butterflies in the conservatory, but after a while my legs were killing me.

"Hey, Agent Double J, I'm ready to call it a day." I forced a smile.

"Good idea," she replied. We found a small hotel, and thankfully there were two rooms available. We booked them and checked in for the night.

"I'll see you in the morning; let's meet at the breakfast bar," waved Agent Double J as we both stepped off the elevator. My room was a few doors down from hers. Once I was in my room, I got situated and fell asleep. It had been quite the day.

Location: Hotel_

I woke early the next morning to the buzzing alarm clock. It was six a.m. Apparently, the person before me was not courteous enough to turn the alarm off when they left. I rubbed my eyes and looked out the window. The sun was just coming up dusting the sky with pink and orange.

I decided to get up, because it would have been no use trying to fall back asleep. Instead of counting sheep, I flipped on the TV. A news report was on, talking about the Spartan base we had just escaped from. The authorities had heard the commotion and decided to investigate shortly after Agent Double J and I had left.

The building was scoured, but there was no one there. After hearing the report, I assumed that the Spartans had fled to Alberta. Thankfully, our flight was today. We would hopefully figure out just what was going on. I showered and dressed in the spare pair of gear I always brought on missions. After I freshened up, I walked downstairs to the breakfast bar to meet Agent Double J.

There were a few early risers sitting around the tables drinking coffee. I looked over the breakfast options to see nothing special, just the regular continental breakfast. I waited for quite a while. Agent Double J was always very presentable, so it took her a bit longer than most people to get ready in the morning. Eventually, she appeared.

"Good morning, Sir Alexander," she trilled.

"Good morning, do you want a roll or something for breakfast?" I asked.

"No thanks, I think I will just have some cereal," she replied, pouring herself a bowl. We ate our breakfast quickly even though we had plenty of time to get to the airport. As I was eating, I noticed a figure in dark red sitting in the corner with a hat covering his face. My muscles tensed.

"Do you see that guy over at the table in the corner?" I whispered to Agent Double J.

"Yes. I think now would be a great time to head for the airport," she replied. We both ran to get our belongings from our rooms. When I opened my door, I noticed a red piece of paper on the floor. My heart stopped. I called Agent Double J and she came running.

"Look what I found," I said, holding up the note.

"Read it," exclaimed Agent Double J. I unfolded the piece of paper. In very bad handwriting were the words,

"What could the Spartans be planning?" inquired Agent Double J.

"We better get out of here fast," I replied. We both started to quickly make our way down the hallway. Agent Double J pressed the button on the elevator, and it turned red. We waited and waited but the doors never opened.

"I wonder if the elevator is broken?" I questioned aloud.

"Let's just take the stairs," concluded Agent Double J. We walked over to the door labeled *stairs* only to find it locked.

"We should report that to the management." said Agent Double J. "It's certainly a fire hazard." We made our way back to the elevator. I looked at the doors hard willing them to open, when I noticed that the elevator button did not have an up or down arrow. It had the letter "S".

"Look at the button on the elevator," I motioned to Agent Double J. Her eyes widened. We were trapped again.

"I wonder where the Spartans are? They usually attack at this point," I commented.

"I bet you they're trying to get us to miss our flight," exclaimed Agent Double J. We both started to look for a way out. There happened to be a fire escape at the end of the hallway. The door read *Alarm Will Sound*, but with a bit of rewiring I rigged the door, so it opened with no sound at all. Agent Double J and I ran to the road and caught a taxi to the airport. It was nine-thirty a.m.

Location: Airport (Departure) _

We arrived not a moment too late and barely caught our flight. On the plane, I started to relax a bit. I felt good that we were leaving the Spartans behind. Halfway through the flight, the flight attendants came around with beverages. I ordered a lemon lime soda. The flight attendant poured my beverage and handed me a note.

"The man in seat twenty-two wanted me to give this to you," she said. It was another red piece of paper. Agent Double J almost spilled her drink when she saw it. I opened it up and read the same terrible handwriting:

YOU ARE BETTER THAN WE THOUGHT, BUT DON'T WORRY, YOU WILL NEVER MAKE IT TO ALBERTA...

We did not know what to think. There was a Spartan on the plane with us as we were reading the note. We needed to find out if he was planning on altering the flight. We both quickly disguised ourselves as flight attendants.

"I brought these along," said Agent Double J, pulling out two small chips. "The technology department designed them; they are holographic disguises. These will alter the look of our faces just like masks, but they should look completely realistic. I thought it would be a good time to try them out." I pushed a button on the device and selected a different face.

"You simply put the device in your pocket," said a young woman sitting next to me. She had brown hair and was wearing a flight attendant outfit. It dawned on me it was Agent Double J.

"Wow you look totally different," I said.

"So, do you," she replied, "You have blonde hair and glasses." We both walked up to the front of the plane and showed our badges to the other crew members and explained our situation. We both brought a tray of drugged beverages to the Spartan. When he consumed one, he would fall asleep for the duration of the flight. When we arrived at his seat, I recognized him. He happened to be the same Spartan we saw at the hotel.

"Would you like a refill?" asked Agent Double J. The Spartan agreed, and Agent Double J handed him a drugged drink. He downed the whole thing in a few gulps.

"Enjoy your flight," I said as he nodded off. The rest of the flight was uneventful.

Location: Calgary International Airport_

"I'm glad we look like ourselves again," I commented as we exited the plane. Calgary International Airport was smaller than other airports we had traveled through, but it still had the futuristic airport look. Out in the atrium of the airport, Agent Double J and I hid behind one of the plants and waited for the Spartan to walk by. He emerged from around the corner, yawning and rubbing his eyes. After he passed by, Agent Double J and I slipped behind him but kept our distance. The Spartan caught a taxi, and we hopped into one right behind him.

"Can you follow that taxi?" I asked the driver.

"Sure, but you still have to pay," he joked as we drove off. The ride was rather uneventful as we drove through the industrial outskirts of Calgary. After our rather boring ride, we started to see large skyscrapers. The Spartan's taxi stopped in a small square in the city. Our taxi driver stopped as well and dropped us off. I gave him a generous tip considering he was willing to put up with the "follow that taxi" situation. My eyes followed the skyscrapers all the way to the top. The Spartan headed for a dark-colored building with white bars that created triangular looking windows. The curved front of the building looked rather professional. I nodded to Agent Double J and we both entered the edifice. I looked at the directory on the wall. There were many different businesses housed in the skyscraper.

"Great, how are we going to find out which one belongs to the Spartans?" I inquired.

"Let's ask the woman at the front desk," suggested Agent Double J.

"That could backfire, she may be working with them," I cautioned. We decided to ask other people who were standing in the lobby if they had seen anything suspicious. I walked up to an older gentleman.

"Hello, we are private investigators working on a case, would you be willing to answer a few questions?" I asked showing him my badge.

"Sure," he replied, "what do you need to know?" I asked if he had seen anything suspicious around the building or if there was a business that used a lot of red color.

"There is this one business called Dark Crimson Enterprise. All the employees wear maroon gear and often wear dark glasses. I have always found it suspicious, but never really thought anything of it," recalled the man. "They all have a similar dress code. Not to sound too out there, but they look like secret agents with their maroon suits and dark sunglasses." Other patrons around the building mentioned the same place. Agent Double J and I looked at the directory and found that the business on floor twenty. We headed for the elevator.

Location: Office Building in Calgary_

The numbers lit up as we ascended the building, 17... 18... 19... 20. The doors opened, and we stepped into a dark red hallway. Tinted windows overlooked the city below, and recessed lighting added to the mysterious atmosphere. Silver letters on the wall read: Dark Crimson Enterprise. I held my breath as we approached the large, dark wooden doors.

"What do you think this place is?" I asked Agent Double J.

"Why don't we ask them and pretend to be regular patrons of the building," she replied as we forced the heavy doors open. Inside was a large reception area that reached all the way to the other side of the building. One could see the windows from the other side along the back of the space. Even with the large windows, the room still appeared relatively dark.

"How may I help you?" droned a man dressed in a maroon cloak behind the desk.

"We noticed your business and wondered what exactly you guys do," probed Agent Double J.

"We buy and sell property. Are you interested?" asked the Spartan nervously.

"As a matter of fact, we are," I faked. "What do you have available?" I wanted to see what exactly the Spartans were up to with buying property.

"We will have to get back to you on that, you see since we are a newer business we don't have as many spaces available," he said slowly. I knew they were up to no good. I wondered what they might be acquiring property for.

"Would you be willing to give us a tour of your facility? It is quite magnificent," said Agent Double J.

"I'm sorry, madam, but we don't do tours," replied the Spartan. We both exited to the elevator to discuss what we wanted to do.

"Clearly they are trying to hide something, not only from us, but also from the general public," I stated.

"We need to find a way in," contemplated Agent Double J. Nothing was coming to mind, so we decided to sit in the buildings main atrium and do some research on Dark Crimson Enterprise.

Location: Dark Crimson Enterprise_

I pulled out my laptop as Agent Double J and I sat at a table. I navigated to the web and did a quick search. The company had an official website.

"Interesting. It looks like their website is just as helpful as that Spartan we just talked to," sighed Agent Double J. The website gave no indication of what the company really did. I did another search to find out what property belonged to Dark Crimson Enterprise. Surprisingly, there was a large amount of property all over the world that belonged to the company. I noticed that much of the property belonged to former Spartan bases we had visited.

"Agent Double J, I think we stumbled onto a much bigger case than we thought," I commented nervously. We had just found one of the Spartan's most valuable assets. Taking the company down would not happen without heavy resistance.

Agent Double J and I went back into Dark Crimson Enterprise disguised as Spartans. We gained entry easily and immediately started snooping around. There were records of all the Spartan bases and which ones the ICPA had conquered.

"I bet we can find out where they are holding Nick," I whispered to Agent Double J. We found an empty office and locked ourselves inside.

"We won't have much time before whoever works here comes back," cautioned Agent Double J. "I'll keep watch." I started going through files in the drawers of the room, but there were no clues. I decided to sit at the computer and see what I could find. There was a map showing all the Spartan bases, and a log of prisoners. Nicks name appeared at a facility about two miles away.

"I found him," I whispered triumphantly. "He is at a facility not too far from here."

"That's great, Sir Alexander, but I believe the owner of this office has returned," whispered Agent Double J. I heard heavy footsteps outside and the handle on the door rattling. Agent Double J and I crouched in the corners of the room on the wall with the door so we would not be seen upon entry. With a loud crash, the door flew into splintering pieces and a Spartan stepped in. Agent Double J was one step ahead and shot him with a dart. I then deployed a fog detonator. I loved to use fog detonators, because they allowed only ICPA agents with visors to see in the thick mist, but Spartans became blind and confused. A group of Spartans came running when they heard the noise.

"I bet you there are ICPA agents in there," I heard a voice caution.

"You can never be too safe," commented another. I saw a detonator roll onto the floor. Agent Double J and I quickly used our grappling hooks to scale the walls up away from the floor using the lamp. I braced myself for the blow; the detonator was a short-range bomb. The room shook and black smoke filled the air. I held onto my rope as tightly as I could. Unfortunately, the bomb cleared our fog detonator's effects; we were in plain sight.

"Look, there they are!" I heard one of the Spartans shout. With our ropes cut, we both fell to the blackened floor as soot flew into the air. As the soot was clearing, I saw a dark figure emerge from the doorway. It was Mac.

"Impressive," smirked Mac. "I never thought you would have found this facility."

"Nevertheless, here we are. Where's Nick?" I wasn't taking any of Mac's jest today.

"Why don't we pay him a visit?" laughed Mac. I froze in fear. We were being taken to the true Spartan detainment center.

"Guards! Take them away," commanded Mac. Two Spartans dressed in dark red armor emerged with electric blades. Agent Double J and I prepared to defend ourselves. I threw a sleep detonator, but it had no effect on them. The guards were wearing masks.

"Any ideas?" I gasped.

"Nope, I'm totally lost on this one," replied Agent Double J quietly. The guards came closer, and we inched farther into the corner. Pretty soon, there was nowhere to go. The guards latched onto us and dragged us over to Mac.

"The guards will be using an injection to knock you out. Don't worry, it's not fatal; I still need to question you after you wake up," said Mac. I felt a prick in my arm and the room started to go black. The guard draped me over his shoulder, and we headed for the door. The last thing I remembered was seeing Agent Double J drop a small device onto the ground.

Location: Somewhere in Canada_

I heard a loud clanking noise and noticed a door in the distance. I tried to reach for it, but I was simply floating in midair. I reached again and started to fall and fall and fall. I almost hit the ground when I woke up. Apparently, the drugs injected into our bodies were harmless, but they still caused a bit of hallucination. I was in a small cage hanging in what appeared to be a van. I felt the movement of the vehicle as my cage swayed back and forth. It was pitch black. I heard other movement.

"Agent Double J? Is that you?" I whispered.

"Yes, it's me. I'm fine. Are you okay?" she asked.

"I'm fine, but where are we?"

"My guess is as good as yours," she replied. The vehicle we were in lurched and halted. I started to take in my surroundings. There was something around my wrists, and I felt a collar around my neck and a harness on my back. I heard a lock click and bright light flooded into the van. I could now clearly see that I was in a cage, and I was completely restrained with metal chains.

"All right boss, here they are," a Spartan said.

"Good bring them into the center. I want them in the highest security room. You have no clue what these two are capable of," Mac's voice replied. Lifting our cages out of the vehicle, the Spartans carried us toward a large menacing building.

"You should let us go now, or you will regret it later," I warned the Spartan carrying my cage. He did not respond. I poked my finger through one of the slats and poked him in the side.

"Did you hear me?" I asked. Still no response. Eventually, we reached the high security room. I noticed Nick right away; he was in a cage hanging from the edge of an overhang. A force field surrounded his chamber. The Spartans also hooked our cages to the edge of the overhang near Nick's. Mac looked down on us from above.

"I suggest you cooperate and let us interrogate you," he yelled.

"Not today!" I yelled back up.

"Your choice," shrugged Mac. He and his guards vanished behind the edge of the ledge. I immediately turned to Nick.

"Are you okay? I asked.

"Yes, I'm fine. You must let them interrogate you. It's our only hope of escape," Nick warned.

We were in a very sticky situation, but I wasn't about to give up. Even if I wasn't a full field agent, I had now had my fair share of difficult situations. Now was the time to think like a field agent and be fearless.

"What do you think?" I said to Agent Double J.

"Why not?" came her reply. I looked around for a way to call them in, and I noticed a small call button in my cage. I pressed the button, and Spartans peeked over the edge.

"We are ready to be questioned," I yelled. They brought us back up. Nick, Agent Double J, and I entered separate interrogation rooms. Mac entered mine first considering I was one of the top spies.

"Tell me everything you can about the ICPA," he commanded.

"Let's see. Our records are housed on level four in a large safe...or is it level five? Ah yes, level five and when you get to the safe you must, no wait I think its level three. The safe, I mean office... You know what? I can't remember very well in this state. Could you call in Agent Double J? She might be able to help me," I faked.

"We will just ask her," growled Mac.

"She does not know about a lot of the security and secret rooms. Your best bet is to question us together so we can fill in any gaps for each other," I replied.

"Fine," grumbled Mac. Surprisingly, he actually brought in Agent Double J. I noticed she had already somehow managed to steal her guard's weapons. We sat together, and Mac started all over again.

"Make Sir Alexander remember where the files are located," fumed Mac.

"Sure thing, but I have to do something first," she said, shooting Mac and the guard with a light beam, knocking them out.

"Wow, how did you manage that?" I exclaimed.

"Just a little Agent Double J Magic," she smiled. We stole Mac's security card, ran, and saved Nick.

"Let's get out of here," exclaimed Nick. We all hurried straight out the front door, and with the help of Agent Double J's light blaster, we avoided all the guards. Once we were outside, we snagged one of the Spartan's vehicles and sped away. After we had driven for a while, I noticed a red flashing light on the dash.

"Nick, this van is set to self-destruct," I gasped.

"I knew our escape was too easy," frowned Agent Double J.

"This is going to be tough, but I see a river up ahead. We need to jump out, but let the van keep moving so that it lands in the river when it explodes. We have about fifty seconds," Nick instructed. He revved the engine, and we started to travel quickly.

"Now!" yelled Nick. We blasted off the doors with the light gun and jumped. I somersaulted out of the way of an approaching car. It was immensely painful, and I skinned up my arms and knees. The van drove straight into the river and exploded.

"Wow, that was close," I breathed to myself, checking my nasty road rash.

Location: Alberta, Canada - The Side of the Road_

We must have looked strange standing on the side of the road, because a car pulled up and out hopped a lady. When she turned around, I saw it was Amy. We ran over and jumped into her car.

"How did you find us?" I asked.

"It was all thanks to the beacon Agent Double J placed at Dark Crimson Enterprise," said Amy.

"So, that's what I saw right before I blacked out." I said glancing at Agent Double J.

"Yep, I can't believe you were still awake enough to notice," she laughed. With Mac out of the way temporarily, we took over Dark Crimson Enterprise relatively easily with the help of the local authorities. After we finished that task, we headed for the airport.

Location: ICPA HQ_

Back at the ICPA everyone had to hear our story; it was one of the most dramatic missions we had been on.

"So, Ken, how did Denel get in?" I teased. "I thought you were always *watching*." Ken was clearly embarrassed about the whole situation.

"There was a security breech, but I did not want you guys to know for fear of losing credibility, and maybe even my job," he replied sheepishly.

"Hey, back off poor Ken. He has one of the hardest jobs here," joked Veronica.

"Next time, don't be afraid to tell Amy or me. We won't be upset. It's better to know where the intruder is, and then Agent Double J and I won't have to sneak into your office," I said.

"What? You snuck into my office?" exclaimed Ken.

"Remember the marble falling off of your statue?" I asked. "That was us."

"You guys are truly the top spies in the agency. I never thought you could get past me. Don't worry. In the future, I will make sure to report problems," he said.

The ICPA was truly a one big family. We could forgive and forget easily, and we all got along great for the most part.

"What was the Spartan base like? Was it scary? I wish I could have come. Do you think I could be a field agent? What happened to Mac?" Matthew bounced with excitement.

"Calm down, Matthew. After completing all your training, you will get to go on your first mission," I consoled.

"Can I go on a mission with you and Agent Double J, or with Amy?" he asked with glittering eyes.

"Yes, you can come on my next mission with me," I agreed, even though I knew he would be a handful.

"Yes! You have no clue how honored I am, Sir Alexander! Maybe you can teach me both desk and field agent skills!" He said as he shook my hand.

"It looks like you have your work cut out for you," laughed Agent Double J.

"You realize this means you are now his training supervisor," smiled Amy as she walked over.

"I am?" I stammered. "I really need to read the terms and conditions before I agree to something," I laughed. Matthew would make a great agent someday. I knew he would be a challenge to train, but I felt honored that I would pass on my skills to the next generation of ICPA Agents.

AN INVISIBLE ENEMY IN THE OUTBACK: AUSTRALIA

Location: ICPA HQ_

After reading through all the fine print, I signed the papers. I could not believe I was actually accepting the second position of training supervisor for Matthew. I would still be the head desk agent, but I became a mentor as well. Josey had trained a few field agents in her time and had always pushed me to train some desk agents, but I always felt I was too picky to handle training. Now, however, I decided I need to step outside my comfort zone and pass on what I had learned. Amy had also coaxed me a bit by pointing out it was the next phase of the cross-departmental training plan.

"Congratulations, Sir Alexander," beamed Amy after I had finished the stack of paperwork.

"I can't believe I am Matthew's mentor. What have I gotten myself into?" I half-joked. Amy and I walked down the hallway toward the new spy-training center. We arrived at a small conference room with a bunch of spies who were graduating from the training program and getting to meet their mentors. It was just like graduation from university. There were diplomas and the best young spies gave speeches. I watched proudly as Matthew made his way to the stage. I handed him his diploma.

"Matthew, you are assigned to Sir Alexander as your mentor," Amy announced into the microphone. Everyone clapped and many of the other spies gasped, surprised that Matthew would be working with one of the agency's top desk agents and an agent who also never took on trainees at that. After the graduation, Matthew could hardly contain his excitement as we walked through the desk agent area to my office.

"Congratulations, Matthew. We are glad to have you on our team," said Veronica as we walked past her desk. When we arrived at my office, I sat with Matthew so we could start planning his training. Just as I was logging onto my computer, Laurel walked in with a stack of papers.

"I never thought you would take on a training position," she laughed. "I brought these papers for you; they were just faxed over from one of our agents in Antarctica."

"Oh wow. Are we going to Antarctica?" Matthew blurted.

"No, we still need to do your second level training in the mountain course before I am taking you anywhere outside the country," I replied.

"I've heard it's a really hard training course," said Matthew, looking at the floor.

"Don't worry, it's not that bad," said Laurel, patting Matthew on the shoulder. I sifted through the papers Laurel had given me.

"So, Joe thinks he found us a lead? I asked.

"Yes. On the rim of Antarctica are the remains of what we believe to be an oil rig. The clues all point to the Spartans. We think they may be selling oil to pay for their missions, but we are not sure," Laurel stated seriously.

"Thank you, Laurel. Could you file these records?" I asked, handing her a stack of papers from my recent Canadian mission.

"Sure thing," said Laurel walking back into her office.

"Okay, now for your training," I said, turning to Matthew.

Location: ICPA HQ - Training Course_

Bruce flew Matthew and I to the ICPA's covert remote training course in the Rocky Mountains located just outside of our headquarters. Stepping out of the, helicopter the crisp mountain air blew my hair to the side.

"There's nothing here. It's a dead end," said Matthew.

"Have patience, and trust yourself," I replied, walking over to a wall of stones and placing my hand on a boulder in the middle.

The stones started to grind and slide apart to reveal a mountain temple. The temple's doorframe was made out of granite with the ICPA logo carved into the stone. Entering the temple, I could tell Matthew was a bit intimidated. Light filtered through the pine trees above, creating an eerily quiet atmosphere inside the sacred site.

"Here is where your training begins. You must select the tools with which you will complete the course," I instructed. "Will you choose a grappling hook, a laser, camouflage? There are many items stored in this temple in secret places. Find what you need and exit the temple from the door in the back when you are ready. I'll be waiting for you."

After briefing Matthew, I made my way through a shortcut to the start of the training course. I waited for a long time, taking in the mountain scenery and diving back into my memories of completing the training course with Josey when I was a young spy. Here in the secluded mountains, I felt her presence and I felt my heart pang when I thought about losing her, but I knew she would be so proud of me for taking on the training of a young spy. She would have done the same.

In fact, I realized what was holding me back from taking on an apprentice all these years was not the fact that I was picky, but rather that I didn't have enough confidence in myself. Things were starting to change. While I still didn't feel like I completely lived up to the expectations of a field agent, I was getting there. I also had the desk agent side of things completely under control. I was startled back to reality when I noticed Matthew had successfully emerged from the temple.

"Welcome to your second level training. This course will help you with Spartan tactics and survival." I motioned to the next structure in front of us. From where we stood, there only appeared to be a door in the side of a hill similar to the temple. I started to depart after a brief word of encouragement.

"Wait!" yelled Matthew. I turned around to see what the problem was.

"Sir Alexander, I'm really scared. I already struggled to get through the temple and find any tools. I mean it's my first time doing this kind of thing, and what if I mess up, and I don't want to fail, and..." he rambled.

"Don't worry, you are an ICPA spy. You will know what to do," I comforted. "I will be delivering information to you via your wrist communicator from now on." Helicopter blades whirred above us as Bruce ascended to pick me up. I hopped back into the helicopter with Bruce, and we flew off; Matthew got smaller and smaller as we retreated into the sky.

"Do you think he will do okay?" asked Bruce, "That training course is scary."

"Not as scary as the computer simulation," I joked.

"You desk agents are crazy," replied Bruce with a smile. I pulled out my wrist communicator radio and signaled my trainee.

"Matthew, your first objective is to open the door in front of your location," I relayed. Bruce and I landed high on a different mountaintop and entered the command center for the training course. Surveying the security cameras, we saw that Matthew had successfully opened the door.

"Good job. See, I knew you could do it. Now you should be in a grassy meadow. Spartan bombs are hidden underground, make sure to avoid them," I cautioned. Matthew navigated around the bombs.

"Here comes the scary part," Bruce said covering his eyes. To help the spies deal with crazy and dangerous situations we would detonate a bomb at this point and cut off communication to see if the trainees could use problem solving to get through a portion of the course by themselves.

I pressed the button and a bomb exploded near Matthew. He was fine, but I saw his panic as he kept trying to page us on his wrist communicator. Since the command center was a bit of distance away from the training course Bruce and I started the trek down the gray brick hallway to get to the area where we would reunite with Matthew.

We descended many crumbling staircases that spiraled through the mountain. I stopped for a brief moment to peer out a stone outlined window in the wall on one of the landings on our way down. One could clearly see the mountains outside, and small wildflowers had taken up residence between the stones that outlined the window. Their red and yellow petals contrasted with the blue and grey mountain scenery beyond.

Eventually, we made it to the area where Matthew would hopefully appear. It was an open courtyard with overhead access where we could look down to see the trainees. Foliage had grown into the walkways above and dangled into the courtyard. Bruce and I sat on the old concrete. I was always afraid that the supports would collapse due to erosion. After sitting for a while, a door on a gray brick building slid open, and a distraught looking Matthew emerged. I paged his wrist communicator.

"Good job. You made it through the hardest part of the course. We will be here to guide you the rest of the way," I spoke into the device. Matthew noticed us and waved, looking much happier. In no time, Matthew completed the rest of the challenges with ease.

"See, it was not that hard," I said when Matthew reached the end of the training.

"I wasn't scared at all," boasted Matthew. I just laughed. As we were congratulating Matthew, my wrist communicator beeped.

"Sir Alexander here," I answered.

"It's Amy, I wanted to let you know we have just received new intel on a possible Spartan intervention, please return to the base immediately. Amy out," her voice relayed urgently. Bruce, Matthew, and I glanced at each other nervously.

Location: Amy's Office_

We arrived back at the agency, and I immediately ran to Amy's office.

"Sir Alexander, we have a problem. In the past hour, we have been unable to contact Joe. He was heading for Australia. We have a few bases down there, but I don't even have maps to them. The map data seems to have been erased. Also, all records on the computer for the bases in Australia have been deleted. Someone must be after something housed there. I am sending you to Australia tomorrow," she instructed.

"What about Matthew?" I asked.

"He is going with you," said Amy. "Consider it the rest of his training."

Location: Denver International Airport_

The next day Matthew and I boarded a flight to "the land down under".

"I'm so excited for my first mission," said Matthew. He was practically jumping up and down.

"Calm down, we haven't gotten there yet," I sighed, not knowing how to keep him under control. We boarded the international flight. To be nice and make Matthew's fist mission more enjoyable, I had booked us both first class seats.

"You are too awesome," exclaimed Matthew as he stepped into the first-class cabin. After we had taken off, Matthew and I started to go over our objectives for the mission.

"We are going to meet an agent from the base in Australia," I stated, looking over the papers Amy had given me.

"What is his name?" inquired Matthew.

"I'm not sure, Amy's note says, 'You will know who he is; you can't miss him.' whatever that's supposed to mean," I sighed.

"Have you and Amy been all over the world?" asked Matthew.

"I would not say *all over*, but we have been to a fair share of the counties," I said. I stared out the window and wondered who this agent was, and how he would signal us when we arrived. I also contemplated this next chapter of my life as a mentor; would I really be able to handle all of this?

Location: Sydney, Australia_

Matthew and I stepped off the plane in Sydney, Australia after our long flight.

"Wow, it's hot down here," Matthew commented once we were waiting outside the airport for a taxi.

"What did you think it would be like?" I joked. The sun beat down on us until we finally stepped into an air-conditioned vehicle. The city around us was very pretty. I hoped we could stop by the famous opera house during our visit if time allowed.

"The spy said he would meet us at the Shell Café," I told Matthew. "That's where we are headed." The taxi driver drove us through the city streets until we arrived at a small café. The café glinted in the sunlight being almost entirely of glass. It simply seemed to blend in by reflecting the cityscape. Once we walked through the tall, transparent doors the world seemed to transform. The inside of the café had a warm feeling. The ceiling was crafted with wood, and rustic benches lined the room where one could sit and enjoy a cup of coffee. Matthew and I walked in and immediately started to look for our contact. I saw what Amy meant when she said he was going to be hard to miss. In the corner of the café sat a man dressed in safari gear. He stood out from the other regularly dressed patrons. Matthew and I made our way to the table inconspicuously.

"Hi, I am Sir Alexander, and this is Matthew." I extended my hand. The man glanced up from underneath his hat and smiled. He recognized our names.

"I am Neil," he replied. Neil led us out around the back of the building where his safari vehicle was waiting.

"Good to meet you two. I wanted us to do our introductions where we could be certain there were no Spartans. So, I'll start. I'm Neil, head of exploration at the ICPA. I feel bad that I have never been able to meet you guys from the main part of the agency, but as my title implies, I'm always searching for new land and new places we can set up camp." Neil smiled often and spoke with an Australian accent.

"I am Sir Alexander—"

"Oh yes, Amy has told me all about you, the head desk agent who became a desk-field-mentor agent. Boy, you sure have your plate full. Your business card must have a lot of positions listed on it," laughed

Neil. "We could really use a desk agent on this mission." I wondered what he meant as we exited the café and headed his Jeep.

"I'm Matthew, and I am Sir Alexander's spy intern," Matthew stated proudly.

"You got yourself a fine mentor," said Neil. He started the car's engine, and we were off to the base. After arriving at a small checkpoint, we transitioned to a helicopter for the rest of the journey.

"We can talk while I fly. Now, Sir Alexander, fill me in on what has been going on at your end of the spectrum," said Neil thought our headsets.

"Someone stole all of the records for the Australian bases and deleted information from our computers and archives," I sighed.

"Don't you worry, I know my way," said Neil. "The Spartans have taken over the base and locked us out, that's why you couldn't contact Joe. I need someone with good computer skills, such as yourself, to unlock the security system, so we can get in and see what is really going on," said Neil. We flew along for what seemed like an eternity into the arid landscape of Australia. The land was rather barren but after a while a large rock appeared in the distance.

"Don't tell me you were able to establish a base underneath Ayers rock," I laughed.

"Not exactly underneath, but nearby," replied Neil. "Also, the real name of the rock is Uluru given by the Pitjantjatjara people. We worked with the government and aboriginal leaders to create a fake area of protected land nearby for the ICPA base to keep it hidden."

"Wow, that thing is huge," said Matthew as we flew by over the rock.

It appeared very large even from the air. Neil landed the helicopter near a fake ranger station, where he slid his card into a security reader and the ground started to shake. We descended as the ground cracked apart, revealing a small lift.

"I thought you said the base was locked down," I commented.

"This is as far as we can go without alerting them," responded Neil. We ran down an underground tunnel until we made it to a locked door.

"We can't go in that way; it is far too obvious. We need to use the labyrinth of tunnels around us to find another way in," I said. We searched the tunnels, and finally Matthew found a door that Neil said led to a supply closet. I pulled out my laptop and plugged it into the lock on the door. I ran a few codes and quickly opened the door without alerting the security system.

"You have to teach me that," pleaded Matthew.

"I will, but right now we are kind of in the middle of something," I replied. We snuck into the base quietly, and I pointed up above us.

"Look, this base is equipped with catwalks for maintenance," I whispered. "We can use them to navigate the hallways without being noticed. I shot my grappling hook and line, which we used to climb onto the catwalk. We tiptoed our way past many Spartans until we reached the main control room.

"Perfect," we overheard Mac's voice. "Everything is going as planned. They better not send Sir Alexander or any of his accomplices to come thwart our progress. I am sick and tired of it. For years I come to within a couple steps of from global control, and then Sir Alexander comes along and ruins everything. But this time, it will be different."

"That is what you say every time, boss," replied one of the other Spartans, "By the way, we finished engineering the bacteria as you requested."

Matthew, Neil, and I glanced at each other in alarm. The Spartans were kicking things up a notch. Bacteria would most likely be aimed at harming the general civilian population. We had to stop them before it was too late.

Location: ICPA Australia Base_

We kept tiptoeing along the catwalks until we found the lab where the Spartans were engineering the bacteria. Canisters of liquid sat in boxes around the room.

"I bet those are the bacteria," said Matthew.

I pulled out my electromagnetic binoculars and zoomed in for a closer look. "Yep, you are right. They have already made a huge supply of it," I whispered. After the scientists had left, we swooped down off the catwalk and took a closer look. "Here, put these on." I offered everyone oxygen mask. "Just in case."

"The good thing is, it looks like the bacteria is not airborne, and it's curable if we kill it in the bottles by adding harsh chemicals," said Neil.

"Then what are we waiting for? Let's get those chemicals," Matthew replied.

Location: Sydney, Australia_

We escaped the base and flew back into the city.

"We need to find a pharmacy where we can purchase antibiotics. We can make them stronger by adding powdered silver," suggested Neil.

"I'm sure we can find a pharmacy, but I doubt we can find powdered silver that easily," I commented. Our group decided to go to the industrial part of the city to see if we could find any powdered silver. We came upon many scrap-metal stores but none of them had what we were looking for. Finally, one of the owners suggested we visit the university's science department, so we all headed to The University of Sydney.

The campus featured ornate buildings that looked to have been around for ages judging by the weathered stone. The ornate gothic style architecture contrasted beautifully with the perfectly mowed grass. The emerald green of the grass caught me off guard and I wondered how much they had to pay in water bills to keep the campus so lush. We walked up to the front desk and got directions to the science department where we purchased a large amount of powdered silver for an "experiment" we were doing.

"Thank you so much for letting us purchase your supply," I said to the professor.

"No problem at all. What kind of experiment are you doing?" he asked.

"We are using antibiotics and powdered silver to see if it helps increase the effectiveness of the antibiotic," I said. We quickly made our way to the pharmacy.

"I'm sorry sir, but you need a prescription for any large amount of antibiotic." I whipped out my badge.

"All right, just be very careful with the dosage," warned the pharmacist as we purchased a large amount of the product.

"Don't worry, we won't be taking it ourselves," I said. We all hopped back into Neil's helicopter and sped back to Uluru.

Location: ICPA Australia Base_

We entered the base the same way we did the first time, easily avoiding all the Spartans. Once we were over the lab, we waited for the scientists to exit and jumped into the room.

We put on our oxygen masks and gloves. There were some syringes in a cabinet we could use to insert the silver and antibiotic mixture into the bacteria containers. We mixed up the silver and liquid antibiotic and started to dispense the liquid into the containers. It turned the mixture gray so we could easily tell which canisters we finished. As we were filling up the canisters, I heard footsteps outside the door.

"Guys, we have company," I hissed. We quickly hid underneath one of the lab stations.

"What happened to these canisters?" asked one of the Spartans.

"They have turned all gray, let's analyze the contents," replied the other. After looking at the solution under a microscope, the one Spartan gasped.

"The bacteria in the gray canisters are dead!" he exclaimed, "There appears to be a mixture of silver and antibiotics in here that was strong enough to wipe out these bacteria, even though we thought they were resistant."

"We have to tell the boss," replied the other in a rough voice. They both exited the room. After they left, we resumed filling the canisters with our mixture.

"Sir Alexander, it looks like we are running low," said Neil. Again, we heard footsteps in the hallway. That time we were able to make it back up onto the catwalk.

"What is going on here?" yelled Mac. He ran over to the canisters. "Oh no, have the bacteria been doing this on their own?" he asked.

"At first, we thought a chemical reaction had occurred, but after analyzing the substance, we believe something had to be inserted by a human. The substance is killing the bacteria," informed the Spartan.

"I bet the ICPA is behind this. I want patrols up here now," yelled Mac storming out of the room. We kept up our pattern and filled up a few more canisters before the patrols arrived.

Entering the room Mac glanced around. "Would you look at that, there seem to be even more canisters filled since the last time we were in here," he growled, "I bet the intruders are nearby." As Mac was walking out the door, I rolled a sleep detonator out onto the floor and knocked out the two guards.

"Perfect. You did it," exclaimed Matthew.

"Yes, but we are running terribly low on our antibiotic solution," I sighed.

"This is an ICPA base, right?" asked Matthew.

"Yes, it is. What do you have in mind?" I replied.

"If we can find the supply room, we should have all the chemicals we need on hand to make more of our mixture," said Matthew.

"I never would have thought of that. Good quick plan," I complimented. "To the supply room." We searched all over the base from the catwalks, but there was no sign of the supply room.

"It's here, I remember the scientists talking about it," recalled Neil.

"What we really need is a map," I said.

"Matthew and I will make our way to the control room while you keep filling those canisters," I commanded. Matthew and I quietly scooted along the catwalks to see if we could locate a map.

Location: ICPA Australia Base_

"Look," pointed Matthew. There on the wall was the security map. I once again used my binoculars to get a better look.

"It seems to me that the supply closet is in the west wing," I whispered.

"Yes, it is, but sadly, you will never make it there," sneered Mac. Matthew and I turned to see Mac standing on the catwalk with Neil handcuffed.

"You thought you could just sneak in and ruin my entire plan but think again. I am having you all sent far away from here," Mac laughed. "Guards, take care of them." We were placed into a box and carried away by a helicopter. Both Matthew and Neil were afraid of heights and passed out about halfway through our voyage. The

Spartans dropped us off somewhere in the middle of the desert. I heard the helicopter fly into the distance.

"Wake up guys; we have arrived," I said, shaking Matthew and Neil.

"Are we on the ground?" asked Matthew.

"Yes. I don't know where, but we are on the ground," I replied.

"For all we know they could have dropped us off in another country," scowled Neil.

"Not to worry, I stayed awake for the whole flight. We are still in Australia," I said. We all decided that it would be good to find the nearest civilization possible and get some drinking water. After we had walked for a little while, Neil started to slow down.

"Are you okay?" I asked.

"I'm fine," he replied. He then proceeded to double over and throw up.

"I bet Mac poisoned him with the bacteria solution," I said in shock, "You stay here with him, Matthew, and I will go look for help. Make sure to wear your oxygen mask." I started to walk quickly. I did not want to run for fear of dehydrating myself. I had made my way about a mile when I saw a small village. I ran to the first house I saw and knocked on the door. A young lady, who looked to be in her twenties, opened the door.

"Hi ma'am. We were out in the desert and one of our men fell sick. If you, or someone here, could lend a hand we would be most grateful," I asked.

"Of course, I would be willing to help. Let me get my husband, and we will ride out to them in our dune buggy," she replied without hesitation. The next thing I knew, we were racing over the arid planes. I guided the driver the best I could, and eventually, we saw two figures on the horizon.

"There they are!" I exclaimed. We sped toward Matthew and Neil.

"What happened to your friend?" asked the young lady.

"He drank contaminated water," I replied. I remembered I still had a small amount of the silver solution in my back pocket.

"This should solve the problem, but I don't know the correct dosage," I sighed, showing the lady the medication I had.

"My husband is a doctor; you would know, right honey?" she asked turning to her husband.

"What kind of medication is it?" he asked.

"Penicillin enhanced with silver powder," I replied, hoping we could use it to save Neil.

Location: Sydney, Australia_

Neil was back up and going in about two days. We had made it to a hotel where he could recover, but we had lost a significant amount of time. I sat outside Neil's room. My mind was racing. There was no telling how much more bacteria the Spartans had been able to manufacture during the time we were away. Also, there was a deadly bacterium in mass production. I felt like everything was slipping through my fingers.

"I think Amy needs to know about what is going on," I said to my team.

I got out my wrist communicator and a hologram of Amy appeared.

"Is everything okay? I was not expecting your call."

"Not really. Neil was poisoned, but he is just about recovered. I am at a loss as to what to do. We need to stop the Spartans, but I don't want to put my team in danger," I sighed.

"If you can send me a blood sample, we can analyze the bacteria and create a strong antidote," reassured Amy. My wrist communicator displayed a picture of a blood sampling kit with an arrow pointing to it.

"Just reach into the hologram and take it. Laurel made a new app for the wrist communicators," came Amy's voice. I did as I was told and reached into the transparent picture. I felt the kit assemble in my hand, and suddenly, I was holding the blood sample kit itself. I looked at it closely to make sure it was real. It did not seem possible but there it was.

I took the blood sample then sent it back to Amy. Feeling the kit disappear from my hand was just as strange as when it appeared.

Location: Australian Outback_

Matthew, Neil, and I decided that the best tactic was to go back to the base and make another attempt to get rid of the bacterial disease the Spartans had created. I hoped that the lab team would be able to find an antidote, because working around the bacteria was risky. After another helicopter ride, Neil raced the dune buggy along. I felt my hair whipping in the wind.

"Can you slow down a bit? We might crash at this rate," I yelled.

"Don't worry, we're almost there," came his reply, buffeted by the wind.

We reached our destination in only ten minutes thanks to Neil's crazy driving, and then we infiltrated the base with ease.

"Strange, there is no one here to stop us," whispered Matthew.

"It could be a trap," I cautioned.

We walked along waiting for a Spartan to jump out any minute, but no one did.

"Look!" gasped Matthew. "All of their equipment is gone; the place is empty."

After searching the base, we found no trace of the Spartans.

"This could mean one of two things: they have relocated, or they are done making the bacteria and are distributing it," pondered Neil. I plugged my laptop into the mainframe of the system to see what I could find.

"Just what I was afraid of," I sighed. Neil and Matthew looked over my shoulders. There was a note from Mac in the system.

TOO LATE, SIR ALEXANDER. I HAVE ALREADY SHIPPED MY BACTERIA SOLUTION TO COUNTRIES AROUND THE WORLD! NOT YOU, AMY, OR AGENT DOUBLE J CAN STOP ME NOW!

-MAC

"I guess we should call Amy..." I trailed off.

Location: Classified Flight to ICPA Island_

The next thing I knew we were on a flight to a secret island in the Pacific Ocean.

"Why do you think Amy called us to some random island when we gave her the news?" asked Matthew.

"Sometimes, it is better just to follow the orders, Matthew. You will learn that after a while," I replied. Our pilot dropped us off on a runway near a jungle. There were no buildings in sight.

"All right, here you are. I am surprised there is actually a runway here," commented the pilot. We paid him, and he was on his way. I looked around, but there was no sign of anyone. I was beginning to think that we had just walked into another trap when my wrist communicator started to beep. I pressed the button, and a map displayed our destination. Neil, Matthew, and I hiked about a mile, before we saw a small glass structure built into one of the hills.

We made our way over, but there did not seem to be a way in.

"What was that?" whispered Matthew. There was a crumbling sound as a large rock slid aside to reveal a steel door.

"This day keeps getting more and more interesting," I said as we entered the secret base.

Location: ICPA Secret Base_

Amy was waiting for us inside.

"Sir Alexander, I have called upon agents from every country; we are currently doing our best to track all Mac's shipments of the bacteria," she reported as we walked in.

"Feeling better, Neil?" asked Amy. Neil nodded, but I could tell he was still not one hundred percent. In the glass room we had seen from outside was a large banquet table with spies from many countries lined up along its perimeter. The room was rather dark, despite the long windows, and candles sat as centerpieces to provide some extra light.

"Thank you, fellow spies, for coming to this very important meeting. Mac has taken it to the next level, and there are currently over five hundred cases of harmful bacteria traveling to their final destinations. We cannot allow this. We must...we *shall* stop Mac from succeeding," said Amy. "In Mac's note he said that *I* could not stop him, *Sir Alexander* could not stop him, and *Agent Double J* could not stop him. The thing he forgot was that we have someone else on our team, someone who he does not even know about who *can* stop him. Agent A. Since we can't spare any extra agents for this mission, Agent A has volunteered to help."

Most of the agents did not know of Agent A. She lived and studied outside of the ICPA headquarters, and only stepped in to help if the agency was in dire need. Now was one of those times. I recalled how fun my last mission was with Agent A in Spain. Crawling through secret tunnels and trapping the Spartan's was a highlight of my experience as a spy. The doors slid open and in walked Agent A dressed in a navy-blue cloak with a dark brown top and pants. The room filled with awe.

"May I present Agent A, our secret weapon," said Amy. The room erupted in applause.

After a planning session with various groups of spies Amy came over to our table with Agent A.

"Thank you all for being here. I am so glad that you saved Neil even if it complicated things," said Amy. "That is why we have Agent A. Our next plan is to track Mac's shipments of the bacteria."

"The bacteria can't have gotten too far, due to the fact that it was only shipped yesterday," pondered Agent A. "We will still have time to cut off the shipments before they reach their destination. The hard part will be stopping them."

"I have located the port they left from," said Matthew.

"Good work, Matthew. Looks like the desk agent skills I taught you have paid off," I said.

"It looks like our first step is searching the docks," concluded Agent A. At that moment, I heard a familiar voice.

"Oh, Sir Alexander," called Agent Double J, "I made you all some great new outfits that are resistant to the bacteria."

"Boy, am I glad to see you, Agent Double J. You never fail to amaze me. Fashionable and functional," I said.

"I am so glad we have this island to house our International Emergency Conference Center," commented Agent Double J.

"So, that's what this place is," I laughed. "I didn't even know we had one."

"Jeez, keep up with the times," teased Agent Double J.

"Are you two done catching up?" inquired Agent A. "We don't have much time."

I said my farewells and soon Matthew, Agent A, and I were off to Australia. Neil stayed behind to recover.

Location: The Docks_

We all headed to the docks. Not a place for the faint of heart; it smelled salty like the ocean, and shady characters hung around the various crates that created a maze.

"Okay, we need to find the export log. I am guessing that it is in that building over there," directed Agent A pointing to a tall tower. "Be careful, this is a perfect setting for something to go wrong." We all walked along, quietly avoiding eye contact with any of the shady figures. After a lot of walking, we seemed to be going in circles and the tower never really got any closer.

"Maybe we could go up in the crane over there and see the whole area, or even move some boxes if needed," offered Matthew. We all agreed and climbed up the crane.

"Look, guys," I exclaimed once we were inside, "A map!" On the digital map we saw the whole area.

"It looks like this is the best way," commented Agent A as she acquired the data from the map using her wrist communicator. We now saw ourselves moving on the map through the maze of crates on the hologram.

"Watch out!" Matthew yelled. A falling crate nearly knocked me into the deep water on the side of the walkway. Agent A helped me back up onto the wharf.

"Someone else must be here," she cautioned.

"They must really want to get that bacteria distributed," I said.

As I walked along, I felt like someone was following us.

"Shhhh, I think someone is following us," I whispered to my colleagues. We all walked quietly and in pace with each other. Sure, enough there was another set of footsteps close behind.

"I bet we are walking into a trap," whispered Agent A. We walked a bit further before I turned quickly and sprayed a figure dressed in black with sleeping mist.

"Oops, I don't think this is a Spartan," I smiled clearly embarrassed. We took a closer look and noticed whoever was following us had an automatic rifle and a handheld radio.

"I bet we can use this to figure out who he is," said Matthew as he pressed the call button, "I lost them, what now?"

"You fool," a voice yelled through the radio. "We are not paying you anymore; we will find them ourselves."

"That could be Spartans, or it could be someone else," said Agent A. "What we know is they must be close by, so we better keep moving." We picked up our pace and eventually made it to the control building. We cut our way inside and slid behind some crates.

Location: The Docks Control Tower_

"What now?" asked Matthew.

We glanced around at the surroundings and decided taking the stairs was our best bet, since most people take the elevator. As we snuck up the stairs, I wondered if we were again walking into another trap. At the top of the stairs, Agent A stopped us.

"I think there are Spartans in there," she whispered. We peeked through the window on the door and sure enough, Spartans filled the room.

"They must have trapped the staff somewhere and are monitoring the shipments of the bacteria," I whispered. We burst into the room and started to take out the Spartans one by one. While my team was at work, I snuck over to the computer system and stopped all movement of cargo on the docs. Soon, we had captured all the Spartans and released the staff members.

"It looks like the boxes that have a red "X" on the side have the bacteria. They are being loaded onto multiple ships and some are headed to the airport," I sighed. The situation was getting complicated.

We were too late; much of the bacteria had already shipped off according to the logs.

"It's probably best if we separate and each head to nearby airports; we can hopefully cut off much of the bacteria once we get there."

Location: Sydney International Airport_

I went to Sydney International Airport to investigate. After making my way through security, I sat in a waiting area and perused the other passengers for any suspicious characters. One person seemed to stand out. He sat diagonally to my right, dressed all in red, and had on military boots. While we were waiting, I casually walked by and snagged his laptop while he was looking for something in his other bag. I hacked in and found that this indeed was the flight that was shipping the bacteria. The shipment was bound for Japan and would arrive the next day. I knew I could not let that happen.

"We will begin boarding immediately," an electronic voice drawled over the loudspeaker. I followed the red figure into the plane and sat right behind him in hopes of finding out a bit more information.

For a large portion of the flight, the Spartan sat in silence until he noticed that he was bereft of his laptop. I pressed the button on my earpiece to tap into his radio transmission.

"Mac, things just got complicated. Someone stole my laptop. If an ICPA agent finds it, our plans may be foiled."

"Find that laptop. We have received intel that the ICPA may be following you, we intercepted a coded transmission at the docks. We were able to unscramble a portion. Be wary, the ICPA is composed of weaklings, but they are smart weaklings."

I waited for the Spartan to act. He seemed rather nervous and held a small remote in his hand. It could be for one of two things: to release the crates of bacteria, or to blow up the plane. I knew I could not allow either plan to come to fruition. At that moment, I jumped up, knocking the remote out of the Spartan's hand. I used my scanner to deactivate it. The plane erupted into chaos. I ran down the aisle to the bathroom. Inside, I activated a secret hatch and parachuted out. To my surprise, boxes of bacteria with a red "X" were parachuting down with me. The Spartans must have tricked me into deactivating a fake remote.

I shed my parachute and activated a hang glider. Soaring at high speed, I whipped out my grappling hook and used it as a sort of lasso to the best of my ability. I was able to collect the boxes fairly quickly using this method. The extra weight immediately made me start to lose altitude. I noticed a Spartan plane behind me. It dawned on me that the Spartans were aiming to switch the cargo from one plane to another. The day kept seeming to get harder, with one obstacle after another.

The plane came in near and tried to shoot me down. I was fine thanks to Agent Double J's bullet proof outfit, but my hang glider was not. I started to fall and landed on top of the Spartan plane. Sliding off the plane, I started a free-fall. My ears popped as I descended. It took a lot of strength while falling, but I managed to press my wrist communicator to signal any ICPA planes that were nearby. I expected to have to use my backup parachute and land, but an ICPA jet swooped out of nowhere, and I landed in the docking bay with the crates.

"Glad I could stop by," a voice came through my earpiece.

"Bruce, how did you end up in Australia? I thought you were back at the base."

"Amy thought you may run into some trouble and sent me down; looks like I was just in time."

Location: ICPA HQ_

Bruce and I flew back to the main ICPA base and met Matthew and Agent A. Thankfully, everyone had retrieved their shipments of the bacteria. We locked them in one of the many ICPA safes. Another successful mission. I went back to my office and greeted Laurel. She was glad to have me back as when I was out, many of the office tasks fell to her. I sat at my desk and sighed. There were a few papers for filing and some encryption modules that needed encoding. As I sat and coded the encryption modules, I heard a knock at my door.

"Look who's back from another adventure." Kai leaned against the doorframe.

"Yes, and thankfully in one piece. I don't know how field agents go out there every day and do daring things. Free-falling from a plane is not fun, even if I can do it now."

"Come on, free-falling is super fun, I love the adrenaline rush." Kai sat across from me. He fiddled with the other encryption module. "You've gotta teach me how to do these sometime, in exchange for what I taught you."

"Of course," I smiled. "It's actually not too hard, just plug the purple wire into the circuit board, and then—"

My phone rang interrupting our lesson.

"Hey Sir Alexander, it's Amy, something is not right. I need you to come to my office now."

Kai and I ran to Amy's office, and she filled us in on the unfortunate news. The bacteria boxes had hidden bombs that would detonate in a few hours. We raced to get as many spies as possible to disable the bombs. Many of us had training to disable weapons, so there were quite a few spies available. We ran into the vault and started disabling bomb after bomb. I opened a crate and a hologram emerged. It was Mac.

"Enjoy your victory, ICPA, the bombs are not my only weapon; things are about to get messy!"

Location: ICPA HQ_

"What did he mean by that?" I inquired aloud.

"I don't know, but I feel like we are in for more trouble," groaned Amy.

After a few minutes, we got news of the trouble we were in for. The Spartans were preparing to infiltrate the ICPA base, and not one or two Spartans, but an army.

The next thing I knew, we were standing around a table in the briefing room with a hologram of our base floating in the middle. The blue light from the hologram illuminated everyone's faces in the otherwise dark chamber.

"We will have to send a large number of our agents to secure the perimeter, but some will have to stay here to keep disabling the bombs," directed Amy. "Sir Alexander, I need you to go between both teams to monitor the situation and notify us of any attacks in case our communication system is knocked out for any reason. As you all know, the ICPA abstains from violence in any way, so we are on the extreme defensive this time. Don't let that get you down. We can do this."

Leaving the briefing room, I checked the security systems, put the base into lockdown, and activated the switch to close the heavy blast doors over the mountain entrance. The base rumbled as the heavy lead doors ground shut. Since most of the base was inside of the mountain, we were relatively safe. I glanced at a security monitor to see the large army approaching. The intercom chimed and I answered. It was from the front door.

"Hey everyone, it's Mac! Are you ready? We are. Now come out here and fight us, don't hide. You are all such weaklings."

I ignored the call and instead went back to the vault to check on the progress of my fellow spies. The team was diligently working on disarming the bombs quickly, but still had a bit more to go. As we were working the ground shook, and I heard a loud crash. My radio crackled to life.

"They have entered the base, repeat, the Spartans have entered the base!"

Amy and I glanced at each other.

"I'll go check it out," I offered.

"Don't go alone, it is far too dangerous," cautioned Amy.

Kai volunteered to come with me. "How bad do you think it is?" he asked.

"I'm pretty sure that they have only broken into an isolated area. Since the base is locked down, it will be hard for them to move about freely without encountering many locked doors. Thanks for coming with, you are far better trained in combat than I am."

We walked to the security camera monitors and found my hypothesis to be correct; the Spartans had only entered the front room. They were preparing to break down the next door. Our relief was only temporary. The security system sounded, and the display showed breeches in multiple areas all closing in on...the bombs. I pulled out my radio, "Amy, the Spartans are closing in on the bombs, seal off the vault!"

"If we don't engage, we are going to be sitting ducks," warned Kai.

"You are right; we need to do something now," I called the few free spies we could spare and alerted them that we needed to start fending off the Spartans, because they were closing in from multiple avenues. Kai and I ran down the hallway to the hangar. As we approached, we were thrown down the corridor by a blast. Kai caught me in his arms, shielding me from the flying debris as the whole room shook. The Spartans had blown a hole in the rock wall.

"How are we going to get to the hangar? It has most of our weapons and fighter jets," exclaimed one of the spies with us.

"Don't worry, we can use the secret passages, we will just have to be careful as they are rather treacherous; they're only meant for emergency access," I replied.

Location: ICPA HQ - Secret Passageways_

Kai and I, as well as some other spies we picked up along the way to help, ran to a decorative plant in the corner of a dark hallway in our base and opened the passage from behind the decoration.

"Here it goes," said Kai. "I don't think we have done maintenance on these passages in years."

"Kai is right... these passageways are rarely used. Please stick right behind us so no one gets lost," I cautioned.

I pulled a lever on the wall to activate the emergency lighting, so we could more easily see where we were going. A dim light lit up the space from some sparse industrial lights strung along the passageway, most of which were no longer operational. We all slid along rusty narrow catwalks and over deep pools of water hundreds of feet below. I shuddered as a stone went clattering down into the abyss.

We then climbed up narrow passageways with sharp rocks and slid along on our stomachs through some small tunnels. We had to brush spiderwebs out of the way and watch for other critters that had taken up residence in the time that the passages had gone unused. At last, we arrived at the hangar. I pressed a button and a door slid away. We exited out of a decorative panel on the wall.

"Everyone to your jets!" I yelled. All the spies ran to the available jets, helicopters, and other vehicles. Kai and I hopped in a jet with Bruce.

"Are you guys ready?" he asked.

Location: Fighter Jet_

We took off out of the side of the mountain, meeting heavy Spartan fire.

"I am going to need you two to operate the turrets," yelled Bruce. I looked at Kai with surprise; I had never operated a turret before. He gave me a small nod of encouragement. We jumped into the seats and threw on headsets so we could communicate, because each turret was on opposite sides of the jet.

"Alex, you can use these turrets to fire sleep detonators and electromagnetic pulses," Kai instructed. "We can fire them into the groups of Spartans below."

We both started firing the detonators into the Spartan's ground troops. Even from the air, we saw the blasts of purple mist. Other ICPA agents were defending the base to the best of their ability as well. Some threw detonators from the tops of hills, others drove in land rovers shooting tranquilizer darts, and some flew jets and helicopters to deter the Spartan planes.

"We need to take out Mac," I yelled into my headset. "Without him, the Spartans won't be able to do much." Bruce did a bank turn in the plane and headed for a large military looking helicopter. Mac was standing in the door.

"You guys are going to have to board the helicopter," Bruce yelled over the headsets.

Kai and I shot our grappling hooks into the bottom of our jet and swung down onto Mac's helicopter.

"Well, well, well, Sir Alexander now has a handsome bodyguard," sneered Mac. "You two will soon be captured as you are no match against my Spartan warriors. Brains may have gotten you this far, but you need more strength than a sole bodyguard to win this battle."

What the Spartan's did not account for was Agent Double J's gear that we were both wearing. We were protected from bullets, chemicals, and many other elements. We both turned on the camouflage mode that allowed our outfits to perfectly match the background behind us. It did not make us invisible, but we were much harder to see. I tripped a few Spartans while Kai knocked out a few more with his bare hands. Pretty soon, we had cleared the entire helicopter except for Mac.

"You are weak!" shouted Mac, even though we had taken out all his bodyguards. He then proceeded to jump out of the helicopter. Kai and I watched Mac land on a nearby Spartan plane and speed away. The helicopter we were in started to spin out of control as well, because the pilot had fled. Kai took the controls and landed the helicopter.

"That was close," I gasped.

Location: ICPA HQ_

Without Mac, the Spartans were lost, confused, and they ended up retreating. In all the chaos, Agent A had captured Denel, Mac's assistant. We were able to get quite a bit of valuable information out of her before her release. Amy hoped she would lead us back to Mac.

"It looks like we were victorious in our first battle," said Amy.

Everyone was content, even though Mac escaped; we had saved many lives by stopping the bacteria and being victorious in battle against the Spartans as well as disabling the bombs inside.

When we asked Matthew about his first mission his response was, "Way too cool, but now I have to clean up the base. Those Spartans sure are sloppy. They left such a mess."

We were all thankful that our hopes had been fulfilled. Neil was well again, and our agency resumed its regular state.

YOU'RE GETTING WARMER: ANTARCTICA & ARGENTINA

Location: Antarctica - The
Middle of Nowhere_

I stepped off the jet into the freezing air. Why the Spartans would have come here was beyond me. I scanned the desolate horizon for any signs of life.

"Do you think they lured us here to send us on a wild goose chase?" asked Matthew.

"No, I can tell that there is something wrong, something different." I could feel it in my bones. It wasn't just the cold. Something much colder, much more sinister was in the air.

"Like what? I hate to tell you, Sir Alexander, but I think we are the only ones down here." Right after Matthew had finished his thought, I heard a sound. It was far away, but it was decipherable. A motor.

"You hear that?"

"Yeah, but it could be one of a billion different things. I think you are overanalyzing this whole situation." I did not wait for Matthew to finish; I had already hopped on my purple snowmobile and motioned him over.

"We are following that sound," I commanded.

Matthew reluctantly hopped on the snowmobile behind me, and we sped off. I locked my radar onto the sound that was just a bit ahead of us.

"I think we are almost there," I yelled.

We pulled up onto a ridge covered with snow. There ahead of us was a red snowmobile barreling across the ice-covered terrain. I tuned to Matthew with a smirk.

"Fine, you told me so."

We got off our snowmobiles to walk on foot.

"We have to follow their tracks. If they hear another snowmobile, they will know there is someone following them," I said.

Matthew and I walked for what seemed like miles. My toes and fingers started to go numb. I thought my nose had frost bite, and Matthew was falling behind. I was contemplating turning back when I saw steam spiraling into the sky.

"There, that is our destination."

"Thank goodness. If you would have made me walk any further, I think I would have asked for a new mentor!"

I pressed a button on my wrist communicator and my snowmobile autopiloted itself to us.

"They are far enough ahead now that we don't need to worry about the engine's noise."

We zipped across the frozen wasteland headed toward the shoreline. On the horizon appeared an oil rig with steam billowing out of its vents.

"Do you think they saw us?"

"No, we're too small to be picked up on their scanners."

An oil rig was an interesting development. If the Spartans were selling oil, it would be a great source of income for their operation and would make our job that much harder.

"I must say the Spartans are good at making money one way or another," I commented to Matthew.

We shot our grappling hooks onto the structure and began to ascend the building floating just off the coast.

"Remember, Matthew, this is going to be a stealth mission, so don't go in guns a blazing."

"Got it. Get in, get out, and don't be noticed."

"And don't die," I added jokingly.

When we had made it to the bottom of the stilted structure. I used my laser to cut a hole that we climbed through.

"I can't see a thing. It's so dark."

"We are probably in the cargo hold, remember your training."

Matthew and I crawled along, feeling our way through the dark. I finally spotted light coming through a vent above us. I peered through to see a break room.

"This is the perfect place to get some information," I commented.

I waited and listened. Nothing. We slipped up into the room and looked around. Red uniforms were strewn about as well as lunch boxes and other personal items. I started to search through the pockets of the coats and found a few IDs and a keycard that I was sure would come in handy. As I was searching the next coat, I heard footsteps.

"Quick, Matthew, we have company."

I dove into the vent quickly, Matthew hot on my heels. I then used my sound amplification device to see if I could catch a bit of the conversation.

"The facility is on alert; we tracked a plane landing not far from our location. From the markings it appeared to be associated with the ICPA," came a muffled voice.

"We can't let them find our operation here. It generates considerable revenue for the Spartan Clan."

I glanced over at Matthew. It looked like we had a clue that could lead us to a bigger picture.

Location: Exiting the Spartan Oil Rig_

Back on the barren snow-covered plains, we trudged back to where we had left our snowmobiles.

"They're gone," cried Matthew.

Sadly, he was correct. Both of our snowmobiles were missing. I guessed the Spartans must have found them.

"We will have to find place to hide where I can send out a distress signal for a plane or helicopter to come pick us up."

We made our way to a glacier in the distance. To our luck, there were plenty of crevices and nooks where one could hide. We got out of the wind, and I pressed my wrist communicator to call for a plane. That was one thing that I still hadn't gotten used to. On missions with Matthew, I not only had to prove to myself that I could handle difficult situations. I also had to be a good mentor and set a good example.

"I encrypted the signal, but no promises. That plane better get here before the Spartans figure out what's up."

Matthew nodded. We waited for what seemed like an eternity. Even out of the wind the temperature was well in the negative digits. At last, I spotted a plane on the horizon.

"There! That's our ride."

I motioned Matthew to follow me out of the glacier so we could depart from Antarctica. We ran out of our hiding place waving our arms.

"Sir Alexander, watch out!"

I looked over to see Spartans barreling toward us on red snowmobiles and in the distance another plane approached.

"I think they are onto us," I yelled. "Our plane will not be able to make a pass if they are engaged with that Spartan plane. We will have to take it out."

"Are you crazy, Sir Alexander? You're never this daring."

"Sometimes, you have to be, especially when there is a herd of Spartans rapidly approaching."

I activated my jetpack, much to Matthew's surprise. He did the same, and we soared up toward the Spartan plane.

"Hey Bruce," I yelled into my wrist communicator, "would you mind flying a bit lower to see if you can get that Spartan plane to follow you? My jetpack can't gain much more altitude."

"Copy that, Sir Alexander. I must say, I think you've lost your mind."

"I think I can argue that I am a much smaller target that is harder to hit."

Bruce swooped the plane down and the black Spartan plane followed suit. I soared as high as I could and threw an electronic detonator at the plane with all my might. It looked like it would not make it, thankfully Matthew had my back and was able to get his to attach.

"Decrease altitude," I gasped.

Matthew and I fell from the sky onto Bruce's plane and attached to the top with our magnetic boots. The Spartan plane swooped through the air and suddenly burst forth with blue electric bolts. The engines died and the plane went down. We boarded Bruce's jet and flew quickly away from the scene.

Location: Antarctica - In Transit Back to ICPA HQ_

The lounge onboard was a nice contrast to the frigid weather outside. Plush seats surrounded a mahogany table and various refreshments from tea to hot chocolate were available, but there wasn't time to partake in a beverage at that moment.

"We will have to tell Amy what is developing; this could really be an issue. The income from oil is extensive. With more income, the Spartans can easily complete their missions and establish new well-guarded bases. They could also hire mercenaries," I contemplated.

"You will have to wait to tell Amy the news, we have to stop to refuel in Argentina on the way back," called Bruce from the cockpit.

It was not long before we landed in Buenos Aires. The city had an eclectic feel with modern architecture mixed in with colonial style buildings. Even these buildings had a sort of unique flair with some of them being painted in bright colors. Overall, the city was quite vibrant and lively giving it a playful and welcoming vibe.

I decided to have a break in a coffee shop not far from the airport. I sat, gazing at the people and cars zoom past on the street below. I encrypted my Internet connection and sent an email to Amy regarding the recent development. As I sat sipping my maté, I became aware that someone or something was wrong.

I cannot explain how the phenomenon works, but as a spy, there is a feeling one gets right before something bad is going to happen. I set down my dink and glanced around. Nothing. Suddenly, a police officer approached the table.

"Sir, I need you to come with me."

I followed cautiously. I felt that same feeling from earlier in Antarctica. Something was not right. The second we got outside the building, a group of Spartans pounced on me. I did my best to break free but due to the surprise attack, I was not able to escape.

"I should have known. What is Mac up to now?" I sighed.

"Why don't you join us to find out," said the leader of the group.

Location: Buenos Aires, Argentina_

I was bereft of my wrist communicator and had no connection to Bruce and Matthew. Hopefully, they would be able to find me and get me out of this situation before it was too late. The Spartans forced me into a car, and we drove toward the coast. It was dusk at this point, and I could see nothing. We boarded a small boat and sped into the ocean. My odds of rescue kept decreasing.

"So, I see that you have expanded to Antarctica. Not a wise move. The secluded area makes it the perfect place to monitor," I said, trying to break the silence.

"Mac has ordered us not to talk to you; your mind powers are too strong."

I smiled. Apparently, Mac had classified me as enough of a threat that his men were no longer allowed to converse with me. Soon, I saw a small light on the horizon, an island perhaps? No, as we approached, I could tell that it was another oil rig. The situation had just become a lot more complicated. The Spartans seemed to have oil rigs in multiple locations. Inside, they chained me to a chair, as usual. I waited for quite a while in a dark room with a spotlight focused on me.

"Do I believe my eyes? It looks like Sir Alexander, and he is alone," laughed Mac.

"You are quite rude to have kept me waiting so long," I retorted.

"If you are so eager to see me, I will give you a nice long talk about my new empire."

I rolled my eyes.

"You see, the world right now is obsessed with oil and will pay just about anything to get it. So I, Mac, have stolen a few oil rigs from various locations. The revenue they produce is considerable, much more than we have made in the past allowing us to open new bases, design new technologies, and ultimately take control."

"Do you realize how much you monologue?" I groaned.

"Men, gag him; I am tired of his sass."

Two Spartans came over and tied a piece of fabric over my mouth.

"I think it is a pretty brilliant plan, what do you think?" he laughed, "With you out of the picture I don't see much room for failure. Put him in front of that screen over there where he can watch our revenue gain."

The guards placed me in front of a screen that displayed an exponential growth pattern of revenue. It was a typical move for Mac, always trying to be the stereotypical villain. I often wondered why he didn't just shoot me.

"When we reach another million dollars, the hatch below your chair will open and drop you into the ocean - enjoy the show," laughed Mac as he walked out of the room.

There was nothing I could do but watch the screen and my impending doom. $500,000 dollars more and I would be in the ocean tied to a chair unable to swim. I hoped that the chair might float; however, I doubted the Spartans would have installed a seat cushion flotation device. $700,000 dollars, $750,000 then $800,000. I felt hopeless. All of the confidence I had gained as a field agent was gone, just like that. Try as I might to think of how a field agent would handle the situation, I came up with nothing.

I was sure Mac was enjoying watching me from his office. $900,000 dollars, $950,000, I was toast. I could already imagine falling. I heard a crash and closed my eyes, but strangely I did not fall. I glanced around but did not see anything. $985,000 and at last $1,000,000 dollars, I was done for. The hatch creaked open, and I fell. The air was cold as it rushed past me. Suddenly, I landed and bounced off something. I passed out.

Location and Time UNKNOWN_

I woke in a dark room still tied to the chair. I pondered to myself whether or not I was even alive. Surely, I should have drowned by now. A dim light illuminated the room. I peered out of the cell to get a better idea of where I was being detained. The space seemed to have originally been some sort of office. Remnants of cubicles were scattered about, and computer parts sat piled on tables.

"He lived," stated a masked character dressed in black including a cape. A group of people dressed in gray with their faces covered surrounded who I assumed was the leader.

They removed my gag.

"Where am I?" I asked. My head was pounding.

"You are under our protection. Don't worry, we don't want to hurt you," came the voice of the leader.

I was then untied from the chair and pushed into a makeshift cell. Normally, I would have been able to easily break out, but without my tools I was stuck. It was cold and dark. I saw the main room dimly illuminated outside of the iron bars. My captors gave me food, which I ate each day, even though it may have been poison; I was just too hungry, and the food turned out to be fine.

Here I was, supposed field and desk agent trapped in a cell. I felt I had been overconfident. I thought I was finally getting the hang of things, but that was not the case. I thought about the other field agents easily escaping from captivity and felt small and hopeless. I curled up in the corner of the cell. After what I assumed was three days from counting the cycles of the sun a cloaked member came and escorted me from my cell.

It appeared that we were inside some sort of old building that was on the brink of falling apart. It surprised me that there was even electricity, however it did not do much good with all the dim light bulbs hardly illuminating the hallways. We eventually arrived at a makeshift office where the person dressed in black awaited.

"Leave us," they commanded.

I sat across from them at a desk. The office was much brighter, and I saw the sun rising outside of the window.

"You are Sir Alexander, is that correct?"

"Yes, you have the right person."

"We need your help."

"After you kept me in a cell for three days, I don't know how inclined I feel about helping you."

"We wanted to see if we could trust you not to escape or call for help. As far as the world is concerned, you are dead to both Spartans and the ICPA. This gives you and us a major advantage."

"You told the ICPA that I am dead?"

"No, Mac did. He sent them this video."

A cracked monitor illuminated. I watched myself fall through the hatch in the floor of the oil rig.

"What do you need?" I asked.

"We need help defeating the Spartans."

Location: Resistance Force Base_

The request surprised me, but I agreed to help on the condition that as soon as the mission finished my friends and family would know that I was alive.

The team outfitted me in a gray cloak with a face covering and a slit that only let my eyes show. To my surprise, the cloak had purple embroidery. I decided that the group couldn't be that bad if they had added that personal touch. Later that day, I sat in a dark damp mess hall eating my lunch when another cloaked figure approached me.

"Hi, my name is Amelia, and I made your cloak. I hope you like it. I know Agent Double J makes such beautiful clothing that this must seem horrible, but I did my best."

I smiled, although one could not tell.

"I love it, you did an amazing job, and the purple embroidery is such a nice touch. Can you maybe give me a better idea as to what's going on here?"

"I cannot, but the leader can; she is glad that you offered to help us."

Later that day, as promised, I met with the leader.

"Okay, now that we are officially working together, can I get an idea of who you are?" I asked.

"We are an underground resistance force against the Spartans in this area. I guess you could say we are a spy agency like the ICPA, but without the funding."

I could tell the leader was smiling under her face covering.

"Why do we have to wear such secretive clothing?" I asked.

The leader laughed.

"We don't wear these outfits at all times; only when we're on duty. Tonight, no one will be wearing them. We are all having dinner together. This group is like a family."

"Lastly, how do you all know so much about the ICPA?"

"We look up to your organization and monitor what you do, your strategies, your structure, all that kind of information. We then use it to help us defeat the Spartans. Sure, we have our own take on how a spy agency is run, but you are our role model."

Location: Resistance Force Mess Hall_

That night, we removed our cloaks and sat around a large table. It was amazing to see everyone without such mysterious clothing. Amelia turned out to be to have blonde hair, angular features, and a great sense of humor. We enjoyed talking about Agent Double J's designs.

Amy had talked about partnering with an agency in Mexico that was much like our very own ICPA, but the group I was with now was so different; they resembled much more a resistance force than a spy agency. I wondered if with some help and funding from the ICPA this group would be able to take off.

"I am glad we all got to sit down as a family tonight for dinner, but training for our mission starts tomorrow, so I want you all in bed early tonight," stated the leader. It turned out her name was Angie. She was like a mother to the whole resistance force. To my surprise, I felt rather at home despite the strange circumstances.

Location: Resistance Force Base_

The next day, I woke and put on my cloak and mask. It was time to start training. I exited the building and found that it was an abandoned factory on the docks. The factory surrounded a center courtyard that the group used for practice. Thanks to my spy training from the past, I was able to pass all the tests, from explosives to melee fighting.

"I believe you are all ready to put our plan into action," said Angie at the end of the day.

"What exactly do you have planned?" I inquired.

"The plan is complicated and involves many steps so please listen closely. The first phase of the plan is to gather intel on how widespread oil production is for the Spartans. For this portion of the mission, I have assigned you and Amelia. Go to the Spartan oil rig where they are currently headquartered and extract data from their computer system."

Angie continued to explain the rest of the plan. We were all ready for anything.

Location: The Docks_

Amelia and I snuck around the docks and took a boat to the large Spartan owned and operated oil rig.

"I bet this is not exactly where you wanted to come after almost dying here," said Amelia.

The oil rig loomed above us.

"Not exactly, but this time we can work together, and we'll be fine."

"How do you plan to enter?"

I pulled out the Spartan key cards I had stolen from the base in Antarctica. The Spartans were so sure of my demise that they hadn't even bothered to search me.

"We will give these a try," I said.

Amelia and I found a small maintenance door, and to our surprise the cards worked.

"This will give us a lot of mobility around the base, but I doubt the cards will get us into the computer server room, so we will have to find an alternate way to enter," I commented.

We freely snuck about the rig thanks to the key cards and finally made our way to the server room.

"I think I'll have to hotwire this door," I sighed.

"I've got your back," said Amelia.

I pulled the panel off the wall and started moving some wires.

"Sir Alexander, someone is coming."

We both dove around the corner of the hallway and listened to the voices.

"Well, it seems that...wait, this panel looks like it has been tampered with."

"Better let Mac know to be on guard. I'll stay in the server room while you alert him."

Amelia and I glanced at each other. That would complicate things a bit.

"I bet he's the only one in there. If I get the door, you can take him out," I offered.

We both decided that my plan was our best bet. I finished hotwiring the door and Amelia rushed in, knocking over the Spartan. I pulled out a sleeping dart and shot him square in the arm.

"He will be out for a while. Jam the door while we work."

I pulled out a flash drive and plugged it into the mainframe. The screen read *ten minutes to download data.*

"It is going to take ten minutes for this thing to download," I warned, "If anyone comes back, we will have to do our best to fight them off."

We stared at the screen, willing it to go faster. Hearing footsteps in the hallway, we quickly turned.

"I have an idea. Amelia, put on that Spartan gear and distract the patrol. They can't know I am alive or the whole mission will be compromised."

Amelia threw on the gear hanging on the nearby wall and exited into the hall. I heard her through the door.

"Good afternoon."

"Good afternoon sir, all systems normal. I was sent here by Mac. It seems like something fishy is going on."

"What do you mean?"

"Oh, it looked as if this panel on the wall had been tampered with. I searched the room, and all systems were normal. Thankfully, it appears whoever tried to enter, failed."

Five more minutes, and I would have all the data downloaded.

"Do you think there is ICPA activity?"

"Most likely. We know the ICPA's tactics; the tampering is their style."

"What is your ID number?"

"Umm..."

I heard the Spartan's body hit the floor. The door opened and Amelia drug in his unconscious body.

"Well, he was rather boring to talk to anyway," she said.

"There are only three minutes left on the download."

"I hope that's enough time. If someone was expecting this guy anytime soon, we may have company."

The alarm system went off and the lighting turned red. The computer must have had a failsafe.

"How prophetic," I stated.

Thankfully, to our advantage, the door to the server room sealed itself locking with a click. We waited for the download to complete. To our surprise, as we were going to exit, the door to the room opened and in walked Mac. I should have known that he could override the system and enter. I grabbed the flash drive out of the computer; whatever data we had would have to do. Amelia had already cut a hole in the floor. We both jumped down and fell into the boat we had arrived in and sped away.

Location: Resistance Force Base_

We returned to Angie with the flash drive.

"We're so sorry, but this is all we were able to retrieve," I sighed.

"It's better than nothing at all. In fact, it looks like you got quite a bit of data," said Angie as she looked at her computer screen.

"Phase one is complete, however I do have some bad news. The Spartan oil production is much larger than we predicted. There are oil rigs all over the world under their ownership according to this data," sighed Angie.

"One step at a time," I added. "If we can take care of the main rig with the headquarters, the other Spartans will be thrown into confusion. In that time, we can send in ICPA agents or local authorities. My guess is that if Mac is here, we have already found their HQ."

The data proved my hypothesis correct. It was time to put phase two of the plan into action. The attack.

Location: Resistance Force Base_

Angie stood before us in a large room in the dilapidated factory.

"All right, team, this is the day. We have trained for months to overthrow the Spartans and now is our chance. Each of you has an important job, and what one person does can affect the entire group, and the mission. Do your best, help each other, and remember life is more important than victory. If we have to try again because it means keeping the team alive, we will, but for now we shall charge forward."

Angie proceeded to go over the whole plan. Her unique strategy focused on using one hundred percent of the group's resources for the one attack. Each member had a job, even if it was simply pulling a lever or sending a code. That allowed the steps of the plan to be executed very quickly, hopefully allowing the strike to take place before the Spartans even knew what had happened.

"Your primary target is Mac. He needs to be taken out of the game once and for all. A nice long prison sentence should do him good," said Angie.

We pulled our cloaks over our heads and became figures lacking identity to the outside world; however, we each knew exactly who was who, giving us another advantage. We could easily switch places making it harder to track us from the Spartan's perspective.

For the attack, I was on a submarine that would allow us to enter through one of the oil rig's supports. I boarded and we plunged below the surface of the sea. I waited as the welding team made a hole in the support that allowed us to enter. Once inside it was my job to lead the purple team up through the pillar.

"All right, does everyone have their magnets ready? It's going to be a long climb up!" I yelled over the roar of the engine.

We used our magnets and climbed the walls until we reached the top, where our goal was to cut a hole in the floor to enter. Teams would enter from all four pillars as well as from the air and sea.

I pulled out my laser and cut a hole. The alarm system went off.

"This is where the fun begins!"

We all piled into the room as Spartans entered from all directions.

"Who are these guys? Not ICPA? What's happening?" I heard the Spartans yelling.

I whipped out some sleep detonators, my favorite weapon, and got to work. With a large team behind me, it was not too long before we had a room full of sleeping Spartans.

"Come on, we have to make it to Mac's office; it is on the top floor!" I instructed.

We made our way through the base fighting off groups of Spartans here and there. As I ran down the hall, the whole building shook, and I fell to the floor.

"That does not sound good. What is going on? Contact Angie," I said.

Amelia got on her wrist communicator to see what was happening.

"Spartan reinforcements have arrived, I repeat, Spartan reinforcements have arrived," came Angie's voice.

"I wonder how many people they brought?" pondered Amelia.

"I think we just found out," I gasped as figures clad in red poured through doors, vents, and down the stairway.

Location: Spartan Oil Rig_

"What are we going to do?" exclaimed Amelia.

"We are going to fight as long as we can," I shouted over the noise.

The room erupted in a chaotic blend of gray and red as the groups fought against each other. Sadly, the Spartans largely outnumbered us, and while we did take out a significant number of the troops, they ended up capturing our team.

As if scheduled, Mac appeared.

"Whoa, what is going on here? ICPA? No? What! Another group is onto us. Thankfully it looks like they are amateurs, and we have won, again," laughed Mac sarcastically. "You look like you are special judging by your outfit." Mac walked toward me. I realized I was the only one with an embroidered pattern.

"Are you the leader?"

"No, I am more like a manager."

"You all seem to be hiding your faces; let's see who you really are..."

My eyes widened.

"Yes, I know it is you, Sir Alexander. I know you didn't die. I can't believe you would stoop to the level of helping this resistance group. Did you really think this whole scheme of yours was going to work? I'm not stupid. I simply thought you would give up."

Mac pulled down my face covering. "See, I knew it was you. This time I am going to make sure you are really dead," Mac pulled out a large knife. "Over the years, I always thought to myself after I captured you, I would take the time to question and interrogate to see what information I could gain regarding the ICPA, but every time you manage to get away. Now, I have decided I am just plain tired of dealing with you." Mac raised the knife to my neck. "It looks like my news is about to come true. The ICPA will really be without Sir Alexander."

I closed my eyes. The building suddenly shook again, and I heard the knife drop to the floor. A frenzy of activity swarmed about me, and the next thing I knew I was being carried away quickly. One of my team members sat me down on a bench in the hall.

"Sir Alexander, are you okay?"

"I am fine. I thought I died there for a second. Don't waste time, let's go!"

We ran outside onto the walkway, and to my surprise, Amy swooped down next to us.

"Who are you? Identify yourselves," she shouted, pointing a gun toward us.

"We are members of the resistance force against the Spartans, Mac is just down the hall." I knew what I had to do. "The code word is Colorado!"

"Colorado" was our code word for when ICPA contacts met. Amy glanced at me strangely and ran inside.

"What was that about?" my teammate asked.

"No time to explain."

We ran after Amy. She charged Mac, but a group of burly Spartan thugs blocked her way. Mac quickly used a laser to cut a hole in the ceiling and jet packed through.

The building shook again, violently. I felt the room turn, the floor proceeded to tilt, and everyone in the hallway slid.

"Quick, grab onto this rope," I yelled, shooting my grappling hook to what was now the top of the hallway.

Amy and my team members grabbed on, and we worked our way up to the walkway. Standing on the wall we could then see that the Spartan ships had taken out one of the oil rig's supports and the whole rig was sinking.

I sprang into action and shot another rope to an ICPA helicopter. I made sure everyone got out, and I climbed up the rope last. I had almost reached the top where again another surprise awaited me, Agent Double J. I reached my hand to her, but a shot from a Spartan plane hit my rope and I fell. Thankfully, Agent Double J caught my cloak and pulled me aboard. I stood up and my face covering fell off due to a rip caused by Agent Double J's save. She stood in shock.

Location: ICPA Helicopter_

"There is no time to explain, we have to capture Mac,"

I ran to the cockpit and directed the pilot to follow Mac's black getaway helicopter. We took a sharp turn and sped up. Mac must have noticed us since his helicopter took a turn as well and fired at us.

"We have put in way too much effort to let Mac get away this time," I said. "I have a plan that may allow us to capture him. A helicopter fight might be just the thing. Man-to-man but not with the 'copters. We can use the jetpacks aboard to get over to his helicopter as long as we are close."

The pilot did his best and got us closer. We activated our jetpacks and soared over to Mac's military helicopter. I slid down the side and used my magnets to cling on. The wind blew strongly through my hair. I reached for the handle when suddenly the door fell toward me. Plummeting toward the cold ocean below, I used my grappling hook to latch onto the bottom of the 'copter and pulled my way up.

"I thought you were dead again!" exclaimed Agent Double J.

"For the second time," I joked.

"Ahh, Sir Alexander, Agent Double J, we meet again," scowled Mac.

"Do you have any idea how cliché you sound?" I retorted.

Mac lunged at us with a few of his Spartan bodyguards. The Spartan helicopter pilot did not make our lives any easier by swaying the vehicle to try to get us to fall out.

"Do you really think you can capture me? How many times have you failed?" yelled Mac.

"Have you ever thought that there is a strategy in that?" I bluffed.

"Would you two pull yourselves together?" scolded Agent Double J, "While you were arguing the pilot jumped out of the helicopter. We are headed straight for another oil rig."

"Take the controls!" I yelled to Agent Double J.

Mac took that time to make his departure.

"Oh no, you don't," I gasped, using my grappling cable to snatch his ankle.

We were in quite the predicament. Mac dangled from the helicopter, as I clung on for dear life, while Agent Double J careened the helicopter away from the oil rig. To my dismay, Mac dragged me down, so I was hanging off the helicopter as well.

"You really thought you could get away with this!" laughed Mac, cutting the wire and freefalling to a Spartan plane that whizzed by. I flipped back up into the helicopter and ran to the cockpit.

"Agent Double J, watch out. I bet that plane is going to try to engage us."

I hopped into the copilot chair, and we got ready. Sure, enough the plane did a quick bank turn and shot a few missiles.

"I see them," yelled Agent Double J as she let the helicopter drop. The missiles collided above us in a fiery inferno.

Mac's plane soared off into the distance.

"I guess he was right; he got away," I sighed.

"Don't worry, there will be a next time. I'm sure of it. You and Mac tend to run into each other quite a bit," said Agent Double J.

"Not that I like it. I fear that some time I might actually end up disappearing due to him."

"Speaking of that, you have some explaining to do," frowned Agent Double J.

Location: Resistance Force Base_

Back at the resistance's base, another battle was taking place.

"I can't believe that you would not tell us Sir Alexander was alive," shouted Amy.

"We needed the advantage," defended Angie.

"Oh, so you thought that was more important than telling people that really care about him!"

"Keep in mind, we did save his life."

"Is this true?" Amy turned to me.

"Yes, it is," I stated. "In fact, I was thinking more along the lines of friendship rather than being at arms with each other."

After some mediation Amy and Angie were able to come to terms with the situation and Amy granted an official application for a partnership.

Later, we exited to the run-down hall where the resistance group and a few ICPA spies gathered.

"It has been decided that the ICPA will partner with your group in order to better combat the Spartan clan," I said.

Everyone cheered.

Location: ICPA HQ_

Back at the base, everyone was relieved to find out I was alive.

"I think this is the most daring thing you've done yet," said Veronica. "You really are becoming more like a field agent. I would have never expected you to fake your own death."

"Unprecedented situations call for unprecedented tactics," I replied. "Even after this recent mission, I still feel like my place is in the office."

"Well, look who's here," Veronica nodded subtly prompting me to turn around.

Kai came rushing into the office.

"You have no idea how worried I was," he said, embracing me in one of his bearhugs. "I know I have encouraged you to be a field agent, but you didn't have to take it to the extent of faking your own death!" I could tell he was teasing me but still genuinely relieved to know I was okay. "Next time you go on a mission that dangerous, please bring me along."

At the end of the day as I was cleaning up my office, I realized a big shift in my life had taken place. I could confidently say I wasn't just a desk agent anymore. I was able to think and act like a field agent when I needed to. With this newly found confidence, I was ready to take on whatever the next mission would be.

JUST BEING ALEX: CHINA

It was a monumental occasion; Amy had called a special meeting. We all sat in the banquet hall with a panoramic view of the Rocky Mountains as the backdrop to the special event.

"Spies, I would like to introduce our new partnership with..." Amy paused. "You need a name."

Angie smiled and took the microphone.

"Thank you all for allowing us to partner with your agency. We have looked up to your organization since we started and thanks to your partnership, we can now better control the Spartan Clan. At first, we did not have a name, but thanks to this turn of events we are now Team Acacia."

The room applauded. After the official meeting Amy called me to her office.

"What do you think of this turn of events, Sir Alexander?"

"I don't know. I remember watching the screen of the Spartan's revenue from the oil. They are gaining millions and millions of dollars, and Mac escaped, allowing them to use the money they have gained to create more havoc around the globe."

"This is truly troubling. We will double our efforts and maybe even start splitting into committees to allow us to better monitor criminal activity."

"Why split into committees? We are all fighting a common enemy; is not unity what we seek?"

"Sir Alexander, these are troubling times, and sometimes friend and foe are very similar. The Spartans, yes, are still who we are trying to stop, but they are not the only criminals out there."

"What are you trying to say?"

"You know what? I just need a minute," Amy sighed, "Let's meet tomorrow, and we can discuss this in greater detail."

"Sure, of course."

I left Amy's office feeling very confused. What could she be talking about? Committees, criminals, and what else? As I was walking down the hallway in deep thought, I ran into Amelia.

"Hey, what are you doing here?" I asked.

"Guess what? I am the official liaison between Team Acacia and the ICPA."

"Congratulations!"

"I am so excited, and we will still get to see each other here and there."

"By the way, thanks again for the cloak," I smiled, pulling it out of my satchel

and draping it over my head. It was a very special privilege to be part of two agencies.

Location: ICPA HQ - Desk
Agent Department_

Everyone at the Agency was in frenzy. Laurel and Nick had decided to get married. It had officially been two years since they met. Along with our usual duties, we were all helping plan the wedding. Laurel had taken time off to plan as well, so I was without an assistant for a few weeks.

"Sir Alexander, come over to see these dress designs Laurel chose for her bridesmaids," came Agent Double J's voice through my intercom.

"I'll be over in just a second."

One thing was for sure, weddings took a lot of planning. It made me realize that being single for the time being did have some perks. I stepped out of my office into the Desk Agent Suite.

"Let Laurel know we have just mailed out the last of her invitations," chirped Veronica as I walked through the office.

Location: Denver, Colorado USA_

The day of the wedding came way faster than we were all planning. My job was making the guest list and seating guests for the reception after the wedding. Agent A tapped me on the shoulder.

"You doing okay?"

"Yes. I just can't believe Laurel is getting married. I think she might be planning to leave the agency and pursue her dream of becoming a teacher. I don't know how I feel about losing her as my assistant. No one else will ever file things right," I tried to chuckle.

"I am sure she will come back to visit," consoled Agent A.

The ceremony was beautiful, and everything came together very nicely. Laurel had chosen a gorgeous venue for her reception, the upper levels of one of Denver's skyscrapers. The room was decorated with flowers in pinks and whites while tables illuminated with soft lighting sat around a dance floor. The tables had tall, glass centerpieces that spiraled upward giving the whole space an elevated vibe. Guests danced away and sat chatting at the tables.

The reception was in full swing, and I had just seated the last few guests on the list. I felt a bit uneasy, however, this time it was not because of the changes in the agency. There was someone present who was not on the list. He had said he was a cousin of Nick's who had decided to drop in at the last minute. Nick had told me the guy looked familiar and to let him in.

I glanced around nervously as it dawned on me that the man was wearing a red bow tie. I tried to talk myself out of it, after all not *everything* that was red had to do with the Spartans. I decided I would follow the mysterious guest after he darted down the hallway at the back of the room. I turned down the hall as well and followed closely behind. I peered around the corner as the guest pulled off a ventilation grate on the wall.

"So, how are you related to Nick again?" I asked.

The man whirled around.

"I am one of Nick's Spartan brothers. I don't know how you weak-minded fools were able to get him to join the ICPA. Now, he has to go."

"I wouldn't be so sure of that."

I pressed the button on my wrist communicator and Amy ran down the hall to meet me.

"Can't even fight one on one, can you Sir Alexander?" laughed the Spartan.

"If we did not have to fight it would be even better," I retorted.

The Spartan, instead of fighting, laughed, pulled out a sniper rifle, and headed up the ventilation shaft before we could tackle him.

"We have to stop him. He is after Nick!"

Amy nodded. I activated a holo-map of the building's ventilation system.

"I think I have a plan, Amy. The Spartan is heading back to the ballroom to snipe Nick; if that is his course, he can only go this way.

To reach the ballroom he must pass over this room, here. If we cut the grate in the ceiling of this room he will fall and we can capture him, hopefully without alerting the guests."

"Got it," said Amy.

We ran into a small side room and used our lasers to cut the grate enough that it would fall if pressure came from above. We both pressed ourselves against the wall so he would not see us while passing over. Crashing through the grate, the Spartan entered the room with a cloud of dust.

"Not so fast," shouted Amy as she shocked the Spartan.

Thankfully, he passed out, and we were able to remove him before the cutting of the cake. The rest of the night proceeded without a hitch.

Location: ICPA HQ - My Office_

The next day, Laurel got a kick out of the story.

"Thank you for saving Nick and making sure the Spartans did not crash my reception."

I hung up the phone. I could not believe that it was true Laurel would now be an elementary school teacher. Quite a shift from working in a spy agency. Even though I was excited for her, I was sad to lose my assistant.

As I was nostalgically recalling Laurel renovating her office a few years ago, my phone rang again.

"Hi Amy, how can I help you?"

"Would you mind stopping by my office? I have a few things I would like to discuss with you."

Location: ICPA HQ - Amy's Office_

I arrived at Amy's office on the upper floor and took a seat.

"So, I have been thinking, Sir Alexander, for years and years we have been after the Spartans, and again and again Mac seems to escape. In fact, we have no idea where he is right now."

"Yes, Amy, but that does not mean that we need to give up."

"No, however I have many other things I need to look into, in fact some have been criticizing our agency for the fact that we focus too much on the Spartans and ignore other crime syndicates. I don't know, Sir Alexander; I just feel like I have led us in the wrong direction."

"Nonsense. We have a successful agency, one of the most successful in the world. Don't let whoever is criticizing you to get you down."

I left feeling rather strange about Amy's comments, and I wondered who would have criticized the ICPA's practices.

Location: ICPA HQ - Desk Agent Department_

The next day, I arrived at work feeling rather discombobulated because Laurel was not there helping me keep everything on track. Files had already piled up on her desk and the phone showed that there were callers waiting on hold. I sighed as I scooped up some files off her desk and placed them in the correct baskets. I couldn't understand why people didn't follow the posted instructions on filing. Just because Laurel wasn't with us anymore didn't mean they could just throw them on her desk, although that appeared to be what was happening. Kai stopped by while I was organizing. His presence had become a usual part of the desk agent department since he came to visit so often.

"Good morning," he smiled as he entered. "You look like you've got your hands full now that Laurel is gone. Need any help?"

"Thanks, that would be great. The files in the blue folders need to be separated out and put into the grey cabinet. Can you mark them off this list too? Veronica put it together. They're all in alphabetical order."

"No problem, anything for you." Kai flashed me a smile.

"How do you have time to help me with this, aren't there classes and training programs you need to take care of? I don't want to be taking you away from that."

"There aren't any active combat missions at the moment, just intel which of course falls to your department."

I was lucky to have connected with Kai. Not only had he helped me gain confidence in the field, but he was also kind enough to visit and help me out now that Laurel had left. As we worked, Amy poked her head through the open door.

"Sorry to bother you two, but I was wondering if Sir Alexander and I could go over a quick briefing. Some stuff has come up in China,"

"Go ahead, I'll finish up the files," said Kai.

I headed out with Amy to her office.

"I think you have unintentionally made Kai a cross-departmental spy. He has practically filled in for Laurel since she has been gone," said Amy.

"I can't thank him enough. We really need to get another intern to keep things running.

After we arrived at Amy's office, we sat at her desk.

"Sir Alexander, there has been a recent development at one of our bases in China. Some of our scouts reported that the Spartans are constructing mining operations to extract rare earth metals. We believe that the extracted metals are now being sold on the black market."

"I am ready to go," I said. Hopefully, the mission would get my mind off all that was going on at the agency.

"Sir Alexander, you have proven yourself in the field, so this time I would like you to go alone. No need to bring Matthew this time either. I need all of your focus on the mission."

I was honored that Amy felt I was ready to do missions alone, but I felt a bit nervous as it was my first fully solo field assignment. Instead of taking an ICPA jet Laurel had scheduled me for a regular flight to Beijing before she had left the agency. Things just did not feel right. I knew I could do a mission solo, but I was so used to having someone along.

Location: ICPA HQ - Agent Double J's Design Studio_

I decided to make my usual trip over to Agent Double J for some new gear for the trip. After all, every mission required a different sort of outfit.

"Good afternoon," I chirped.

"Sir Alexander, it is so good to see you. I have already begun working on your outfit for this mission. It has some of the usual features; however, for this mission I added radioactive resistance. If the Spartans are extracting rare earth metals, they may have some that are radioactive."

"Very true. Good call."

Agent Double J pulled out the black and purple outfit, which was almost complete. All that was left to add were the details like buttons and zippers.

"I stuck to black as the main color; we don't want you standing out too much."

The gear for the mission was nondescript overall and would blend in nicely with the current fashion trends in China.

Location: Denver International Airport_

I left, feeling even more uneasy than usual as I threw my new outfit into my suitcase and headed to the airport. There was so much change happening in the agency. I knew it was impossible for things to remain the same forever, but it was still uncomfortable to handle so many changes with such little notice. I pushed the thoughts aside as I boarded the tram at Denver International Airport.

The flight to Beijing had one stop, and I was very glad when I finally arrived. Stepping into the hotel room, I let out a long sigh, threw myself on the bed, and fell asleep.

Location: Beijing China - The Trip to Fushun_

My alarm buzzed loudly. I could not believe it was already six in the morning. I threw on my gear and decided to just start working without breakfast, which was rather uncharacteristic of me. I downloaded the list of maps Laurel had put together before she had left. The Spartan facility appeared to be in Fushun, a coal-mining city.

I decided to make my way back over to the airport. The flight would take about an hour, so I brought along some research materials to hopefully find out what the Spartans might be up to. The early morning light filtered through the smog that covered Beijing like a blanket. The sheer number of people on the streets was surprising for the early time of day. I arrived at the airport and sat at my gate to wait.

My suit started to beep, and I looked at the notification on my phone. The app read: *Your suit is blocking radiation from nearby source.* I glanced around. It was odd that the suit was detecting enough radiation to alert me. I decided to walk around and see if I could pinpoint the nearby source. It appeared to be one of the signs with schedules; the closer I got the higher the level of radiation. Then it dawned on me, it was not the sign, but the person next to it. He wore miners work clothes with red suspenders. I had found my lead.

During the flight, I watched him closely. I was able to hack into his tablet over the free Wi-Fi on the plane. I found that the location of the mine he was working at was just on the outskirts of Fushun. I tagged the location on my wrist communicator. When we arrived, the Spartan slipped into the crowd before I could follow him. I decided to call it a day and check into my hotel.

Location: Fushun - Touring the City_

The next day, I decided to take a walk around Fushun to get a feel for the area and maybe dig up some more clues. The city was overall industrial in style and shared the same thick smog as Beijing. It was a big enough city that I certainly did not feel like I was in a more remote part of China despite the fact that the city was nestled in the northern part of the country closer to North Korea. I made my way to a park to see the one of the city's main architectural attractions, the Ring of Life. The ring contrasted with the rest of the city's boxier concrete architecture.

I pondered the Spartan encounter as I meandered through the small park at the base of the silver ring. Fushun's claim to fame was coal mining, so I found it interesting that I was picking up radiation from the Spartan since coal was not a highly radioactive material. In fact, after some research, it didn't appear that mining of radioactive materials was much of an industry in the area at all.

I caught a taxi to take me near the outskirts of the city. After walking for a bit, I found what I was looking for—a coal mine. The strange thing was, my suit did not seem to be blocking any radiation. I snooped around the entrance of the mine. It appeared abandoned. Rather than following my usual cautious procedures, I decided to just take a look inside.

Creeping down into the mine I followed the two barely visible mine cart tracks. I felt as though I was walking into some sort of void as the darkness encompassed my body. I flipped on my flashlight; however, it didn't do me much good considering how much rust was on the tracks. I kept walking, carefully placing my feet down lightly in case there were rotten floorboards or holes in the ground. I thought I saw something move to my right. I jumped. What could be lurking in the darkness? Probably just a bat, I reassured myself as I moved forward. My suit started beeping wildly, *radiation at critical level*, came the warning.

I jumped back to see if it was the area in which I was standing, but the suit kept issuing the same warning. I twirled the flashlight to see if there was anything, or anyone near my position, but nothing showed up.

"Whoever you are, I don't want any trouble."

I heard a horrible screeching sound echo down the mineshaft. I slowly started to back up toward the entrance when something grabbed my ankle. I latched onto the rotting wooden slats between the tracks and struggled to pull myself away. Thankfully, the rotten boards were strong enough that whatever had a hold of me let go and skittered off into the darkness. I barely glimpsed two glowing green eyes before I ran back to safety outside the mine.

Location: Shanghai - Another Adventure

Safely back at the hotel, I gave the ICPA lab in Shanghai a call.

"Hi, its Sir Alexander. I have a development to report..."

The next thing I knew, I was on another flight to the Shanghai lab. It was getting to be nighttime, and I could see the shimmering city in the distance with its unique skyscrapers as we came in for our landing.

I shuffled through the crowded streets with lanterns illuminating the ground. The slightly wet asphalt reflected the light in an eerie way, and the smell of noodles wafted by me as I passed a small street food stand. I quickly ducked into an alley and knocked on a small door. It opened, and I slipped into the warm kitchen of one of the restaurants. The owners, former ICPA agents, allowed us to install our lab above their business.

"Hi, Biyu, how is the business doing?"

"Oh, Sir Alexander, so good to see you. You poor thing, you look starved. Here, have something to eat."

"I would love to, but I really need to get up to the la—"

"No, no, you can eat first here." Biyu brought out some noodles and soup.

"Thank you," I said as I sat, knowing I could not deny Biyu's hospitality. It was great to know that she cared that I was doing okay.

After my dinner, I pushed aside the refrigerator to reveal an elevator up to the lab. When the curved white doors slid to the side, it felt like a whole different world.

"Good to see you, Sir Alexander," said the lab assistant. "What have you brought us?"

"While I was inspecting an abandoned mine shaft that I believe may be a link to a current Spartan plot, someone – or something - grabbed me. Whatever it was it was highly radioactive. I brought in my gear for you to scan."

While the lab team ran various tests on the gear, I looked out the window. What was in that mine? Recalling the green eyes were enough to make me shiver.

"Sir Alexander, the analysis is complete."

"What did you find?"

"We found some hair on your suit that had a radioactive isotope present. We were able to extract the DNA and it appears to be for a rat. The strange thing is the DNA has been highly altered by the radiation, but not in a way that is degenerative, but rather it has altered the DNA to be more robust. After running a simulation of what the alterations in the DNA would cause we came up with this." The lab assistant motioned to a computer screen that showed an overly large green-eyed rat.

"I am very glad I did not actually have to see it," I replied.

"Good luck, Sir Alexander, and make sure to keep that radioactive suit on, there is no doubt it saved you from contamination."

Location: Fushun - Back to the Mine_

The next day I was back in Fushun. I wanted to get a better idea of what the mine might be hiding, or what was hiding within it. I reluctantly returned to the site of my near-death experience. That time, I simply hid nearby and looked to see if I could catch anyone going in or out. Sure enough, after about an hour a group of red clad miners entered the main door. I quickly snuck in behind them. I followed very cautiously glancing around for any green eyes.

"I really don't know how I feel about this whole thing. I usually don't question the boss, but I think this is getting out of hand. One of them almost got out yesterday."

I hid behind a stalagmite as the Spartans approached a hidden door.

"Another day of radiation, thankfully none of us have gotten sick yet."

I again slipped through the door as it was closing. On the opposite side I found myself in a lab. I quickly activated some magnets and clung to the metal ceiling. I scooted over to get a better view of what was going on. In a cage across the room was a set of gigantic rats with glowing green eyes. As I watched, the Spartans injected a small rat with a substance, and it immediately grew and gained green eyes. I had to stop myself from gasping. The DNA was not accidentally altered; it was a plot.

"Wait, be careful!"

Before my eyes, one of the Spartans accidentally spilled some of the radioactive liquid on his hand. The effect took place immediately, he grew, just like the rat, to three times his size and acquired glowing green eyes. I clung to the ceiling in horror as the lab below erupted into chaos, converting more Spartans, and to my dismay, releasing the captive rats. I quickly deployed some sleep detonators, and the room became quieter, but the contaminated rats and Spartans did not fall asleep, instead they simply became slower.

I dropped from the ceiling and ran as fast as I could out of the mine. Once outside, I closed the door. I looked at the panel to see if I could jam it. To my luck there was a button labeled "lockdown." I pressed the button and an alarm started to sound and to my relief, a large lock sealed the door.

Location: Fushun - Back at the Hotel_

I sat on the bed at the hotel and tried to recollect my thoughts. This was quite a lot for my first solo mission, but I wasn't going to give up. I decided to give Amy a call and fill her in on the development.

"I don't know Amy; they have some kind of radioactive elixir that turns anything into some sort of beast. Not even my sleep detonators could stop them."

"Calm down, Sir Alexander. All we need to do is give the lab a bit more time. They said that they should be able to find an antidote by speeding up the radioactive half-life of the isotope. That should return the rats and humans back to normal unharmed."

"I sure hope that is the case, Amy. I have put the Spartan lab in lockdown so all of whatever is in there will stay there at least until we find the antidote."

"Sounds good."

After I hung up, my phone immediately rang again. I did not recognize the number, but I answered anyway.

"Sir Alexander here."

"Sir Alexander, so you are still alive?"

"Who is this?" I asked feeling the voice was familiar.

"What? Don't you have me in your contacts? It's Mac! I caught you on surveillance locking down the Spartan lab. I will play your little game. You see the radioactive elixir is contagious and any contact with it, or a contaminated being will have the same effect you witnessed. At this moment, I have sent a team to break open the vault door and release these new beasts into Fushun. It is up to you to stop them; you would not want to be responsible, I'm sure."

"Mac, what do you stand to gain from this grotesque, and might I mention poorly designed, experiment?"

"Oh yes, always sarcastic even in danger; that is the Sir Alexander I know. With this new threat the only one with the ability to save the world is me. After I save the population from this threat, I will get all the glory and gain leverage and credibility."

"As usual, a bit of a stretch, but I see where you are going. Well, the joke is on you. I will go stop your men!" I yelled as I slammed the phone down.

However, the way I planned to stop them did not involve force, after all I was on a solo mission. I needed to find where Mac was keeping the antidote, however all my research led me to dead ends. Things were really falling apart. I was running low on time while Mac had already sent men to release the terrible monsters in the mine into society.

As I researched, I thought about the fact that although I was on a solo mission, that didn't mean I couldn't ask for help. I needed help from a friend. I pulled out my personal smartphone and dialed a number.

"What a pleasant surprise - how are you, Alex?" came Jaemin's voice.

"To be honest, I've been better; I'm struggling to find information on Mac's location without using the ICPA network. I don't want to raise any red flags."

"I've got you covered," said Jaemin. He had access though a diplomatic agreement to some databases in China.

"I've found it, Sir Alexander. Mac appears to have a penthouse in Beijing. That's your best bet."

Location: Beijing - Mac's Penthouse_

"You are certain that the location is correct?"

"Yes, Alex. Mac is currently in Beijing. Thankfully, it is only a quick flight from where you are," said Jaemin through my earpiece.

"Get me there quick, but keep in mind right now a mob of angry Spartans is probably chiseling away at the vault door to the lab."

I grabbed my coat and ran out the door. I could hardly sit still on the flight over, but thankfully, I was in Beijing before I knew it. I located the coordinates on my wrist communicator and stared up at the skyscraper. It was a building made of tan brick with a penthouse at the top covered by a garden. Gold gargoyles protected the edifice. Knowing Mac, he was probably in the penthouse, I thought as I shot my grappling hook.

Once at the top, I cut a hole in one of the windows and jumped in. To my surprise, it was quiet and clear. I tiptoed through the various rooms, trying to find the vault in which I believed Mac had a pre-made antidote of his own.

"Welcome."

I spun to see Mac smirking at me.

"I thought you might stop by."

Guards appeared out of thin air and shoved me into a chair.

"Is this what you were looking for?" asked Mac tauntingly swirling a vile of pink liquid in front of my face.

"No, as a matter of fact I was stopping in to admire your penthouse," I said while rolling my eyes.

"While you are here you might as well have dinner with me. I can tell you all of my future plans for the spread of these rats."

I was forced into a chair and held at gunpoint. Dinner was indeed served, but I didn't eat a bite off the gold-plated dishes. Mac droned on as I stared at the vile of liquid just in front of me on the table. Mac was taunting me. The thing I needed was just out of reach. I needed to get rid of the guards. As long as I was held at gunpoint there was not much I could do. I pressed my wrist communicator button.

Shortly after, an explosion rocked the building. I was sure Jaemin found a way to overcharge the power transformers. The lights blinked off and I took my chance, grabbing the vile of antidote. I ran across the room and kicked out the window before the lights even came back on. Free falling from the penthouse, I activated my glider and sailed across the city.

Location: Fushun - The Mine_

Back at the mine, I heard screeching and banging coming from inside. I grappled my way up on top of the door to see if I could get a better look. To my surprise, the banging sound was not from the creatures inside the base, it was Spartans on the outside trying to break in. I realized exactly what they were up to; they were trying to break out the creatures inside.

"Oh no, you don't," I yelled, dropping onto the ground. I engaged the Spartans in hand-to-hand combat and was able to take out the small group. Just when I thought I was the victor, I heard a motor in the distance. A few SUV's with bright headlights bounced over the hill and Spartans piled out.

I brought out my sleeping spray and eliminated a few in the front of the hoard charging toward me. I was able to take out a few more with my wrist dart gun, but there were far too many to defeat alone. To my surprise, the Spartans did not attack me, but rather they ran toward the mine's door and started to pry it open.

I watched helplessly as huge, ugly, green-eyed rats poured out of the opening. As they scratched the Spartans around the door, those Spartans gained green eyes and became very violent. I started to run; there was nothing I could do but go get help. I heard a screeching sound and felt a claw catch my arm. The world started to turn green. I knew I had Mac's antidote, so I quickly downed it. As the world started to fade, I felt something drag me away.

Location: UNKNOWN_

I woke up in what appeared to be a hospital bed; however, I could not tell where I was.

"He will make a full recovery, the newer antidote we made is much stronger," I heard a voice say in the distance.

"How are you feeling?" Mac stepped out of the shadows.

I tried to run, but I was far too weak to even move my legs.

"Don't worry. I'm not here to hurt you. In fact, you are in the Spartan medical facility. I was able to get you here after you passed out."

"Why did you save me? I thought your goal was to get rid of me?"

"Well, Sir Alexander," Mac said putting his arm around me, "you are my nemesis, but I will let you in on a little secret. I really enjoy all of our fights, your sarcastic remarks every time I catch you, and how you have helped me in a roundabout way get better at taking over the world."

I tried to hide my smile.

"You know what, Mac, I cannot deny that the past six years have been quite a blast. I would not trade you for another nemesis any day."

"So, after you are back up on your feet you better get yourself in gear. A rogue group of rats is now attacking the city."

"Who said I have to wait until I am back up on my feet?"

"That is the Sir Alexander I know."

"Mac, I can tell things got out of hand for you this time, so instead of working against each other it might be best if we work together to get rid of this issue. Without control of this situation, you are not going to be able to take over anything, let alone the world."

"As much as I hate that idea, I think you are right. My men have found a way to return the rats to normal with the antidote as well as cure infected people."

"How about the Spartans treat the rats and the ICPA can treat the people?" I suggested.

"Don't expect my help in the future, but considering my original plan failed, I'll help you this time."

While I knew I could never trust Mac, I knew he would follow through since he would never want to jeopardize his future chances of taking over the world or whatever he was scheming.

Location: Fushun - Medial Mission_

"Amy, I need a group of agents here stat. Mac released the rats on the city, and I stole an antidote that will allow us to cure any affected people."

"Good work, Sir Alexander. I have sent over a team of our best field agents in the area. They will meet you at the hospital."

At the hospital, I sent out a team to other medical facilities in Fushun. The hospital staff were struggling to restrain the violent green-eyed victims, however by pouring the antidote in the cuts on the victims they fell asleep and would wake up back to normal within a few hours.

"What about the rats, Sir Alexander?" asked my teammate.

"One thing at a time," I said, seeing a Spartan cure a rat outside the hospital window.

After a few days we had made our way through the city and cured all the victims and the rats had "mysteriously" disappeared. I made sure not to tell anyone since I did not want anyone to find out the Spartans and ICPA had cooperated on a task.

It felt strange stepping back onto the plane to go home after the whole ordeal. Things just were not the same.

Location: ICPA HQ_

Back at the ICPA base, I gave everyone my recount of the events, leaving out the part about Mac saving me. It was exciting to get to see all my team again. As I sat at my desk trying to figure out where things had been filed, Amy paged me to her office. I made my way over quickly.

"Sir Alexander, another job well done. In fact, you have done so well that I would like to promote you to the head of the agency."

"Amy! That is only something that you can do. You have been the head of the agency for six years now, it is not just something that you can hand over."

"Sir Alexander, six years is a long time, and it is time for me to move on. I am going back to school. I feel like my passion for psychology has always been there, but I never really followed my dream, plus the Spartans just seem to crop up over and over again no matter what we do."

"It is like a game Amy; we make a move and then they do. Even if it is stressful, it is rather fun, right?"

"After six years, I am not so sure."

"Amy, you can't just go."

"I'm sorry, Sir Alexander, I need to go my own way, and there is no one I trust more than you to take over the agency for me. I have my official resignation ceremony scheduled for tomorrow."

"Thank you, Amy."

Location: ICPA HQ - My Office_

I ran back to my office and burst into tears. Veronica and Kai peeked in to comfort me.

"I just heard the news. Don't worry, I think you will make a great head agent."

"I don't think I can do it, Veronica."

"We all believe in you," Kai smiled.

The next few hours were very hard as the desk agent team put together the details for Amy's departure. Per the ICPA tradition, we ordered gray and white decorations to signal the departure. Agent Double J measured me for a new gray suit, and I ordered a set of white flowers for table centerpieces.

"Why would she just leave, Double J?"

"She was ready; it is not something you could have changed. Don't worry, you will do fine, and she will be happy."

That night I sat in bed unable to sleep. I tossed and turned going over the events in my mind. I decided to call Eunhyuk again to get the opinion of someone who wasn't associated with the agency.

"Hi Eunhyuk...I remembered you told me to count on my friends when I need help, and I am really in need of help."

"I'm proud of you, Alex. That's what friends are for. You don't have to go through this alone. In my opinion, you have to follow your heart," he said reassuringly.

"I know, Eunhyuk, but to be honest I'm scared. The ICPA has been all I've known for such a long time."

There was a pause on the line and then he continued, "You were able to take up the challenge of becoming a field agent. As your friend, I think it is time for you to take up the challenge of becoming yourself."

After the call, I sat curled up on my couch trying to sort out my feelings. I had been Sir Alexander for so long that I realized I didn't really know who I was outside of that role. I finally came to the conclusion that if Amy was not going to stay, I was not going to stay either. It was time for me to start a new chapter of my life.

Location: ICPA HQ - Banquet Hall_

It was the official day of departure for Amy. All the tables sat perfectly arranged with gray tablecloths and white lily centerpieces. The spies sat murmuring to each other, clad in the same color palette. As Amy got up onto the stage to make her remarks, I felt Kai put his arm around me, trying to calm me down.

"Good afternoon, fellow spies. Please do not think of this as a somber moment, but an exciting one. I have enjoyed running this agency and appreciate all that each and every one of you does, but it is time for change." Amy's voice cracked a bit as she held back her emotions. "I know change can be painful at first, but it can bring something even more amazing. After careful consideration, I have chosen Sir Alexander to be the new head of the agency. I know he will lead you all into a successful future."

Kai patted me on the back and nodded toward the stage with a look of encouragement. I stood up with tears in my eyes and took the microphone as everyone applauded.

"I know that I have been at the agency for a long time, but I decline to take the position of head spy. I give this position to Matthew, my apprentice. He is an honest, organized, and enthusiastic spy. He knows the agency and has been able to participate in very important missions during his tenure here. I am stepping down from head desk agent as well and award my position to Veronica, who has been there for me since the beginning as a fellow desk agent."

The room was completely silent. A weak applause broke out.

Location: Tokyo, Japan – Yuki's Apartment_

To my surprise, after I announced my departure Kai confided in me that he had been on the fence about all the changes and decided to end his contract with the ICPA too.

The two of us returned to Tokyo together. I could not decide what to do with myself. Thankfully, with Kai at my side and my best friend Yuki nearby I had the support I needed.

"I don't know what to do, Yuki. I stepped down from the ICPA as head desk agent."

"What happened?" Yuki asked, sitting next to me and Kai on the couch.

"Well, a lot of things. Amy stepped down as the head of the agency, and I realized that I didn't really know who I was anymore. Sure, I gained confidence, but in the end the ICPA defined me to the point that I couldn't define myself without it."

"This just means you have a new beginning. You don't have to be Sir Alexander anymore; you can just be Alex now."

I burst into tears as Kai and Yuki did their best to comfort me. I wanted to be Alex, but I didn't know how since I had been Sir Alexander for so long. As Tokyo tower lit up the room, Kai departed for the evening and Yuki covered me with a blanket as she headed off to bed.

"Alex, just remember this is a new beginning. See you in the morning."

Location: Tokyo, Japan - A new beginning_

A few months later, I was getting used to the idea of a new beginning. I had acquired a job at the embassy in Tokyo, and I loved every bit of it. Kai ended up sharing my apartment in Shinjuku, which was near where he had taken up work as a personal trainer. After the day was over, I walked to a small café to unwind.

"How was your day at the embassy?"

I looked up from my coffee to see Kai's familiar face. "It was nice. Nothing crazy happened, and I am completely okay with that. Any new members at the gym?"

"I signed a few more, hopefully they stick around. I heard the ICPA is doing well. Matthew really knows what he's doing."

"I knew he could handle it, plus I know Veronica has the desk agents very organized and efficient. Even more so than when I was there."

"You know Matthew has allowed a lot of cross training so that there are many more agents that were like you, both at the desk and in the field. You should be proud of what you started."

"I couldn't have done it alone. Thanks to you and everyone else who helped me believe in myself, I was able to accomplish what I started."

Amy and I would visit whenever she was on a school break and Agent Double J kept me decked out in the most fashionable clothes. Laurel kept me posted on what she was up to with teaching. While most of my original team had gone their separate ways, I knew that one day we would all see each other again. But for now, I would focus on just being Alex.

www.ingramcontent.com/pod-product-compliance
Lightning Source LLC
Chambersburg PA
CBHW032034240626
47154CB00003B/907